Alaric Alfred Watts

Alaric Watts, a narrative of his life

Vol. I

Alaric Alfred Watts

Alaric Watts, a narrative of his life
Vol. I

ISBN/EAN: 9783337056056

Printed in Europe, USA, Canada, Australia, Japan

Cover: Foto ©Raphael Reischuk / pixelio.de

More available books at **www.hansebooks.com**

ALARIC WATTS.

A Narrative of His Life.

BY

HIS SON,

ALARIC ALFRED WATTS.

'Les luttes et les souffrances de chaque homme sont pour
l'enseignment de tous.'

GEORGE SAND.

WITH PORTRAITS.

IN TWO VOLUMES.

VOL. I.

LONDON:

RICHARD BENTLEY AND SON,

Publishers in Ordinary to Her Majesty the Queen.

1884.

[All Rights Reserved.]

To

ZILLAH,

THIS NARRATIVE OF THEIR FATHER'S LIFE,

Is lovingly Inscribed

BY HER

BROTHER.

19, CHEYNE WALK,
  CHELSEA, S.W.
Christmas Day, 1883.

CONTENTS OF VOL. I.

CHAPTER I.

PAGE

Introductory.—The Age of Sentiment - - - 1

CHAPTER II.

Family History.—Childhood - - - - 15

CHAPTER III.

Youth.—Wye College.—Ashford - - - 25

CHAPTER IV.

Mr. Crabb's Academy.—The Circle of the Ruspinis, and Life in Pall Mall.—Interview with Lord Byron - - - - - .. - 37

CHAPTER V.

Runcorn.—'New Monthly Magazine' - - - 50

CHAPTER VI.

Maturin, the Author of 'Melmoth.'—Bringing out a New Play - - - - - - 62

CHAPTER VII.

Woburn - - - - - - - 72

CHAPTER VIII.

PAGE

Priscilla Maden Wiffen - - - - - 84

CHAPTER IX.

Illustrative Correspondence, 1819-20 - - - 94

CHAPTER X.

The 'Literary Gazette' - - - - 107

CHAPTER XI.

Hurst, Robinson and Company.—Marriage - - 119

CHAPTER XII.

Early Married Life.—Rev. William Lisle Bowles and
the Popeian Controversy - - - - 133

CHAPTER XIII.

Further Developments of the Age of Sentiment.—
Publication of 'Poetical Sketches.'—Opinions of
Lamb and Coleridge - - - - 145

CHAPTER XIV.

Leeds - - - - - - - 155

CHAPTER XV.

The Annuals.—' The Literary Souvenir ' - - 167

CHAPTER XVI.

Maria Jane Jewsbury - - - - - 178

CHAPTER XVII.

Miscellaneous Correspondence - - - - 189

CHAPTER XVIII.

PAGE

The Blues - - - - - - 204

CHAPTER XIX.

'The Literary Souvenir' for 1826. — Panic of 1825,
and Failure of Hurst, Robinson and Co. - - 214

CHAPTER XX.

Letters of Alaric Watts, 1822-26 - - - 227

CHAPTER XXI.

Wordsworth and Coleridge - - - - 235

CHAPTER XXII.

'Literary Souvenir,' 1827.—The Editor's Diary - 248

CHAPTER XXIII.

The 'Standard' Newspaper.—Politics of the Poets - 260

CHAPTER XXIV.

'The Literary Souvenir' for 1828.—Mr. T. K. Hervey 268

CHAPTER XXV.

Letters of Wordsworth and Coleridge, 1825-28 - 281

CHAPTER XXVI.

Paris.—The Romanticists - - - - 294

CHAPTER XXVII.

'The Literary Souvenir,' 1829.—'Christopher North'
and 'The Shepherd' thereupon.—The 'New Year's
Gift' - - - - - - 305

CHAPTER XXVIII.

William Sidney Walker, and Winthrop Mackworth Praed — 314

CHAPTER XXIX.

Selections from Poems of Earlier Life — 327

ALARIC WATTS:

A NARRATIVE OF HIS LIFE.

CHAPTER I.

INTRODUCTORY.—THE AGE OF SENTIMENT.

'THE necessity,' says Dr. Johnson, 'of complying with times and of sparing persons is the great obstacle to biography.' If we may judge from some recent examples, we must assume that biographers and editors of correspondence, at the present day, are more solicitous to comply with the former of these requisites than the latter. It is on the whole the safer alternative, if it be needful, as sometimes it may, that the one be sacrificed to the other; but it is not in this modest biography proposed to adopt it. The writer trusts to give pain to no person, but dares not indulge the hope of absolutely complying in it with the times to which he seeks to address himself.

Notwithstanding the opinion of an eminent leader of modern thought,* that of three great evils of the day, one is sentimentalism, the writer must admit himself far from feeling assured of the sympathy of the age he is seeking to interest, with the spirit of sentiment which prevailed at the time of which he is to speak. The habit of thought of the present day has given, as he ventures to think, too much encouragement to the idea that strength of character is the exclusive property of the intellect, and that to be susceptible to feeling and to display such susceptibility is to be weak. There is surely no graver error. It is only that which is affected, whether it be affected sensibility or sentimentalism, or affected intellect or intellectualism, that is feeble.

The Age of Sentiment had its origin broadly in this wise.

The aspirations for fuller freedom which were

* Professor Huxley.

agitating, in England, the closing years of the last century, were not confined to the domain of action or politics; they displayed themselves in the republic of letters, or thought; and, it may be added, even in the realm of fashion in dress. The necessity had begun to be more and more recognised, especially in refined natures, for fuller freedom in the cultivation and manifestation of feeling, for liberty to express emotion with greater openness, and, as a consequence, in more familiar and natural language, in poetry and literature generally, than had prevailed in that, or immediately preceding ages. This was not a new condition of the public mind. The same spirit had characterized the earlier years of the preceding century, imparting an exquisite grace and tenderness to the poetry of the age of the early Stuarts, maintaining its influence with ever-increasing difficulty through the fanaticism of the Commonwealth and the license of the Restoration. The intellectual spirit in Pope to which it finally succumbed, like an extinct volcano, had ceased either to vivify or illuminate, when the genius of Sterne, pro-

minent amidst co-operating influences, arose
once more to liberate the emotions.   The
spirit of the age, long groaning under the
despotism of mere formal intellectualism, responded with enthusiasm to the appeal to its
feelings to arise and be free.   Even Johnson,
no lover of innovation, and assuredly no senti-
mentalist, was found complaining that the
conversation of his oldest friend, Garrick, gay
as it was and full of good things, had not solid
merit, from its deficiency in 'sentiment,'—
that quality which he had himself insensibly
assimilated, and was displaying not ungrace-
fully to congenial associates in his altered
mode of address from 'Sir,' or 'Dear sir,' to
'My Baretti,' and 'My dear Mr. Warton.'
   Freedom of feeling, as needful to human
happiness and progress as freedom of action
or freedom of thought, having definitively
asserted its right to exist, a spirit of sentiment
which is perhaps the first stage or spring-tide
of feeling,—the perception of it as something
not hitherto realized to the mind rather than
feeling in the fulness of activity,—began to
characterize predominantly all the literature,

especially the poetical literature, of the age. In poetry it assumed three aspects, or flowed into three channels : the romantic ; the familiar ; and the pensive. The romantic, as displayed in Gray's 'Bard,' Percy's 'Reliques of Early English Poetry,' Macpherson's 'Ossian,' and the quasi 'Rowley Revivals' of Chatterton ; the familiar, in the poems of Cowper ; and the pensive, in those of Thomas Warton. These three phases of sentiment in poetry, though distinct in themselves, are more or less traceable in the writings of all the poets of that time, sometimes one, sometimes another predominating. The romantic element, for example, was to be found in Warton, as well as the pensive ; the familiar as well as the romantic in Gray ; and the pensive as well as the familiar in the 'divine chit-chat' of Cowper.

The influence of a spirit of tender, rather mournful sentiment more or less pervaded the whole of English literature, and became more and more accentuated as the century approached its end. Nor was this spirit confined to England. It was influencing also the literature of the Continent, in France, Germany, and Italy. It was, in truth, the vivifying spirit of a new era,—a distinct stage of advance in human nature and human civilization.

The spirit of an age that in any direction encourages Freedom, can scarcely avoid affording also occasion for license. When people are invited by public sentiment to explore their emotions and express them without fear, very surprising discoveries and utterances are likely to respond to the invitation. Much genuine feeling was now evoked, but a considerable quantity came to the surface in a very mixed condition; and as taste, which is the touchstone of feeling, requires experience and observation to develop, much folly and false sentiment began, and continued for a season, to pervade the popular poetical literature of the day. The age was somewhat in the condition of the honest German whom Boswell describes as having been surprised when jumping over chairs in his bedroom, and who excused himself for being discovered in so ludicrous an exercise with the explanation, ' J'apprends d'être vif.'

By degrees, sentimentalism, that is exaggerated or untrue sentiment, false imagery, silly redundances, inapt allusions, and defective taste of every description, Gallicisms, Italicisms, especially the latter, began more and more to adulterate and corrupt the popular literature of the day.

> ' Abortive thoughts, that right and wrong confound;
>   Truth sacrificed to letters—sense to sound;
>   False glare, incongruous images combine,
>   And noise and nonsense clatter through the line.'

Satire now interposed,

> ' To hiss preposterous fustian from the stage !'

The Sewards and Hayleys, who were really cultivated people, and susceptible to true sentiment, were warned that the republic of letters was not a mutual admiration society, that

> ' Ode didactic, epic, sonnet,
>   Mr. Hayley, you're divine !
>   Ma'am, I'll take my oath upon it,
>   You yourself are all the Nine,'

would not do any longer ; and that people who were able to write, and write well, should express themselves with moderation, judgment, and good taste.   While, Della Crusca and Rosa

Matilda, the Lauras and the Theodores, who had been complimenting each other in the newspapers in false sentiment and bad English, by dozens, were ridiculed into giving up writing and encouraged to take to reading instead. The laurels of Lady Miller's Vase at Batheaston, and of the Florentine 'Accademia,' with their prizes to competitive sentimentalism of wreaths and diplomas, never recovered from the effects of the satire of Gifford and Mathias; but the spirit of true sentiment suffered not a whit. By it, the age was softened, coarseness of manners was restrained, and sensitive natures were protected and encouraged not to be fearful of the truth that was in them. Sympathy began to be not only felt but avowed for the criminal and the prostitute; and even the animal race was allowed to possess claims to be treated with humanity. To this spirit of sentiment we are indebted for the emancipation of the slave; the reformation of the lunatic asylum; the mitigation of the criminal code; and every humanizing and progressive movement which has given sweetness, grace, dignity, and beauty to the age in which we live.

It was towards the close of the earlier period of development of this spirit in English literature, viz., in 1791, that a young gentleman presented himself to Mr. Cruttwell, a printer at Bath, with fourteen sonnets, written chiefly in picturesque spots during a journey, with the profits to be derived from which he indulged himself in the hopes of paying a mercer's bill at Oxford. Mr. Cruttwell could hold out no encouragement favourable to the prospects of the mercer. He had strong doubts whether the publication would even repay the expense of printing,—about five pounds ; but he either suffered himself to be persuaded, or, more probably, the five pounds were forthcoming, for a hundred copies in quarto were struck off. Six months later, the author was agreeably surprised by a letter from the printer, informing him that the hundred copies had all been sold, and that if five hundred had been printed, they would have, no doubt, been sold also. Five hundred more copies were accordingly produced, and sold they were. Soon after, —the sale had been rapid,—seven hundred and fifty more copies were printed and sold likewise. In 1805 a ninth edition was called for. How many editions of these poems, with additions introduced from time to time, were published between 1805 and the last edition, 1837, this writer is unable to say.

The young gentleman in question was Mr. William Lisle Bowles, afterwards the Rev. W. Lisle Bowles, Rector of Bremhill and Canon of Salisbury.

. The publication of these fourteen sonnets may be taken as the starting-point of the second period of the Poetry of Sentiment in England.

They were received with enthusiasm, as something quite new and animating, by a little circle of young men who were themselves destined to carry on the spirit of sentiment, familiar, romantic, and pathetic, and much more, into the literature of succeeding ages.

'Soon after the publication of the third edition,' says Mr. Bowles in his introduction to the edition of 1837, 'two strangers, one a particularly handsome youth, lately from Westminster School, called upon Mr. Cruttwell, and spoke in high commendation of my volume.

Who the young men were, I knew not at the time, nor until I received a visit at my parsonage, some forty years afterwards, from one of them,—it was Robert Southey.'

At the same time another young writer, whose work it was to delight and purify the heart by establishing the compatibility of the tenderest sentiment with the truest humour, was writing to a young friend about to make an experiment upon the town with his first volume of poetical ' effusions.' 'I love you,' says Charles Lamb, to his friend, ' for dedicating your poetry to Bowles.' In the preface to this little book—'·Poems on Various Subjects, by S. T. Coleridge, late of Jesus College, Cambridge '—the writer assigns as a reason for not describing these poems as ' sonnets,' the fear of reminding the reader of the poems of the Rev. W. L. Bowles, a comparison with which he deprecates very earnestly and in terms of touching modesty ; and in his 'Autobiography,' published some fifty years later, Coleridge speaks with gratitude of the benefit which he had derived ' from the genial influence of poetry so tender and yet so manly,

so natural and real and yet so dignified and
harmonious ;' and mentions that 'when the
sonnets of Mr. Bowles, twenty in number,
published in a quarto pamphlet, were made
known to him, he made, within less than a
year and a half, more than forty transcriptions
of them ;' he was too poor to buy them ' to
give to his friends.' These sonnets, it may be
added, the subjects of which are chiefly river
scenery, were published ten years before those
of Wordsworth on the river Duddon.

It is not easy, perhaps, now, at first sight, to
discover what was the new spirit which had
arrested the attention of these young writers,
and been so deeply felt, in these poems. Their
sentiment, their pathos, what was romantic in
them, the love of nature which they displayed,
and their pensive individualism, were all, in a
greater or less degree, characteristic of the
poetry of the age.   What was it then that was
new?   What it was, has become fused into and
incorporated with the sentiment of a later age,
and it is not easy to resolve that sentiment
into its primal elements.   The charm, perhaps,
was a certain definiteness of aim in each com-

position, a harmony both of thought and expression, an instinctive attention to accuracy in the illustrations and imagery; in fact, a happy combination of those qualities, the absence of which had been the glaring defect of the poetry of the Della Cruscan period. In a word, it was Taste. That divine quality, only perceived by those who possess it; because, like 'Love' as defined by the Apostle, it is manifested mainly in negatives,—in what it does not do, rather than in what it does.

The first period of the Age of Sentiment had been marked in poetry by the vindication of Liberty; the second period was to be characterized by its submission to rational Law,—the unwritten and unwritable law of refinement and propriety of judgment.

The poetry of the period from the rise of Bowles to the rise of Tennyson was the poetry of an often powerful, but always refined and cultivated sentiment. It was, in all its variations, in the best sense, the poetry of Taste; and those who read it, even in those masters of the lyre who made the most claim to the free spirit, will find on reflection how rare are the deviations from the predominating and abiding influence of this purifying quality.

Of the development of the Age of Taste, by which it led into two distinct, and in a certain sense opposite directions, the poetry of imagination and the poetry of outer art, the parent of modern Æstheticism, the following pages may, it is hoped, supply some illustrations.

CHAPTER II.

'THE child,' which Mr. Wordsworth reminds us is 'father to the man,' is itself the offspring of many fathers ; the representative expression of many co-operating and conflicting characters and characteristics. Irrespective of its natural parents, by whose virtues it profits and whose errors it bears upon its brow, a little scapegoat in a great wilderness, it is the child also of antagonistic or propitious circumstance in the lives which have preceded it, as well as of the predominant principles of thought, not always readily understood in a later day, of the age out of which it is born.

Of the last-mentioned of these influences, I have given some account in the preceding introductory chapter. It may be needful to take some further note of it, as it affects the subject of this memoir, when referring later to the work by which he rendered himself of utility in his day and generation, and which, it is hoped to show, has given him a title to be kindly remembered when the time, probably not far distant, shall arrive for doing justice to the services rendered by that day to the progress in this country of artistic and poetical taste.

Of the two other influences combining to mould the character of the child, and thus in some degree to fashion its destinies, viz., the nature of its antecedents, personal and circumstantial, some notice may be allowed to introduce this biography, which the writer asks permission to set forth in his own person simply and unaffectedly, as a son may most easily to himself, and probably therefore also to his hearers, narrate the history of a father's life.

Alaric Alexander Watts was the youngest child of the marriage of Mr. John Mosley Watts with Sarah, daughter of Mr. Samuel Bolton, of Fair Mile, near Henley-on-Thames, and was born in London on the 16th March, 1797. Mr. Mosley Watts was the representative of a family of somewhat more than respectable antiquity, which had been settled in the midland counties for some three centuries, originally at Beby, in Leicestershire; subsequently at Blakesley in Northamptonshire, of which it had held the manor, with a fair estate; and, from the close of the seventeenth century, at Danetts Hall, near Leicester. Some account of this family may be found by the curious in Baker's 'County History of Northamptonshire,' in Throsby's 'Select Views of the Seats of the Nobility and Gentry of the County of Leicester,' and in Nichols' 'History' of that county; but, with its fortunes and genealogies, however respectable and interesting to those immediately concerned, the reader will not care that this narrative should be encumbered. It is now represented by my cousin, Mr. Frederick Mosley Watts.

John Mosley Watts was the only son of Dr. William Watts, a physician at Leicester, originally of Danetts Hall near that town, by Mary, daughter of George Whalley, Esq., of

Norton, of the family of Whalley the Regicide. Dr. Watts was a man of piety and sensibility at a time when the latter quality was less general than it became later. 'He was,' says Nichols, 'chiefly instrumental in the foundation of that valuable institution, the Leicester Infirmary,' of the need for which he had acquired experience in the practice of his profession. In later life he took Orders ; not, I imagine, with any view to preferment, but rather for the purpose of qualifying himself, as he believed only thus he could, for he was of an enthusiastic and mystical temperament, for ministering to the spiritual as well as temporal disorders of his neighbours.

Of John Mosley Watts, having nothing to record to his credit, I desire to say little. He was neither a good son nor a good husband. His children were indebted to him for little but existence ; and those who represent them will probably best discharge that limited obligation by not needlessly withdrawing him from oblivion. It is, however, perhaps just to add, having said so much, that he behaved, on the whole, in his later days with more moderation and sense of justice than might have been anticipated from his earlier career ; and that, although no direct intercourse with him took place on the part of his family, the close of a stormy life was passed by him not unwatched or uncared for by the dutiful solicitude of his elder son.

It was thus 'amidst the disadvantages of a house divided against itself, and narrow means, that my father's childhood was passed. Fortunately, whatever may be the influence upon later life of unprosperity in youth, childhood adapts itself readily to the condition of things around it ; and sunshine which it does not know, it does not miss. Mrs. Mosley Watts was a woman of capacity and cultivation, according to the measure of that day, and a strong, if somewhat saturnine nature. She did, I believe, the best in her power for her family ; and she was permitted to survive to witness its fortunes repaired in the person of her elder son, and some credit and distinction given to it in another way by the subject of this memoir.

After residing for a time at Leicester under

the protection of her husband's friends, she removed to London, where a presentation at Christ's Hospital had been secured for the elder boy, and took up her residence in Great Portland Street. This street and its immediate neighbourhood was much occupied at that time by the better class of the French *émigrés*, who had been driven to this country by the Revolution; those who were less prosperous occupying the purlieus of Somers Town. There were at that time in England no less than six thousand emigrant priests, to whom the British Government made for some time an allowance of six shillings a week to each person. One of my father's earliest recollections was of one of these ecclesiastics, whose dignified and placid benignity greatly impressed and attracted him; and a shadowy recollection of words of deep personal interest and import, addressed to him by the good father in a little garden with rockwork and a fountain, was impressed so deeply on his mind that he made more than one attempt in after-life to discover the spot where this interview had taken place.

One of these *émigrés*, this very ecclesiastic, I have reason to believe, who had returned to France after the Revolution, came over again to England during the short interval of peace which succeeded the Treaty of Amiens, renewed his acquaintance with the family, and proposed to take charge of the child; and this was not the last occasion on which he evinced an interest in its welfare. The following extract from a letter addressed to my father by the late Miss Anastasia Watts, relates to him at this period, and to this incident :

'Old Dame Carrington, quite a gentlewoman in her poverty, taught you to read, and pronounced you a child of ability at five years old. A very marked characteristic of your early years was your indignation at tyranny, and the fearlessness with which you expressed it. I remember once, when I had placed a pair of new shoes too near the fire and a hot cinder caused a hole in one of them, mother was much displeased, and expressed herself with more severity than seemed to you to be warranted by the circumstance. You were outrageous, and broke out with all the contempt in your face conceivable, and desired her not to scold me so, for she knew I was a good girl; and that these particular shoes moreover, as it happened,

had been purchased with my own money, so that,
you said, it was no concern of hers if they were
injured. Your face was full of scorn. You were
then quite a child. You were, nevertheless,
tenderly attached to her ; for when, about this time,
a friend of our family who resided abroad, much
taken with your promising and manly behaviour,
proposed to take charge of you, to send you to
college in France, and to provide for your future,
you declined to have anything to do with him, or
even to speak decently to the poor gentleman ; and
as mother had no desire to part with you, the idea
was abandoned.'

The following autobiographical notes belong
also to this season :

'We lodged,' my father says, 'during a
portion of one summer at the White House
at Islington, a large old mansion, of which a
Mrs. Poe was the proprietress. Mrs. Poe was
a hundred years old, and her daughter, who
lived with her, was in her seventy-first year.
The curtains of my bed and of the windows
were of a description which greatly excited
my imagination. They were of calico, printed
with a representation of Captain Cook's murder
by the natives of Otaheite. The figures were
some seven or eight inches in height, and

printed in dark bistre. When the wind moved them, the savages seemed to my terrified apprehension to be alive, and often deprived me of sleep, or filled it with uneasy dreams. Weird and wan did they look, with the moon-light making ghastly attempts to pass through them. Another subject, I remember, was Penn's Treaty with the Indians, illustrated in the same manner. The White House has long since been demolished, and the site and garden converted into a street. The New River does not seem so bright and pleasant as it used to do when I explored its mazes in search of stickle-backs and crawfish. The old Queen's Head has been rebuilt, and the whole aspect of the neighbourhood altered, if not in my eyes improved.'

While it would be rash to avow with George Sand the belief, surely a noble one, neverthe-less, that everything is significant and emble-matic in what may seem the most fortuitous details of human life, some deductions may be allowed from the few and simple incidents above narrated in the life of this child, where-from to forecast, in some sort, the inevitable in

the life of the man of which it was to be the
father. We seem to find rudimentary evidences
of a nature very expressive and true to itself,
and like every human nature really true to
itself, in a certain sense double, and contra-
dictory; a spirit capable of much generous
voluntary sacrifice and self-devotion, but not
ready with obedient self-repression to the will
of others; an ardent and discriminative sense
of abstract justice, but little veneration for
even just authority; a disposition tender and
engaging, but apt to prove fractious and self-
willed. A character, on the whole, promising
to develop a man feeling, and probably therefore inspiring, deep loves and possibly lively
antipathies. Material here for a poet, if either
breadth of imagination or depth of perception
of its own experiences, out of either of which
poetry evolves, should develop later.

CHAPTER III.

In the year 1808, my father was placed at school at Wye College Grammar School, in Kent. Of these days he spoke always with pleasure in later life. They were, indeed, the only days of his childhood of which he greatly cared to speak, and were probably, therefore, the happiest of those days. He visited Wye several times in later life; the last occasion being a short time only before his death.

Continuing the autobiographical notes from which I have quoted, he says: ' I was placed at school at Wye College Grammar School, in Kent, under the Rev. Mr. Vincer—an amiable and kind-hearted man, though, as the fashion was of that day, a pretty severe disciplinarian.

His wife was some twenty years younger than himself, and a very charming person. She had no children of her own, but treated the youths under her care as though they had been her children. Her kindness · was tenderly reciprocated ; and the boys would delight, in the early mornings, to forage the neighbourhood for flowers to be laid before her on the breakfast-table.'

A picturesque and poetical *alma mater* this Wye College, with a history of its own, if only there were space and time and sufficient relevance to this narrative to warrant the telling it in this place.

> ' Set
> Deep in a garden rank and green,
> It were scarce older now than then ;
> For all the seasons gone between,
> So very hoar the branches spread.'*

Behind a low old stone wall ' facing the street ' (a country road now on the skirts of the little town), and reached by gates through a strip of pleasant bowery garden, stands an antique two-storied building, which might be taken for a prosperous old country parsonage, or the

* ' Songs in a Minor Key,' by Mrs. Riddell.

residence of some master of a college. On the left of the gate, with entrance therefrom into the adjacent churchyard, a small ancient Gothic building, looking like a stranded ark of stone, the ancient schoolroom of the 'master of grammar,' attached for secular uses to the original foundation. Everywhere festooning ivy and vine, jessamine and snap-dragon, mullen and poppy, carnation and straggling rosebush, and grass plots shaggy with unmown grass. Arched windows, with their grey-stone mullions peeping forth along the ground through the pleasant leafiness, with patches visible here and there of ancient stained glass. Above, narrow sash windows, dating from the earlier years of the last century, and dark-red brickwork, which had superseded the old timber of the mediæval period ; and surmounting all, a goodly-tiled roof, with a fair show of chimneys.

The interior, not less picturesque in its way, with its long gallery, into which had opened, in early days, chamber of master and provost, cell of priest and clerk ; and its fair parlour on right of the entrance, oak-panelled, with its large window filled with stained glass, and looking out on the bowery garden. The blood-red hat of Cardinal Kempe, Archbishop of Canterbury, the pious founder, forming an appropriate centre to much coat-armour in brilliant colouring, or more or less bleached and faded flowers such as missal-painters love to illuminate, and also to imagine, for such never grew on earth, and birds, the offspring of similar fantastic idealism.

To point a moral, as it were, against the undue exercise of the imagination and poetic fantasy which all these quaint devices might be calcu-lated to stimulate in the mind of youth, stands forth to the wondering eye a centrepiece in grey and orange, traced with no feeble hand, but bleached and wan, representing an ass seated upon a golden throne, playing upon a golden harp; while from the signboard of the ancient inn just opposite, not more modern than the college itself, Pegasus, in the person of the white horse of Kent, creaks to a different tune.

Amidst these surroundings, the child passed one, if not two, happy years. 'I was boarded,' he says, in the notes from which I have quoted, 'one whole summer holiday, with an honest tailor and his wife in the little town, by whom I was almost killed with kindness. I amused myself chiefly by wandering about the old college and churchyard and over the downs, where there was badger-hunting; sometimes to Colonel Sawbridge's mansion, Olantye House, with its three hundred and sixty-five windows, fifty-two doors, and twelve front doors, as credibly reported, and by me to this day implicitly believed.'

It is easy to picture the solitary lad wandering about amidst all these picturesque surroundings, and the not less picturesque if less cheerful environments of the churchyard. One lofty pyramidal monument, with much florid ornamentation and an inscription in spider-legged Italian text, commemorating the virtues of Chamberlain Godfrey, Esq., and of the fortune which that gentleman had improved by commerce at Leghorn, returning to his native town in 1748, will, it may well be believed, have often filled with speculation the active mind of the young solitary. How happy he would be, he often thinks, could he improve his fortune at Leghorn or elsewhere, and have a pleasant native town to go back to for the holidays, like other boys! Nay, little man, be not disconsolate! solitary as thou art, and with the neighbouring downs for a present limit to thy travels, soon shalt thou make the acquaintance on the most friendly and intimate terms of all sorts of interesting and delightful people; and adventure journeys into 'lands and continents' in comparison with which and with whom, Leghorn is but a graveyard, and Chamberlain Godfrey, Esq., with all his fortune, even of no more account than the rude forefathers of the hamlet so narrowly accommodated around him.

At some time in the year 1810, he says, continuing the autobiographical notes before quoted, 'I was removed from Wye College to an Academy at Ashford, in the same county, kept by the Rev. Alexander Power. The date is fixed in my memory by incidents which made a deep impression on it, the succession of military funerals which, in mournful procession, day after day passed forth from the neighbouring barracks of Brabon Lees, of soldiers who had come home invalided and had succumbed to the terrible ague fever which they had contracted in the disastrous expedition to Walcheren in 1809.

'Mr. Power was a worthy man, but, as were too many of his order in those days, wanting the qualifications for a schoolmaster of the better class. In such elements of knowledge as are now accessible at the most ordinary charity school, he was proficient enough, and skilful to impart what he knew. He was a tolerably well-read English scholar; reading and writing, geography and English history, grammar and the leading rules of arithmetic, he taught well and thoroughly. Beyond these, with the exception of French, I learnt nothing. For French I had a marked natural aptitude, and soon became a favourite with the *émigré* by whom it was taught, and of whom I retain a tender and affectionate recollection. His name was Le Flem. He had served in the miserable expedition to Quiberon Bay, the horrors of which I have never seen so vividly delineated as in his descriptions of them.   He was a good creature, and very kind to me.   At Mr. Power's I suffered much from the tyranny of the elder boys, so much so that I even ran away and got as far as Canterbury before my feelings were sufficiently composed to enable me to perceive that that was not the road out of my difficulties.   I returned in better heart, and my persecutions continuing, I tackled the most terrible of my oppressors, and I am sure, not less to my surprise than that of everyone else, I was fortunate enough to thrash him.   His name was Boucher.   This success elevated me into a sort of champion of oppressed innocence, a dangerous position, of which, fortunately perhaps for the permanence of my reputation, I was deprived by a long and severe illness which necessitated my return home.   The diet of private schools in those days was composed for the most part of bread that was almost always heavy and bad, of milk largely extenuated, the smallest of small beer, and salted meats.   Provisions of all kinds were at war-prices, and were too often as bad as they were dear.   Had it not been that worthy Mr. Power occasionally killed his own mutton and bred his own pigs, it would have gone still harder with us. Even as it was, this condition of things sent me home with a serious affection of the mouth which it took six months' domestic care, and the unremitting attention of our friend and physician, the late Mr. Alfred Shirley, of Islington, wholly to eradicate.'

The name of this kind friend of the family recalls an incident characteristic of the manly and resolute character of the lad. He was making his way one day, at the time of the great Westminster election, to take tea with Mr. Shirley, when he was encountered by a band of young roughs who summoned him, then and there, to stand and join in three cheers for Sir Francis Burdett. To this suggestion he flatly declined to obtemperate, as being inconsistent with his political convictions! whereupon he was threatened by these ardent young patriots with the discipline of the pump. To this argument he was equally impervious, and to the pump he went, a little martyr, reaching his friend's house in a very disconsolate condition of exterior, but with unabated resolu-

tion and the honourable consciousness of
having maintained the integrity of his principles !

To compensate him for the hard fare, if not
recurrence of hard usage, to which he had to
revert on his return to Ashford after the long
holiday enforced by his illness, he was now to
be introduced to those agreeable acquaintances
and lifelong friends, and to make those interesting excursions into 'islands and continents'
the most wonderful and remote to which I have
referred, and which friends and acquaintances,
'islands and continents,' arrived all together
one blissful morning in a hair-trunk from
Canterbury, by favour of the father of one of
the ushers who happened to be a bookseller.

In a short space of time the young schoolboy
had accompanied Mr. Peregrine Pickle, as
have so many excursionists, on that delightful
trip to Paris, during which he behaved to his
tutor and governor with such inexcusable levity;
had participated with much sympathy in the
early struggles of Mr. Random, with whom
he dived for a dinner, not once, but ever and
again, to the latest day of his life, with un-

abated appetite and sense of enjoyment. Nor were his interest and friendship confined to these erratic young persons. He conversed with equal satisfaction, and probably more profit, with the wise and benevolent Dr. Primrose, sympathizing with the mischances of Moses and the troubles of his gallant brother, (especially in his experiences as an usher in a school); and admiring with the fervour of youth the kind-hearted humourist, Mr. Burchell, who never made a visit without providing himself with ginger-bread for the regalement of his young friends. Though interested in the Miss Primroses, and touched by the sorrows of Olivia, his affections became very early engaged, as whose have not? by that charming young person Miss Sophia Western, who has not grown a day older to this hour, and will retain unimpaired all her beauty and attractiveness so long as there remains within us sufficient freshness of heart to appreciate them. He confessed always a mysterious interest also at this time in that unaccountable young lady of 'fashion,' Miss Carolina Wilhelmina Amelia Skeggs; but this may perhaps have been

attributable to his never having been introduced to a 'lady' of 'her fashion' before.

Nor were these all. The cornucopia, in the
prosaic shape of a hair-trunk, had contained
not only Harrison's Novelists' Library, but
Bell's little edition of the British Poets, and
Shakespeare. Now, was opened to the lad a
new world, with which he felt within himself
a certain harmony; which appealed to him as
nothing had appealed to him before; which
was to him new, so wonderfully new, and yet
old, as though he had been in it before; so
marvellous, yet so familiar. Olivia and Nar-
cissa had been, indeed, interesting young
persons, and Sophia Western was the most
charming of girls; but Una and Sabrina,
Titania and Miranda, were creatures of a
different world,—they were not for love, but
for worship.

CHAPTER IV.

MR. CRABB'S ACADEMY.—THE CIRCLE OF THE
RUSPINIS, AND LIFE IN PALL MALL.—INTER-
VIEW WITH LORD BYRON.

AT the Academy of Mr. Power, with all its
deficiencies, my father completed pretty nearly
all the education for which he was destined to
be indebted to others than himself. In the
year 1812 he elected to seek his own fortunes;
and at this date, at the age of fifteen, he may
be considered to have entered upon the practical business of life on his own account. With
no knowledge of the world, save that not unimportant experience which is derived from
witnessing, early in life, the cares of others;
with an education scarcely more than rudimentary, and directed to no special ends;
without connections, and almost without

friends ; he determined to apply himself, in the first instance, to that occupation for which his limited training had best fitted him. In addition to present independence, this might afford him an opportunity of continuing his studies and acquiring that further mental cultivation which he knew must be the only capital on which he could depend for the furtherance of his uncertain fortunes.

He accepted an engagement as usher in a school at Fulham, conducted by the Rev. George Crabb, (not to be confounded with the poet), the editor of a 'Technological Dictionary,' 'Dictionary of Synonyms,' and other useful compilations. For a time, so inexperienced did he feel himself, that he deemed it necessary to devote the leisure of his evenings to a study of the lessons which he had to impart to others on the morrow. But with all disadvantages,— possibly by means of them,—his character was strengthening and developing in power and independence. His life was a somewhat rough one, but he was substantially contented and happy, beginning to feel his feet, and making friends and well-wishers in those about him.

Among those to whom he was indebted for kindness at this time, when kindness was very precious, was no less a person than Robert William Elliston, the comedian, who had a son at school at Mr. Crabb's, and who showed him many obliging attentions. Mr. Elliston lived at this time in Stratford Place, where Mrs. Elliston kept a very *recherché* dancing academy, much frequented by the younger members of the aristocracy ; and when they had their son home for a holiday, from the Saturday to Monday, they would frequently include his young tutor, not much older than himself, in the invitation. The programme, I have heard him say, always comprised rather more wine than was necessary, a night at the play, and a guinea apiece when they returned to school in the morning.

On one of his walks in London at this time, he chanced to pick up, in the street, a roll of bank-notes in an open envelope, bearing the name of the Honourable Miss Jenkinson. This lady was sister to Lord Liverpool, at that time Prime Minister. Proceeding to Fife House, and declining, prudently enough, to surrender

his *trouvaille* to ' groom or porter,' he succeeded
in reaching the great man himself. Favourably impressed, perhaps, by the ingenuous
demeanour of the youth, my lord hinted
at a disposition to serve him ; to which he, in
return, responded, seeing that no time was
to be lost, by a suggestion that a clerkship in
his lordship's own office would suit him admirably. The Premier laughed, and condescended to explain that it would not be much
more difficult to confer upon him an Irish
peerage.

It is the characteristic of independent and
self-contained natures to lose their interest in
any occupation when they have exhausted the
knowledge and experience which they may
feel it to be capable of affording them. This
is an attribute of a higher quality of nature
than that which can be sustained ' by bread
alone ;' and it is, perhaps, in a recognition of
this fact that we may seek an explanation of
much that has been often attributed, in such
natures, to the variableness of caprice, to
infirmity of purpose, or to an undisciplined
restlessness of will.

I suspect that under no circumstances would my father's sojourn in the establishment of Mr. Crabb have extended long after the realization to his own mind of such a conviction. He had added to the knowledge acquired of Mr. Power a fair acquaintance with the classics, a slight knowledge of Italian, and a taste for music; had acquired, in fact, pretty much all that Mr. Crabb could impart to him, when a proposal was made to him of a private tutorship in the family of Mr. Ruspini, dentist to his Royal Highness the Prince Regent, who maintained a handsome establishment in Pall Mall, immediately opposite the gates of Carlton House.

This was promotion indeed, and varied and interesting were the experiences to which it introduced him.

The Chevalier Ruspini, the father of his patron, who had founded in Pall Mall this very lucrative practice, had been a cadet of an old Italian family. He had been intended for the army, and been educated with that view at the *Ecole Militaire*, in Paris. He was a student there when Garnerin made his famous aeronautic ascent from the gardens of that establishment. One of the students, in some sort a fellow-countryman,—being a Corsican,—was desirous of making the ascent; but not having sufficient money, he sought to borrow it in small sums of his schoolfellows, one of whom only, young Ruspini, was able or willing to accommodate him. The lender was to exchange the profession of arms for that of tooth-drawer to the Prince Regent of England; while the borrower, Napoleon Buonaparte, after gratifying to the full his ambition of rising, was, in process of time, to have his own teeth drawn by that august operator.

The Chevalier Ruspini realized by his profession a considerable fortune. The Chevalier's famous styptic and tooth-powder occupied a place of distinction on the toilet-table of the first gentleman in Europe. They yet exist, and an aroma of fashion clings round them even now. He kept a great deal of company at his house in Pall Mall; and it was there, according to John Taylor, that the unfortunate Dr. Dodd was arrested, just as the party was sitting down to dinner, on the charge of forgery, for which he was to suffer on the scaffold.

Mr. Ruspini, the son and successor, was a hospitable man and of a generous spirit, and in his house my father enjoyed the opportunity of seeing a great deal of society. Indeed, a list of the people whom I have heard him mention as having met in this circle, or indirectly in connection with it, would have a certain affinity with a table of contents to a volume of the 'Eccentric Mirror,' of such varied and incongruous elements was it composed. A list of names, though serviceable in a Court Guide, is not of much value in a biography; but I may note that he visited at this time, out of this circle, Dr. Walcot, the celebrated 'Peter Pindar,' in his squalid lodgings in Somers Town; Mrs. Inchbald, in her apartments over a public-house, I believe, in Kensington; Colton, the author of 'Lacon,' in the very extraordinary abiding-place which he affected over a rag-shop in Pimlico; Lady Hamilton, in the King's Bench Prison; and Lord Byron, in the Albany.

To audience of some of these personages,

he was introduced by a man as interesting in his way as most of them, Mr. John Taylor, oculist to the Prince Regent, but better known as an author, from his humorous poem of 'Monsieur Tonson,' which enjoyed a popularity in its day scarcely inferior to that of Cowper's 'John Gilpin.' John Taylor, who became afterwards, I believe, editor of the *Morning Post,* and more lately proprietor and editor of the *Sun,* an influential Liberal evening newspaper, was much connected with the stage, having married a sister-in-law of Stephen Kemble. By him my father was introduced to Charles Young, Incledon the singer, and many other acquaintances in the dramatic and literary circles of the day. The manly tenderness of sentiment of Incledon, who was a frequent visitor at the Ruspinis', in singing the songs of Charles Dibdin, exercised a fascination over my father's mind which gave to this accomplished vocalist a cherished place in his recollection in after years.

It may be here noted, in passing, that it was an age in which to sing at the dinner-table, without accompaniment, was an accomplishment as much cultivated by gentlemen as it is now to sing at the piano in the drawing-room afterwards; and, though the custom no doubt led to much tipsy conviviality, a manly tone of sentiment, a genuine tenderness of spirit, purifying what was coarse and invigorating what was pure in the age, was awakened and kept alive by it.

Apart from this lively circle, there was the little coterie of gentlemen holding appointments in the Prince's establishment of the same nature as those of Mr. Ruspini and Mr. Taylor, whose father, by the way, had also been a 'Chevalier,' among whom was Mr. Astley Cooper, afterwards the famous surgeon Sir Astley Cooper, then holding the modest appointment of Sergeant-Surgeon of the Household; and Mr. Marrable, afterwards Sir Thomas Marrable, and Privy Purse, or his deputy, to the Prince. Nay, even the gentlemen of the Household of higher rank, in immediate attendance on the Prince's person at Carlton House, and now and then, we may suppose, a little bored with that service, did not disdain to vary the tedium of duty by occasional

intercourse with the lively and improving
society of the little house opposite, contributing to the general entertainment their
Court gossip and songs and 'sentiments,'
patriotic, convivial, and sentimental, over Mr.
Ruspini's best burgundy, and sometimes, I
fear, borrowing the money which his father
the Chevalier had so happily accumulated.

My father was residing in the family of Mr.
Ruspini at the time of the visit of the Allied
Sovereigns to London in 1814; and on the
morning of the great *fête* at Carlton House
he made the acquaintance, on Mr. Ruspini's
balcony, of a young man who was engaged in
painting a transparency to do honour to the
occasion, representing the Sovereigns entering
Leipsic after the great victory of October 13th,
1813, and who was destined for many years
to give enjoyment to far more spectators
than he was that night to interest, in works
of every variety of imagination and humour
—his name, George Cruikshank. This particular work came later into the possession
of the proprietors of Vauxhall Gardens, where
it occupied a position of dignity in the

Rotunda long after the memories of Leipsic had been swallowed up in the glories of Waterloo.

Thus was it that, at the age of seventeen, my father enjoyed an introduction to the world under rather favourable circumstances, a little brightness and colour cast upon a life that had hitherto had in it too little of the cheerful and exhilarating element. No doubt he greatly enjoyed this sunshine. He now took lessons on the flute from the celebrated Nicholson, who lived hard by in Panton Street, and who, I doubt not, tempered in some sort the severity of his usual charge of a guinea a lesson to the modest purse of his young pupil. He made his appearance at this season, for the first and only time, I believe, at a masquerade at the Opera House, in a blue domino, veiling his first pair of tight, black kerseymere pantaloons, tied with ribbon at the ankles. In short, of all the diversions going on around him he partook without stint, being supplied with money, I have heard him say, without much regard to the stipulated stipend, and treated generally by his kind employer and his wife more like a son than a dependent.

He did not, however, confine himself, in his leisure moments, to such amusements. He had long been a student of poetry, and he now began to make some attempts at original composition, not without some gratifying encouragement it may be judged from the following incident, for which I am indebted to his pupil, my friend the late Mr. Bladen Ruspini :

‘ While your father,’ he says in a letter he was good enough to address to me on his friend’s death, ‘ was residing with us in Pall Mall, he addressed a short complimentary poem to Lord Byron, of whose writings he was a devoted and enthusiastic admirer. Lord Byron at once acknowledged the compliment, and requested your father to call on him at the Albany. I accompanied him, and was in the upper part of the large room on the ground-floor when the interesting interview took place. The room had a large screen before the door, and upon being introduced by Fletcher, we found Lord Byron seated at a writing-table with his back to the screen. He arose at once, and offering your father both hands, seated him by his side. After some conversation which I was not close enough to hear, thinking proper to keep at a respectful distance, as one who had no title to be there at all, Lord Byron went to a bookcase, took down a beautifully bound volume of " Childe Harold," and adding an inscription on the flyleaf, presented it to your father. This occurred in 1814 or 1815. I often saw the book afterwards in Pall Mall.'

This book, in the chances and changes of this transitory world, has disappeared. If these lines should meet the eyes of the possessor, this narrator would take it kindly to be permitted a sight of it.

CHAPTER V.

In the year 1816 my father quitted the hospitable roof of Mr. Ruspini to enter upon a clerkship in the office of the Controller of Army Accounts, under Colonel Drinkwater, brother to the historian of the 'Siege of Gibraltar.' Whether this situation was a compromise for that clerkship in the Treasury into which he had proposed, so to speak, to convert Miss Jenkinson's bank-notes, and with which the Premier had so frankly admitted the difficulty of supplying him, or whether he owed it to less influential patronage, I never heard. For the symmetry of my narrative I would assume the former. Whencesoever it originated, however, it was of no long duration. The office collapsed on the reduction of the army establishments consequent on the peace ; and my father, who was, I imagine, only a temporary or extra clerk, disappeared with it.

What wind it was, propitious or otherwise, that blew him at this juncture into the little port of Runcorn, in Cheshire, a rather dreary haven, I have no certain knowledge ; but there I find him at the beginning of the year 1816, once more assistant to 'a dominie, who keepit a scule and caa'd it an Acaudemy,' at that place.

From the cool shady side of Pall Mall this was scarcely a change for the better.

Mr. Green's Boarding Academy for Young Gentlemen was one of a pair of solitary red-brick houses erected about the middle of the last century in the fields then separating the town of Runcorn from the parish church. The church then stood on the banks of the Mersey, overlooking the ferry, to the perils whereof significant testimony is borne by more than one weather-stained lichen-covered stone in the old churchyard. The Mersey, here a broad and sullen stream ; on the other side, then, a large tract of waste land, now more profitably occu-

pied by the important chemical works and
generators of 'Weldon's mud' of Widnes.
Below the churchyard, a dreary strand, along
which were congregated the shipbuilders' yards,
and sailors and fishermen's cottages, with the
small craft of the little port interspersed here
and there, lying at low water high and dry
on the mud. Not cheerful, but not without
a certain poetry of its own,

> ' At the same time the same dull view to see ;
>   The bounding marsh-bank, and the blighted tree ;
>   The water only when the tides were high ;
>   When low, the mud, half covered and half dry ;
>   The sunburnt tar that blisters on the planks,
>   And bankside stakes in their uneven ranks.'

His letters to his mother, from one or two of
which my father may now be allowed to tell
his own story, breathe a cheerful and ingenuous
spirit.

' Runcorn, Cheshire,
' Jan. 7, 1817.

' My dearest Mother,

'I am delighted at the prospect of your
coming to reside at Ambleside, rest and quiet being
so necessary to you. Should you determine to
come to Manchester, I should be gratified beyond
anything to meet you and accompany you to your

new home. As to money, Burgess* obliged me to give him a bill for £10, which I must take up shortly; and I have some other matters of apparel to pay for. You shall have the rest, which cannot be far short of the sum you name. Mrs. Fletcher, since she desires it, shall have, in the handwriting of the writer, a copy of the verses she is so kind as to admire. I shall have much more time next half-year for writing. My sonnet to the memory of poor Kerr was published the other day in the *Chester Chronicle*, which I shall send you. Look in that part of it which contains notices to correspondents, and see what a favourable opinion the editor expresses of it. The Manchester papers have copied the poem. The *Manchester Herald*, about a fortnight ago, copied the stanzas I sent you in the Cheltenham paper, with these words, " We have copied the following exquisite stanzas, stated to have been written by a young gentleman of Runcorn. . . .

' I think it might be possible to obtain this school with a little money, Mr. Green's health being infirm. The concern is lucrative; the last half-year's bills amounted to close upon £700. The boys, of whom there are twenty, breakfast on water-porridge, that is, oatmeal boiled till it is of the consistency almost to be cut, and then sweetened with treacle; dinner, much as usual; supper, a kind of thick gruel with milk in it, called milk-porridge, with pieces of bread. The bread in this part of the country is far from

---

* ' Burgess and Co., my tailor—fashionable, but very dear.'—Mr. Toots.

good; it runs all over the oven when sent to be baked, and cannot be made firm. I have seen bread in this place like a lump of wet dough—you might eat it with a spoon. Ours is better, but coarse and black. Remember me to Mary Heron and all friends. Do not pay the postage of your letters, as though you thought me indifferent to hearing from you; and I entreat you in future to let your health be the first thing of which you write.

' I am, my dearest mother,

' Your affectionate son,

' ALARIC ALEX. WATTS.'

The scheme for purchasing Mr. Green's academy does not come to anything.

'MY DEAR MOTHER,

' Mr. Green has sold the school; and the gentleman who has bought it, who is quite in-experienced, is coming to take part in the business as an assistant. This will leave me more time for the present for pursuing my poetical studies; which, notwithstanding my late close confinement, have produced what was beyond my expectations. There is one disadvantage here; I have no sensible person on whose taste and judgment I can rely for advice, so I do my best by myself. Tell me if Lady Hillary has returned a pamphlet on "Lord Byron's Separation," four of his poems in one volume, and two volumes of " Annual Gleanings;" and has Mr. Warburton sent back my music and books? I shall be left alone in the holidays, as Mr. and Mrs. Green are going into Shropshire ; but solitude I do not mind. I have learned to employ myself in study, and seldom write down anything which I have not previously thought out and altered in my own mind. I fancy I brood too much, for sometimes I become completely stupefied by my own thoughts. I send you some verses, part of a longer poem. You may show them—I think them pretty good.

' Your affectionate son,
' A. A. WATTS.'

The poem from which these stanzas were extracted, ' To Octavia, the infant daughter of John Larking, Esq.,' was published in the month of June, 1818, in the *Edinburgh Magazine*, which, a month or two afterwards, was to exchange its nomenclature for its present time-honoured title of *Blackwood's Magazine*. The lines attracted considerable attention, and were extensively quoted in the newspapers of the day, having been attributed very generally to Lord Byron. The memory of this fact seems to have survived many years, for in a letter which I find among my father's papers from Mr. Rogers, the poet says:

' As you have mentioned your poetry in a manner nobody else would do, you must allow me to tell you with what pleasure I have read it, again and again; though the writer of a poem which has passed with good judges for Lord Byron's can need no testimony of mine in his favour.'

The purchaser of Mr. Green's academy and Mr. Green's assistant not coming to terms, and Runcorn having probably exhausted itself to the latter, which it might easily do, he made another engagement of a more eligible character, and became tutor, living in his own private lodgings, to the son of Mr. Shaw, a Manchester manufacturer, in whose family he was treated with much kindness and affection. He now had leisure to pursue those studies, exercises, and recreations to which he was more and more inclining to devote himself, if thereby only he might secure his bread, as the aim and object of his life. The 'Poet's Corner' of the Chester and Manchester newspapers no longer satisfied his ambition. He had begun to regard them rather as places of sepulture than of honourable monument ; and he now attempted, as I have shown with some success, to find an opening in the magazines of

the day.   With this view he kept up a pretty
active fire of contributions, poetical and critical,
upon the leading periodicals of this description;
until he finally settled down,—by what inter-
mediary negotiations I know not,—as sub-
editor under Dr. Watkins, a venerable garreteer,
and in a month or two, so active and energetic did he show himself, as editor-in-chief,
or more accurately speaking, editor-of-all
work, of the *New Monthly Magazine*.   This
publication had been then recently established,
if I may define its aims in the eloquent
periods of its original editor, Dr. Watkins,
'to counteract the pernicious and anarchical
designs of sedition and infidelity,' as 'a medium
of literary commerce, unsophisticated by em-
piricism, and uncontaminated by blasphemy.'
In less ambitious phraseology, in opposition to
the *Monthly Magazine*, not quite fair to the
latter in the matter of title, founded and
edited by Sir Richard Phillips, a Radical bookseller at Leicester, who enjoyed the honour of
knighthood from having 'gone up' with an
address, and the higher distinction, among
the 'Anarchists,' of having been committed

to gaol for publishing Paine's 'Age of Reason.' I do not imagine that up to that time, under the editorship of Dr. Watkins, this venture of the *New Monthly Magazine* had attained any great measure of success, though novelty would seem to have been assured by its title, and respectability by its principles. Nor can I venture to affirm that my father's editorship, he was in his twenty-second year, was likely to have done much for it in this direc- · tion. He worked hard at it, gaining some valuable experience, the essential results of which he summarized later in a magazine article, which he entitled 'Reminiscences of a Magazine Editor.' 'It was about this time,' he says in this paper, 'that the seeds of that mighty revolution which have since sprung up in magazine literature were beginning to germinate. A more fastidious and intellectual public taste was more and more disclosing itself, and editors could no longer impose upon their readers the sheer nonentities with which they had hitherto sought to satisfy them in such publications. My publisher and I found ourselves compelled, whether we liked it or not, to close accounts with some of the long-winded contributors whom I had inherited with the editorial chair. "Sophonisba's" tale was brought to an end to her advantage, as it would seem, as much as to that of her readers, for she was paid nothing for it; "Philo Logos" was no longer permitted to be wordy in our double columns; the quarrels of "Quince" and "Flute" on the difference between a hawk and a hernshaw were amicably composed; the "Gleaner" had to be admonished to exercise more discrimination in his gatherings, and the "Observer" to look further afield than had hitherto been considered needful in their caterings for the public entertainment.

'To dissolve our little cabinet we found simple enough; but to replace it, except on terms and conditions to which my publisher was wholly unaccustomed, was not so easy. It soon became very apparent that days had arrived in which there was no way of conciliating contributors, capable of conciliating readers, and their, to us, more important equivalent, subscribers, except by addressing

ourselves handsomely to their pockets, as
Mr. Blackwood was doing. To this novel
aspect of things my publisher's mind could
not readily adapt itself, and my position as
the responsible agent for filling the magazine
became every month more and more difficult.
Publishers of periodicals, says Mackenzie, in
one of his papers in the *Mirror*, may be compared to the proprietors of stage-coaches, who
are compelled to run their vehicles with or
without passengers. How to fill mine now
haunted me from morn till night, and often,
indeed, from night to morning. I was young
and fond of society, but I became now so
economical of my pleasures that I could hardly
persuade myself to accept an invitation that
did not seem to promise either material for an
agreeable sketch of society, or an agreeable
sketcher to supply me with one on the very
modest terms, if any, that I could prevail
upon my publisher to pay for it. There were
moments now, and these not infrequent, when
I would thankfully have recalled "Sophonisba"
and her tale; when the words of "Philo Logos,"
—the longer the better,—would have been

perfectly acceptable ; and when, for me, hobby-horses might have ambled through my pages as freely as Mr. O'Connell through an Act of Parliament.'

My father's connection with the *New Monthly Magazine* came to an end early in the year 1819, in consequence of some difference with the publisher arising out of the publication of Dr. Polidori's well-known mystification, 'The Vampyre : a Tale, by Lord Byron,' which first saw the light in the number of that publication for April, 1819. I should be well pleased to find myself in the position to affirm that this breach was attributable to my father's disapprobation of this piece of literary quackery and determination to give it no countenance. I have searched his papers in the hope of warranting myself in this conviction, but not with success. He was always rather reticent on the subject of this 'Vampyre' business, and I incline, on the whole, to follow his example, having indeed nothing certain or definite to record about it.

CHAPTER VI.

IT was about this time that my father made
the acquaintance of that eccentric but remarkable genius the Rev. Charles Robert Maturin.
Mr. Maturin was the author of a tragedy,
'Bertram, or the Castle of St. Angelo,' which
met with great success, and introduced him to
the friendship of both Scott and Byron. It
was severely castigated, on the ground of
the immoral tendency of its incidents, by
Coleridge, who deemed this criticism, as
affecting general principles, of sufficient importance to be reprinted in his 'Biographia
Literaria.'

Maturin is, however, best remembered by
his weird and wonderful romance of ' Melmoth,

the Wanderer,' a tale full of horrible and tragic situations, and displaying a deep, if contracted, vein of genuine and powerful imagination. Maturin was greatly valued in France, and may even claim to have borne some part in the foundation of the Romantic School of fiction, which it may be claimed for him that he in some degree anticipated.

Amable Tastu, the poetess of that school and day, wrote a poem entitled 'La Chambre de la Chatelaine,' which she describes as 'Imitation de Maturin;' and Charles Nodier, in reviewing, in the *Quotidienne*, the then recently published 'Hans d'Iceland' of Victor Hugo, draws a comparison between the young author and Maturin ;

'Le Révérend Mathurin s'est rendu célébre dans cette école par les fables monstrueuses de Melmoth et de Montorio, et l'on croyait que l'auteur avait épuisé dans ces combinaisons atroces toutes les horreurs dont peut épouvanter la pensée. Cependant il s'est trouvé dans cette nouvelle génération de Poétes qui a fait en France la fortune du genre romantique un rival de ce triste romancier Anglais,—l'auteur d'Hans d'Iceland.'

Maturin was doubtless of French extraction,

and there is no doubt, as suggested by Nodier, a certain affinity between his genius and that of Victor Hugo. It displays the same daring disregard of conventional probabilities, something of the same meteoric splendour of fancy, and glow and fervour of expression, though lacking the infinite variety and fertility of that noble enthusiast.

Mr. Maturin's other works were : ' Woman, or Pour et Contre,' a novel of modern life ; a romance of the school of Scott, but with more heat of imagination, entitled 'The Albigenses,' a very noble work, and worthy of being reprinted ; and a tragedy, ' Fredolpho,' of which and its author I will now allow my father, (in some autobiographical notes written in later life), to give his own account :

' I have,' he says, ' no distinct recollection of the occasion of my introduction to this remarkable man ; but I have little doubt that it originated in my having written a memoir of him in the first series of the *New Monthly Magazine*, to accompany a fantastic-looking portrait of him in that periodical. He was at that time in the zenith of his fame.

At all events, I was solicited by him, in 1819, to superintend the production, at Covent Garden Theatre, of a tragedy from his pen, entitled " Fredolpho."

'To stand *in loco parentis* to a new play involves a perplexing responsibility, as the godfather has to satisfy, on the one hand, the author and his immediate friends, and on the other, the actors, two classes of persons whose views and points of view, on such occasions, it is not very easy to reconcile. The cast of the piece was of unusual strength. It included Miss O'Neil, Charles Kemble, Charles Young, Macready, and Yates, who made his first appearance in London on this occasion. "Fredolpho " contained a great many highly poetical passages, but the importance of the principal parts was too nearly equal to satisfy all the distinguished actors who were to fill them! Kemble, Young, and Macready were all more or less dissatisfied ; Yates, I remember, was the only one who seemed at all contented with his *rôle*. A short time before my attendance at the first rehearsal, I received a letter of five closely written folio pages, conveying to me Maturin's wishes and suggestions on the subject, to which, as may be imagined, I found sufficient difficulty in securing attention. Indeed, but for the authority of Fawcett, who, as stage-manager, supported me throughout, I should have been compelled to throw up my office in despair. Nothing could be more friendly, and even affectionate, than the relations of Fawcett with the respective performers. He would not, however, allow himself to be trifled with ; and although he seemed to participate, in some degree, in the prejudices of the principal actors against the play, he did all he could to secure its success.

'As some set-off to the many contrarieties which I experienced in this troublesome affair, I must not omit to recall the gratification which it afforded me of forming an acquaintance, which ripened into intimacy, with several of the most distinguished actors of that day, more especially Charles Young and Macready. I also became acquainted, at the same time and by the same means, with Shiel, the Irish orator, who had just produced his play of " Evadne" on the same boards. Shiel was a brisk, impulsive little man, without the least spice, in private, of the almost frantic acerbity of manner which characterized the democrat of Penenden Heath and the House of Commons.

'But to return to my narrative. My experiences before the curtain had led me to regard Miss O'Neil as little below a goddess, so exquisite was her impersonation of Juliet and Belvidera; and it seemed impossible to my inexperience that she should be other than the most refined and intellectual of her sex. But, I cannot say that a personal acquaintance with her, formed on this occasion, tended greatly to confirm this impression. She had been obviously very imperfectly educated, and, what seemed to me, then, even more strange, appeared to possess little of the poetical taste and discrimination which her performances had led me to anticipate. I will not affirm that she might fairly be compared to Thackeray's 'Miss Fotheringay,' but there were many points of resemblance. This lady was cast for the principal part, but displayed little interest in it, and did not hesitate, some three weeks before the play was produced, to prophesy its failure.

It was little likely to succeed under such unfavourable conditions, for it was upon the
female character that the play mainly turned,
and, it failed accordingly. It would, however,
be unfair to attribute this catastrophe wholly
to a want of interest in the play on the part of
the principal personage, confirmed as her instincts had been by the judgment of other
performers. The immediate cause of its damnation was the exquisitely ridiculous manner
in which one of the inferior actors advanced up
the stage, with the deliberation of an under-
taker, and apprised the audience, with the most
stoical calmness, that his master was at tha
moment perishing in a snow-storm on the
mountains.

' The stolidity of this gentleman, under these
afflicting circumstances, and the sedateness
with which he delivered himself of the following harrowing ejaculation,

"My Lord! my Lord! the storm! He perishes!"
precipitated the audience into a fit of merriment from which it was found impossible to
recover them until, a gallant young officer,
having delivered up his sword to his more

successful antagonist, is slaughtered with it on the spot. This thoroughly un-English incident so revolted the audience as to convert their merriment into indignation, and to not another word would they listen. I had presented to Maturin's notice the danger of this situation; but neither Harris, the manager, nor Macready, who took the part of the assassin, appeared to think much of the objection, and the incident was allowed to remain. With the exception of Frederic Yates, who made an extremely effective part of Berthold, and Macready, always conscientious and thorough, little effort was made for the play, and its failure was irremediable. Maturin, the most impulsive and eccentric of Irishmen, and that is saying a great deal, bore his disappointment with some philosophy.

'He had another tragedy in the hands of Edmund Kean, but on this he could obtain no decision whatever. It was entitled " Osmyn," and is said to have been the most careful and effective of his dramatic compositions. I made many attempts to obtain its restitution, but in vain. On one occasion I attacked Kean before a large party, and dwelt upon the cruel injury which Maturin had sustained from his persistent disregard of the matter. Finally I obtained from him a promise that the MS. should be forthcoming if I would call in Clarges Street for it on the ensuing day. This, of course, I did, but was denied access to Mr. Kean, who was said to be too ill to see me. Beyond the satisfaction which I enjoyed at a later period of telling Mr. Kean what I thought of his conduct, I obtained no redress. Never did I witness so grievous an impersonation of vulgar dissipation as Edmund Kean presented when I last saw him. I dined more than once in his company, and the last time he was lying on a sofa so prostrated as to be unable, until he had taken stimulants, to raise himself up and join the company.'

'To return to Maturin. In private life he appears, apart from some harmless eccentricities, to have been all that could be desired. He married early a sister of the Bishop of Killaloe, with whom he lived on terms of the greatest harmony and affection. She was a Miss Henrietta Kingsbury, and was the granddaughter of that Dr. Kingsbury to whom Swift is stated to have uttered his last rational words.'

My father's editorship of the *New Monthly Magazine*, though of brief duration, was not to be to him wholly barren. In his search after novelty in the direction of poetry, his attention had been arrested by some verses introduced into the preface to a ' Life ' of Howard, the Philanthropist, by Mr. James Baldwin Brown, a young barrister, (the father, I may add, of the distinguished Independent minister of the same name). These lines, with which the biographer stated he had been favoured by a young Friend,. a member of the Society of Friends, Mr. J. H. Wiffen, residing at Woburn, in Bedfordshire, impressed my father as being of exceptional excellence, and led him to desire to know more of the writer.

CHAPTER VII.

IT is needful now to shift the scene of this drama to the little town of Woburn in Bedfordshire, than which, in its way, there is no one more attractive in all the midland counties. Slightly dull now, perhaps, but not so in the year 1819, when more than a hundred coaches passed through it daily, and the first night's resting-place for travellers posting northward from London on this road was usually the 'George' at Woburn. Down to the very entrance of the town had extended, by the improvements of successive generations of the princely house of Bedford, the almost garden-like precincts of the ducal demesne of Woburn Abbey. Temple, and rockwork, and ruin, embowered in ever-greens and overlooking ornamental lakes and islets, feed the eye with beauty in every direction, ensuring to the townspeople, free from arbitrary restriction, all that nature refined by art can present of what is health-giving and purifying to mind and body.

> ' Rich is that varied view, with woods around,
>   Seen from the seat within the shrubbery bound,
>   Where shines the distant lake ; and where appear,
>   From ruins bolting, unmolested deer.'

In the year 1819 there dwelt in this little town, carrying on the trade of an ironmonger, Elizabeth Wiffen, a widow, and a member of the Society of Friends. Her husband, John Wiffen, also a Friend, a man of much sensibility and refinement of nature, but of a somewhat lymphatic temperament, had died early, leaving her the heritage of a good name, some debts, and a family of five children. Elizabeth Wiffen was of an honourable pedigree in the Society of Friends, being the representative of one Miles Pattison, who in the year 1658, shortly after the foundation of the Society, in company with Mary Botham, Sarah Baker of Woburn, and some others, was committed to the common gaol of Bedford, and thence relegated to Bridewell, 'for reproving, in a Scriptural manner, for his evil life, the priest of Risely.'

This Mary Botham was an ancestress of Mary Howitt.

Nor was the faith of her forefathers lacking in Elizabeth Wiffen, as the following anecdote may serve to testify.

Towards the close of the last century an officer in the Navy, a member of an old English family, and a descendant of one of the most, indeed the most, prominent of the members of Parliament who sat on the trial of Charles I., paid a visit with his wife to Woburn on their way to the north. On one of their walks they were attracted to the little meeting-house which, so early as the days of George Fox, had been erected in a hamlet on the confines of the old wood of Aspley, near Woburn, known, from the occupants who in earlier times sought their food in the forest, by the euphonious designation of Hogstyend. Lieutenant B—— wore his uniform and hanger, as the custom was of that day, and no little must the dovecote have been fluttered by so uncongenial an apparition. Impressed by what they saw and heard, they were led to prolong their stay, to attend the meeting again, to make inquiry into the tenets and doctrines of the little flock. Gradually convinced that with his former profession, its ways and its wages, he had no longer anything to do, Lieutenant B—— resigned his commission, and with it a sum of prize-money which, with his new views, he did not feel free to receive ; and, with his wife, to the great displeasure of their family and connections, joined the Society of Friends. He took a cottage and a little land at Crawley, near Woburn, and there settled down, living a retired life, as did indeed the other members of the little community who resided more or less at a distance from each other, forgathering only at their weekly and monthly meetings.

The evening meal was just over at the widow Wiffen's one night at the close of the year, when my grandmother,—for such she was,—to the surprise of her children, bade them put up in a basket a supply of cold meat, bread, butter, and cheese, and a bottle of home-made wine, and announced that she was going to Crawley. It was done as she desired, and she started on her way, sure only that, from some cause which she could not fathom, it was then and there her duty to obey a strange impulse which prompted her to carry to the Friends at Crawley the materials for their evening meal. As she approached the house, after a dreary walk, her courage began to fail her. There was no personal intimacy between her and Mr. and Mrs. B——. They were in some sort in a superior position of life to her own, and she had no reason to suppose that a visit from her would be acceptable at such an hour, still less that they could require anything within her power to communicate. She hesitated, half resolved to return as she came, when she observed a light underneath the door, showing that the family had not retired to rest. She summoned courage, and knocked.

On being admitted, she found the Friends seated by the fire, with the table laid for supper, but no food upon it. 'I have come to take my supper with you,' she said, depositing her basket on the table. They looked at each other, and burst into tears. It subsequently transpired that their little capital had become gradually exhausted; one economy had succeeded another, until on that particular evening, so reduced had they become as to be without food or the means of procuring it. It appeared, on comparing notes, that at about the time the impression had presented itself to my grandmother to start from Woburn with their supper, they, under some corresponding impression, had deliberately prepared the table as usual for their evening meal, and were awaiting the issue.

As years wore on, this excellent woman became more and more the confidante, helper, and sustainer of those who needed comfort in the little town; and did a stranger fall ill at the 'George,' next door, or any other extraordinary catastrophe arise, it was she, as a matter of course, it seemed, who was summoned to deal with it. Her tall, upright, matronly figure, her placid smile, her calm, loving, yet irresistible firmness, her white hair and clear grey eyes, with the old-fashioned Quaker cap, snuff-coloured stuff dress, and high-quartered shoes, are, even yet, remembered with veneration in the pleasant neighbourhood in which were passed, uninterruptedly, almost eighty summers and winters of her well-spent life.

At the time to which my narrative is now to be taken up, Jeremiah Holmes Wiffen, her elder son, had established himself as master of a private school, for sons of members of the Society of Friends, in Leighton Street, in his native town, his youngest sister, Priscilla, keeping his house; while his mother, with the assistance of his younger brother Benjamin, was carrying on business as I have described, her eldest daughters, Mary and Sophia, residing with her, at the corner of Park Street opposite. The family, however, though separated, were not divided. When the duties of the day were over in both houses, the young members of the family used to meet in Leighton Street, to read and discuss new books when they could get them, or old ones over again when they could not, as was, perhaps, more frequently the case. The poets were the especial favourites. Cowper, Langhorne, Falconer, and Macpherson's 'Ossian,' of the old ; and Campbell and Rogers among the moderns. Both the brothers wrote poetry. The elder had, indeed, already taken part with two friends in a published volume of verse. Benjamin Wiffen had contented himself, hitherto, with a more limited circle of readers. The usher in the school, also a member of the Society of Friends, as in duty bound, wrote poetry also, in the style, I have heard, of Mr. Southey's striking, but irregular, epic of ' Thalaba,' and bore the soubriquet, in the circle, of ' Gian-Ben-Gian,' in consequence of the awe-inspiring character of his muse ! I do not know that the sisters wrote original verse, at least at that time, though one of them did later ; indeed, there would not appear to have been much opening for them ; but they copied a great deal into books, and were valuable members of the little coterie, as auditors, and for general purposes of criticism and commendation.

It was at one of these evening gatherings, in the spring of the year 1819, that Jeremiah Wiffen produced a letter which he had received from no less a personage than the editor of the *London New Monthly Maga-zine.*

The writer had been much gratified by the perusal of a poem by Mr. Wiffen, introduced into a recent life of Howard the Philanthropist, by Mr. Baldwin Brown, which had led him to desire to know something more of the productions of its author, and, if agreeable, of the author himself. Hearing that he resided in the country, the writer would esteem himself happy in the opportunity of rendering him any service in his power in relation to literary matters in London. That this communication gave much pleasure, and excited some little curiosity, was suitably responded to, and gave rise to further correspondence, will be readily imagined. My father and his correspondent were of about the same age, of similar literary tastes, and, in some sort, even of professional experiences. It was natural that they should soon become friends. The literary circles of that day, and public opinion generally, had been much divided over the domestic disquietudes of ' a certain noble poet ' and his lady. The correspondents were rejoiced to find, and to be made even more one in the knowledge, that they agreed on this important question. They were both Byronists.

In politics they were not in such entire accord. Mr. Wiffen, as became a son of the soil of Woburn, and the librarian that was to be to one of the Dukes of Bedford, was a steady supporter of 'the cause for which Hampden bled on the field, and Russell on the scaffold.' He had, as was natural, composed a poem on the latter event ; and was to have the honour, at a later period, of figuring,—as one of the judges, unfortunately,—in Sir George Hayter's well-known picture, painted for Woburn Abbey, of Lord Russell's trial. My father, on the other hand, was as staunch an advocate of 'social order against the anarchists,' and was vowed to the support of the 'Throne and the Altar.' Such were the grandiose phrases in which it was the custom, in that day, to express the difference in the opinions of those who hope and those who fear from political change. No embitterment, however, on the score of these political disagreements, arose between the two friends. It is not differences of opinion, but differences of feeling, that divide and estrange. It was not in the region of politics that their friendship originated or was to have its habitation.

The correspondence soon becomes intimate and animated. A lively interchange springs up of favourite books, new and old. Mr. Rogers's ' Human Life,' Crabbe's ' Poems,' and Mr. Peacock's ' Rhododaphne,' among the moderns ; and the Elizabethan and Jacobean poets, introduced by my father, and not hitherto much known in Friendly circles, among the older masters. Albums, not, however, known by that worldly name at Woburn, begin to pass to and fro ; and poetry is exchanged, original and selected. The London correspondent is, or professes to be, skilful in reading characters by the handwriting, and, to that end, it is needful that he should possess suitable specimens of the autographs of the sisters. Everybody writes in everybody else's book,—with one exception. The youngest sister declines to participate in these amicable reciprocities. She has no idea of having her character read through her handwriting, or by any other process. 'She is rather a haughty damsel,' explains the brother to his friend, when they meet in London a little later. Indeed, when the sisters are mentioned in the correspondence, it is as 'Mary,' 'Sophia,' and 'the Lady Priscilla,' that they are referred to.

But this young person has too important a part to play in this drama to be introduced at the end of an act.

CHAPTER VIII.

THE summer holidays arriving, and the boys dismissed to their homes, a visit to Woburn is proposed, and the invitation accepted. The visitor is expected to arrive to a late breakfast, but the coach is more rapid, or he more impatient, than had been anticipated. My father presents himself in Leighton Street from his inn rather earlier than he had been looked for, and is ushered into the wainscoted parlour just at the moment when the youngest sister of his friend, who declines to have her character read in her handwriting, enters the room by the opposite door from the garden, with a basket of roses for the adornment of the breakfast-table.

Priscilla Maden Wiffen had just completed

her twentieth year. She was rather above than under the middle height, and of a comely and gracious figure. ' What shoulders that child has !' the good-natured Duchess Georgina of Bedford, (who herself had very beautiful shoulders, and was a connoisseur therein) had observed to her mother on meeting them once in the park at Woburn,—a remark not lost on the little Quakeress.

' I have seen a lady, to-day, with the most beautiful hands I ever saw !' Sir Thomas Lawrence observed a few years later to Mr. Pickersgill the painter, after having seen her turning over some prints at Hurst and Robinson's print-shop in Pall Mall.

A forehead full and oval, a complexion of exquisite purity and delicacy of colour, large liquid blue eyes, light-brown hair, looking almost golden in the sunlight, as it escaped in little tendrils from the narrow frill of the Quaker cap, combined to give almost a Madonna-like expression to the face. It was, perhaps, that circumstance, rather than mere affectation, which led her young husband, a little later, to transform her second name of

Maden to Madonna, an euphemism whereat, in later days, when he had made unto himself unfriends, as will be disclosed hereafter, the profane made mock.

Extreme tenderness of sensibility had taught her, as necessary to her protection, a reserve and caution not naturally a part of her character, and of which nothing appeared on the surface.

' I never knew a person,' said a friend, (the late Miss Jewsbury, the elder), ' of so frank a manner with so much reserve.' The life within was nervous, the bodily temperament lymphatic, tremulously sensitive underneath, but with absolute and entire self-control.

' " Mistress of herself, though china fall,"

might she be counted upon to display herself in all circumstances.

' She had already fathomed the faith of her sect, probing it out for herself silently and solitarily, for she was of a more self-sustained nature than her elder sisters, and, though she had scarcely as yet owned it to herself, had found it wanting, — wanting, for her. She accepted the spirit of it with her whole being, and never deviated from her regard for it; but of the forms and formulas of its informalism her soul wearied as of a chain which she wondered should seem to sit so lightly on those around her,—whose needs were different. A miniature of her, painted soon after her marriage, and before she had discontinued wearing the Quaker cap, is in existence, and would, I am sure, be regarded as warranting me in describing her, at this time, as, in very truth, a highly attractive and beautiful young woman.'

This may, perhaps, be a fitting place at which to seek to give some idea of the person of my father at this period of his life.

He was in his twenty-third year; in stature rather above the middle height, and of slender figure. The forehead large and well-developed, with strongly marked eyebrows overhanging very expressive brown eyes; the hair profuse and silky, of a dark brown hue approaching to black. The features strongly marked and very distinct in individuality; the mouth rather large, but well cut, and full of expression; the complexion somewhat pallid, not to say sallow, and the face generally of a Southern character, as though he might have in his veins Spanish or French blood.

The features were of extreme mobility, yielding up immediately and irresistibly the secrets of the life within, in the most transparent manner, and which, whatever might be his other defects, rendered hypocrisy impossible to him. The temperament nervobilious, with, however, an intense virility and muscularity of nature lying underneath, to be developed and come to the surface later. He dressed with a somewhat careful indifference, and was certainly an interesting and prepossessing young man, especially to women, whose society he preferred to that of men, and whom he always treated with genuine deference and respect.

Such were the two young people,—the one in her twenty-first, the other in his twenty-third year,—now meeting in the wainscoted parlour, this bright summer morning.

> 'It was the time of roses—
> They plucked them as they passed.'

My father found himself at once, as he had

anticipated, amongst congenial friends; and much pleasant time, as may easily be believed, compressed into four days, the young people spent together.

There are events in life which, when we look back upon them, stand out with especial distinctness, like figures in a dream advancing ever to the front when all the rest is shadow. They seem impressed upon the memory, as it were, with a purpose, and they recur to it, at intervals, with a vividness for which there is nothing satisfactory to the reason to account. Such events will generally be found to represent, like wisdom in an apothegm, some principal or marked characteristic of the life 'writ up in hieroglyphic,' and to have had in them something in the nature of prophecy, faintly read later, and generally too late.

Such an event to one of the little party was a visit which the young people paid, among other excursions at this time, to a rustic cottage, or pleasure-house, in the Thornery of the Park of Woburn. A toy cot embowered in woods, in the centre of a

sequestered enclosure, wherein, when wearied
of the glory and grandeur of the great house,
the good-natured and beauty-loving Duchess
Georgina and a select party might pretend to
take repose in the fine summer weather, and
play at being simple, like Marie Antoinette at
the Trianon.   Entrance it had through rustic
doors into an elegant little hall, drawing-room,
dining-room, library, in one, painted in the
Italian style, with rustic fittings in Swiss
carvings, adorned with old china and cheerful
old chintz-covered settees.   A little library of
Arcadian poets and light meditative philosophy; 'Zimmerman on Solitude,' if that can
be called light, prominent among them, elegantly bound in green morocco, and not bearing signs of having been greatly read.   A
little passage through folding-doors, at the
back, opening upon a miniature picnic kitchen,
in a cave in the side of a little hill, with
vaulted roof and the sides covered with white
Wedgwood tiles bordered with ivy wreath;
covering also a French cooking-stove.   On
picturesque shelves and a mantelpiece, store
of Swiss wood-work, pails, spoons, baskets,

etc; on a long dresser, and in convenient closets, elegant dinner, tea, and dessert services of Wedgwood and Sèvres, and old German and Venetian glass-ware. Hard by, in a romantic nook, a fountain of water pouring into a large white marble shell.

All the elegancies and luxuries of life made to look simple. A baby house on a large scale, so unlike anything but a plaything, but practical withal, idealistically. So inconceivable for any serious uses of life, yet so suggestive of reality and something that might prospectively be attainable. The poetry of real life in an epigram! A little home so elegant that it must be all-satisfying; so simple that it could not be regarded as luxurious; so small that it must be economical.

So thought one of the young people who were visiting it this bright June afternoon; and often, as I have hinted, did it, and the day-dream arising out of it, stand out vividly before her in after-life, and preach its homily to her from the pulpit of experience. Very much the same train of thought was passing through thc mind of another of the party at the same time.

It was the epigraph to an important chapter in the lives of both,—an epitome of the scheme of life which they had in their own minds each pictured as their ideal. Whether they were to realize it; and, if realized, under what conditions, will be revealed in the course of this narrative.

After a delightful holiday, my father returned to town, to resume thc business of life, with hopes and aspirations and a stimulus to exertion such as he had never known before. Impetuous and impatient, ardently to desire and to stretch forth the hand to grasp or do, were with him one process; and he had been but a few days at home when he wrote to ask the youngest sister of his friend to be his wife, taking her brothers into his confidence a little later.

Here is the answer, which has survived the vicissitudes of sixty years, and with which, if not satisfied, he must have been very unreasonable, as perhaps sometimes he was.

‘ Woburn, June 17, 1819.

‘ ESTEEMED FRIEND,

‘ I fear I have caused you some disappointment by not answering your note the day on which
it was received ; but, believe me, it was not in my
power, even if I could have had half an hour's
solitude, and now I am totally at a loss what to say.
The oftener I read your note the more firmly I am
persuaded that it was written at a moment when
Feeling alone was in the ascendant. Reflect on the
short period of our acquaintance, and you must see
the impropriety of desiring so hasty a decision on a
subject of so much importance. Consider, also,
what my friends would think. If you insist on
requiring a definite answer, after only four days'
acquaintance, you must be sensible what that
answer must be. Pray excuse this hasty letter. I
have written unreservedly, as to a friend, and
believe me to remain,

‘ Yours sincerely,

‘ P. M. W.

‘ P.S.—I believe it is J.'s intention to write this
evening. M. S. and B. are well ; I am not altogether
so. I shall take care of the ring till you claim it.
Adieu.’

CHAPTER IX.

THE vicissitudes of my father's courtship, and incidentally the characters of the several parties concerned therein, are very fairly illustrated in the following correspondence. I have already allowed the young lady to speak for herself.

FROM MR. J. H. WIFFEN.

'Woburn, 6th mo., 24, 1819.

'MY DEAR ALARIC,

'From a dim, rainy, and melancholy morning I turn to the gladness which always springs up in my heart when writing to thee, and feel my little pinnace of thoughts and feelings fairly afloat. We received the parcel, and seized upon its contents with avidity. I leave the others to discharge their obligations. I have given thy messages to Mary, Sofia, and the Lady Priscilla. I thank thee for Bonaparte's picture. Pray was there a covert meaning in this gift? Was it in answer to my remarks on Reform? Crabbe I have read with subdued delight.   He will not be loved so much as those who present more pleasing pictures of human life ; but he will instruct more.   I like his sententiousness, and his mannerism is sometimes infinitely amusing. When I say I like, I mean to read, not to imitate. Thy last letter was such an one as pleases me.   It took cognizance of topics ; it answered inquiries ; it conversed,—it was, in fact, a systematic letter.   I send my poem ; I am gratified by thy allowing the dedication. . . .   "Annoy," I judge to be fashionable.   It is often in thy mouth.   I heard it more than once at our first interview, and have heard it at Woburn Abbey.   It is expressive.   I bide thy retaliation.   Farewell.

' Thy affectionate friend,

'J. H. WIFFEN.'

To Mr. J. H. WIFFEN.

'Robert Street, Brompton,

' July 29, 1819.

' MY DEAR FRIEND,

'The welcome packet from Woburn arrived yesterday.   You have seen, then, and are not displeased with the verses I addressed to your sister Priscilla.   It is even so.   At the risk then of incurring, perhaps, the loss of your friendship, I am now to avow to you how deeply I feel myself attached to her.   I will communicate with you at large on this subject later ; in the meantime I beg of you to keep my counsel,—at least, you and your brother Benjamin.   Please give my love to all, and believe me,

' Yours affectionately,

'A. A. WATTS.'

FROM MR. J. H. WIFFEN.

'Woburn, August 2, 1819.

'MY DEAR FRIEND,

'In speaking of thy beautiful verses to my sister, I spoke of them simply as a composition addressed to a sister of mine. Now listen to my words of prudence, my dear Alaric. Hastily, or even gradually, to be indulging prepossessions in the face of many obstacles, and to the endangering the peace of ourselves or others, a wise man will pause before doing. Do not misconstrue what I say into anything but my simple desire to preserve my friend happy. Regard us all in the light of friends; it is the counsel of sincerity and, I think, wisdom. I gave thy parcel to Cilla before I had read thy letter, but I should not have considered it "an impropriety" thy writing to her. I am not an advocate for the doctrine that we are never to write to girls, and that they are not to receive a letter, now and then, on casual subjects; but I think it will be well for thee to write nothing to our sister which she could be interested in concealing from another sister; and mind, my friend, not to be too generous to us. There is my sister Mary, who has had a clasp,—a snap,—what call you it?—sent her, fit for my Lady Duchess. "I can never use this," says she; "it is too expensive for me." By all means come and see us again soon. Mary and Priscilla send kind remembrances. Bion is in a merry case over thy letter to him, laughing like any hedge-pig.

'Thy affectionate friend,

'J. H. WIFFEN.'

FROM MR. B. B. WIFFEN.

' August 16, 1819.

' MY DEAR FRIEND,

'Thy letter to Jeremiah he is obliged, from indisposition, to request me to answer so as not to keep thee in anxious expectation. We are one; what passes in his mind is communicated unreservedly to me, and our sentiments on matters of personal interest are always in unison. We had no doubt that the heart had a share in the lines to Cilla, but how far, it was impossible for us to know, nor could we, with delicacy, precipitate an inquiry. You have misunderstood my brother in supposing him to hint a doubt of your qualities for becoming the guardian of our sister's happiness. So far from it, we sincerely believe, circumstances being favourable, that a person of thy heart and mind would be calculated to guard her present and ensure her future felicity. This is *our* candid opinion; for her own, as we have not mentioned the subject to her, thou canst perhaps be a better judge than we. There are, however, difficulties in the way of an engagement. There is a peremptory law in our society which expressly enjoins, that any person inclinable to marry out of the pale of our sect shall be under the censure, and oversight, visitings, remonstrances, etc., of the worthy elders of our Israel; and, finally, if the connection be persisted in, a process of excommunication issues. This law we,—I mean my brother and myself,—do not think should be a bar to the happiness of two individuals whose affections are centred in each other, and whose comfort and happiness in life are really dependent on union ; but it should prevent any precipitation of a *dénouement* which would involve us and our religious body in a protracted state of disquietude. We would request, therefore, that thou wouldst not write to Priscilla for the present, unless on casual subjects. From what I have said thou wilt be satisfied that our sentiments are entirely what thou wouldst wish. As for our mother's views, although she is a strict supporter of our religious doctrines and practices, I do not think she would oppose anything reasonable in which her daughter's happiness should be essentially concerned. My brother sends love.

'Thine sincerely,

'BENJAMIN B. WIFFEN.'

To MR. J. H. WIFFEN.

'Brompton, Sept. 7, 1819.

'MY DEAR FRIEND,

'As I have the offer of a frank, I take the opportunity of acknowledging your kind letter and Bion's. I have enclosed a few lines for Zilla, and shall write again in my next parcel ; meanwhile, allow me to observe that I see the propriety of most of your remarks, and shall endeavour to conform to your wishes. My desire of corresponding with your sister is natural, inasmuch as it is the only means of communicating I can possibly have with her. It is a privilege I enjoy with Mary, which may be extended to another sister without any breach of decorum. Full explanations you have a right to receive from me on various points; but I can speak better of these things than write about them. I am happy to believe that my desolate situation as to friends may be accepted, when you know all, as affording me an additional claim to your sympathy and friendship.

I shall borrow Crabbe's "Tales" for you, also "Don Juan." It is a most unprincipled performance; and we must henceforth give up all hopes of being able to defend Lord Byron's morality, or to regard him with respect. The exquisite talent displayed in it increases the measure of the offence.

' Ever affectionately yours,

' A. A. WATTS.'

TO MISS PRISCILLA WIFFEN.

' Brompton, April 13, 1820.

' MY DEAREST LOVE,

'I send you Coleridge's "Literary Life," written by himself. You will find much that will give you pleasure in it. The volumes contain much beautiful criticism, especially on Wordsworth, of whom I have recently taught myself to be a very great admirer. Coleridge, as well as Wordsworth, is ever most fervent in praise of our divine Milton. In Coleridge's volume of poetry are several pieces exquisitely tender and pathetic. I will bear in mind the book you wish to see of Hannah More, also Mrs. Tighe's "Psyche," and Bernard Barton. Of Lord Byron's works I have duplicate copies already devoted to thee. You said you should be

7—2

better if I were happy and well. In truth, I am suffering from the effects of disappointment, and annoyance of mind does not contribute to the renovation of health ; still, the anticipation of, I hope, our early happiness is very soothing. I am not avaricious, save in love, and in that I am also a prodigal; all I desire is a moderate competence, my wife, and my friend. I often think of that passage in Coleridge's "Life" in which he pourtrays the domestic comforts of a literary man, who makes literature his amusement only, and other matters his pursuit and particular occupation. When such reflections steal across my mind, how earnestly do I think of thee! I admit that I have been often unkind,—very unkind, and I reflect with pain upon it. Your generosity has not been lost upon me; and whenever I am again fretfully disposed I will remember it, and strive to be silent. Tell me, have you had any further conversation with your mother? and have you yet been *visited ?*

'I am, my dearest girl,

 'Most faithfully and affectionately yours,

   'ALARIC A. WATTS.'

  FROM MR. J. H. WIFFEN.

    'Woburn, May 26, 1820.

'MY DEAR ALARIC,

 'I should have been more happy if I sat down to write to thee under more fortunate circumstances. To say that I regret the turn things have taken here is to express what I feel very faintly. I gave thy letter to my mother on Sunday morning; she showed me the contents, and I expressed to her, undisguisedly, that I should be very glad to have thee for a relation, and that I was of opinion that my sister would be happy in such an union. My mother read the answer she had *then* written, and I was delighted with the neutral situation in which she consented to stand. What was my chagrin when, on returning home late on Tuesday, she called me aside and read me the letter thou hast since received! It seems that Mary thought a more decided answer should be given. When once an objection is started in such a case, it is ten to one that others present themselves. My mother, I know, was not fully satisfied with the letter she sent, but it went; and I knocked up the postmaster, and got back the letter of congratulation, which, under the circumstances, would have had an air of mockery. I would fain, if I could, administer consolation; and if thou art willing for a time to make some sacrifices to conciliate my mother, by suspending thy correspondence with my sister, I shall still have considerable hopes that time and events may alter her opinion. I will gently hint that it will be prudent to abstain in future from any reflections on Methodists and Missions! I will not say that the occasional acerbity of thy remarks on them may not have instilled doubts into the minds of my sisters as to thy religious sentiments! Methodists are collectively a good people, and Missions are good things; and religion may seem to be aimed at even when we blame only individuals. Farewell.

'Thy affectionate friend,

'J. H. WIFFEN.'

FROM MR. J. H. WIFFEN.

'Woburn, June 8, 1820.

'MY DEAR ALARIC,

'I am persuaded that thy having written to my mother has done good. This morning she summoned me into the Tusculum,—thou wilt remember this arbour in her garden,—and gave me thy letter; and as Mary and Priscilla were walking close by, she desired me to call them up also. I then read the letter aloud, and she said she should give thee an interview, represented to Priscilla that the affair was in her own hands, but added, that *she* could not consent to forfeit *her* membership, and must necessarily lay the matter before the monthly meeting next fourth day. I know too well the force of her religious scruples to believe that anything will induce her to act otherwise; and, as Cilla seems fixed in her decision, it must be my care to fortify her against these visits of the meeting, which she so much dreads, and which will be continued, when once begun, either till she abandons the connection, or till it issues in marriage. Whether or not thy interview with my mother will have any effect in preventing this cannot be foreseen; but Cilla seems calmer now that my mother has shown her the letter of invitation down, and now that the first emotions of my mother are somewhat subsided. Thy first care on coming down must be to see my mother, and *to see her first*. I have a comfortable persuasion that if thou doest this, entering into explanations with Mary and Benjamin, and if nothing is left to corrode on the mind of anyone, and if thou becomest the conqueror of thyself so as to temper somewhat,—thou wilt bear it,—of thy natural haughtiness—I say I have a comfortable hope that we shall go on better than we once anticipated. With kind love, in which Priscilla and the rest unite.

'I am, thy affectionate friend,

'J. H. WIFFEN.'

To MISS PRISCILLA WIFFEN.

'Brompton, Wednesday.

'MY DEAREST LOVE,

'You will, I fear, have been disappointed at not having heard ere this. Pray forgive my apparent neglect. I am better, but still unwell. I feel depressed and wretched, I know not why; the vexations of life never disturbed me so much as they have done lately. I will procure for you, dear, Dr. Chalmers. I send you Hannah More, and the "Mysteries of Udolpho;" also a book which has greatly pleased me, "The Sketch Book," by Geoffrey Crayon. The author I chanced to meet once at a friend of Roscoe's, at Liverpool. He is an exceedingly interesting and gentlemanlike young man. His name is Washington Irving. Pray read an essay called "The Wife"! "The Broken Heart," "The Art of Bookmaking," "The Country Church," and "The Widow and her Son," are also very spirited productions.

'I dined on Friday with Croly and his Helen. She seems very amiable, and clever without display, and appears to think her husband glorious Apollo himself. It must be admitted that he is a man of real genius. I was much pleased at being able to tell her of the opinion I had heard Lord Strangford express of " The Angel of the World." On Tuesday I was both at the play and the opera. To the former, because I had an account to give of the new actress ; to the latter, to see the King. It was impossible for anyone to be better received.

'I am, your affectionately attached

'A.'

To Miss Priscilla Wiffen.

'Brompton, Tuesday.

'I write to-day, my dear love, to say that on Saturday, by the Leeds coach, I shall transport myself, and be certainly transported when I get there, to Woburn. I will stop at Leighton Street ; but should the Leeds be full, I will try the Telegraph and Defiance. Be sure of seeing me on that evening. After I have been to Woburn I shall change my abode. I cannot, for good reasons, take a house for a twelvemonth, or a year and a half, so I fear we must abide in apartments at first. I have met with some in the house of a most respectable pair, without children, where there is, or rather will be, no one beside ourselves. I have three rooms, somewhat small, but very pretty, a drawing-room, bedroom, and study. The house is small, but most pleasantly situated just in the King's Road. Here

we shall be most happy—shall we not ?—with our
books, and such occupations and amusements as
are entirely within ourselves. I calculate upon
being obliged to pass the greater part of the day
from you about three times a week; on the other
days I shall be at your disposal. You must not, as
poor Mrs. Pringle is, be jealous of books; for I must
be much occupied this way, and at present read
more than I write. But we will talk much that is
delightful over, when your hand is once more clasped
in mine. As I said before, love, I am, and shall be,
somewhat encumbered for the first eighteen months,
after which my income will, without much exertion,
be at least £300 a year; but payment of a certain
sum out of this, at present, reduces it to a little
above £200, which, however, with economy, will do
very well for us, whose wants are not exorbitant in
anything but love. . . .

'Ever, my dearest, your most affectionate

'A.'

To Miss Priscilla Wiffen.

'Brompton, Tuesday.

'My dearest Zillah,

'I write a few lines to-day, at the hazard of
their arriving before you set out for Leighton.
How happy it makes me to revert to the delightful
moments we passed together during our late happy
fortnight! I was much disappointed at not receiving a few lines to-day. I am so jealous of
every occupation that interferes with our correspondence, that, I protest, I cannot accept, *too often*,
the presence of company as an excuse. . . .

'I saw Charles Lamb yesterday. You would scarcely believe that he is himself the author of the amusing paper in opposition to his own account of Christ's Hospital. I spent this evening with Procter, and a most interesting discussion we had on the merits of our favourite Elizabethans. It is impossible not to be pleased with Procter; he is so gentle and unassuming. His tragedy is just put in rehearsal; it is far superior to mine, both in interest and execution. As for Croly's, mine has certainly more general interest than his, though the language is inferior, as you may naturally expect. But I can do very much better than I have ever yet done.

'I fear that with your " friendly " prejudices you might be inclined to regard my want of success in this particular description of composition with " composure and magnanimity," as Lord Byron has it. By the way, I really begin to suspect Lord Byron to be an absolute power of evil incarnate. He has sent home for publication some compositions absolutely blasphemous. He and Shelley are " magnificent monsters." Does not this letter contain too much incident, and too little sentiment? I fear it does; but this is merely accidental. It is always infinitely more gratifying to talk of what is nearest my heart, than the mere commonplace occurrences that pass through the memory.

'Ever my dearest Zillah's most affectionate

' ALARIC.'

CHAPTER X.

On relinquishing the editorship of the *New Monthly Magazine*, my father associated himself with Mr. William Jerdan, the editor and part-proprietor, with the Longmans, of the *Literary Gazette*, for which he wrote pretty regularly during the following three years. The *Literary Gazette* was the earliest newspaper devoted to the interests of literature and the fine arts that made any impression upon the public. In it, for the first time, were introduced reports of the proceedings of the learned and scientific societies; and by it, also for the first time I think in the newspaper press, note was taken of foreign books and matters of literary and artistic interest abroad. It was in the *Literary Gazette*, as will be remembered, that first appeared the poems of Miss Landon, 'L. E. L.;' and no doubt it was to the discrimination of Mr. Jerdan that we are indebted for the poetry so full of tenderness and spontaneity of her,

> ' Whose was the hand that played for many a year
> Love's silver phrase for England.' *

Jerdan was a man of genuine *bonhomie*, and an able and judicious critic.   In his hands the *Literary Gazette* was conducted in an independent and liberal spirit, unless, perhaps, occasionally, when politics, religious or otherwise, intervened.   There was a powerful clerical pen affected to its service in these days much concerned with the interests of 'the Throne and the Altar,' and very severe in consequence, occasionally, upon ' radicals ' and ' atheists.' But, with all its defects, there is no doubt that the popularization of literature and art in those days was sensibly furthered by the *Literary Gazette.*

Of Mr. Jerdan's intercourse with my father, writing some five-and-thirty years afterwards, he speaks in his ' Autobiography ' in the following terms :

* Mrs. Barrett Browning, ' Lines on L. E. L.'

'Among my earlier coadjutors and friends in the *Literary Gazette* was Mr. Alaric A. Watts, from whom I received many valuable contributions in prose and verse. With my friend, Alaric Watts, I carried on, during many years, an intimate literary intercourse, always benefited by his assistance, and occasionally still more obliged to him for acting in the early days of the *Literary Gazette* as my lieutenant when temporarily absent. He was exceedingly well read, cultivated in taste, superior in talent, and laborious in application. In everything I found him straightforward and honourable. If a little warm sometimes when we happened to differ in opinion, I will venture to record it to the credit of both, that beyond asserting our own convictions of what was due to truth in criticism, we never contravened each other for an hour. In the retrospect of life, there are too often changes to regret more distressing to the mind than the most affecting losses. The latter are inevitable, the conditions of existence; the former are caused by ourselves. Between Alaric Watts and myself no such event ever occurred to be lamented now.'

'Among the contributions,' continues Mr. Jerdan, 'to which I have referred, was a series of articles pointing out the plagiarisms of Lord Byron, which created a considerable sensation at the time.   The French literary journals took it up, and a furious contest ensued.'

I should have hardly ventured to revive the recollection of these ephemeral *criticunculæ*, if they had not had the effect of bringing my father's name prominently before the public for the first time,—he was then in his twenty-fifth year.   They would probably have attracted little attention but for the condition of public feeling, at the time, as respects Lord Byron, arising out of the recent publication of 'Don Juan,' which had greatly revolted the sentiment of the age.   This revulsion of feeling may be worth a moment's attention.

The great mass of the reading public, without much means of information as to the facts, had, up to that time, sided with 'my lord' in his differences with 'my lady.'   The age was not as discriminative of human nature and the consistency of its inconsistencies as is the cultivated society of to-day.   It was impossible for it to believe that the great poet could be other than a man of noble and generous nature, —as he was ; or that a man of such a nature could, in some obscure ignoble property of a very complex organism, behave unworthily to his wife—as he could. They were content to refer the differences between them to an inability on the part of the lady, not absolutely culpable, but unfortunate, to comprehend and make allowance for the venial aberrations of the poetic temperament. The publication of ' Don Juan ' presented to such persons a new and startling aspect of things. It showed that there was a side of this magnificent human being, never before disclosed to them, that was wholly out of harmony with the impressions of his character which they had been led to form from the noble vein of sentiment displayed in his writings ; and which was, moreover, quite consistent with recent rumours floating about to his prejudice. From this revulsion of public feeling he was never, during his lifetime, wholly to recover. It affected for a time, unreasonably enough as it would seem, his reputation as a poet.   Contemporary public opinion is rarely logical, and runs much in extremes; and it was not, perhaps, after all, so wholly unjust that, having appealed so largely as his poetry had done to feeling and personal sympathy, by personal antipathy and feeling it was now to be judged.   The public had a sort of feeling, perhaps, that it had been rather taken in, and this it is rarely ready immediately to forgive.

My father was ardent and impressionable, and was neither of an age nor a temperament to hold abstract opinions.   He was always on one side or the other; and among the hosts of insignificant persons, forming by a certain independence and individuality of character centres of little circles of their own, Lord Byron had had, up to this time, no more enthusiastic devotee and partizan than this young man who was now presuming to assail his poetical reputation.

During the period of ingenuous enthusiasm from which he was now emerging, under these influences, my father had projected and partly completed a work, the original plan of which is now before me, in which he had designed to

do for Lord Byron what had been done for
Pope, Spenser and Milton by the two Wartons,
and Tod. In dealing with each poem, its
subject, origin, structure, and general qualities
and characteristics, space was to be reserved
for the imitations and coincidences in it,
having affinity with passages in the works of
other writers. Jerdan, to whom the work or plan
of it had been submitted, had seen, at a glance,
that very little public interest would be likely
to attach to ' An Essay on the use of Alliteration by Lord Byron ;' ' Remarks on the Octo-
Syllabic Verse, and its superiority for rapid
narrative, as illustrated in Lord Byron's employment of it ;' or ' On the Blank Verse of
Tragedy . in relation to Manfred.' On the
other hand, to have its attention directed to
the similarity in character between the Giaour
and the Schedoni of Mrs. Radcliffe's powerful
romance, the Italian ; between Manfred and
Marlow's Faustus, and Schiller's Moor ; or
between Gulnare and her action in the 'Corsair,'
and the Oberon of Wieland, then recently
translated by Mr. Sotheby, might be expected
to possess for the public a certain interest.

Still more so any 'Imitations and Coincidences' in phrases or isolated passages made apparent by placing the two in juxtaposition.   He accordingly advised my father to disembowel his production, and, casting his criticisms to the winds, or reserving them for future use, to concentrate the 'Imitations and Coincidences' into a series of papers for the *Literary Gazette.* 'Some natural tears he shed,' but he allowed himself to be persuaded.

These papers attracted, mainly I think from the circumstances of the moment, far more attention than they deserved.   Lord Byron condescended to refer to them in his letters; and it is possibly to them that we are indebted for his aphorism that a 'Poet had better borrow anything, except money, than the thoughts of another.   They are sure to be reclaimed.'   The memory of them survived until the publication by Murray of the library edition of Lord Byron's Poems in 1832, wherein a paragraph is devoted by the editor to them.   'These papers,' he remarks, 'are understood to have proceeded from no less a pen than that of Mr. Alaric A. Watts.'   He had omitted to observe that they were avowedly written by my father, whose name they bore. 'I suffered Jerdan,' my father says, in a letter written at the time to Miss Wiffen, 'to give my name to these extracts from my Byron book, because anonymous attacks are cowardly. Lord Byron has never consulted the feelings of other people ; and the subject is one of legitimate public criticism.'

One or two examples of these illustrations may have an interest to collectors of *variorum* notes. A perusal of the whole would probably dispose the judicious reader to adopt the words of Campbell the poet, in relation to a charge advanced against Milton of plagiarizing from Drummond. 'There is no debt,' Campbell elegantly remarks, 'on the part of Milton to the poet of Hawthornden which the former could be in the least impoverished by returning.'

Byron and Madame de Staël.

'Man's love is of man's life a thing apart,
  'Tis woman's whole existence; man may range
The court, camp, church, the vessel and the mart,
  Sword, gown, gain, glory, offer in exchange

Pride, fame, ambition, to fill up his heart,
And few there are whom these cannot estrange:
Men have all these resources; we but one,
To love again—and be again undone.'

Don Juan, c. i., s. 194.

'Que les hommes sont heureux d'aller à la guerre,
d'exposer leur vie, de se livrer a l'enthousiasme de
l'honneur et du danger. Mais il n'y a rien au
dehors qui soulage les femmes.'

Corinne, vol. iii., p. 264.

Byron and Voltaire.

'Commanding, aiding, animating all,
Cheer's Lara's voice and waves or strikes his steel,
Inspiring hope himself has ceased to feel.'

Lara, 1113.

'Il s'excite, il s'empresse, il inspire aux soldats
Cet espoir généreux que lui-méme il n'a pas.'

Henriade.

Byron and Sir William Jones.

'I saw thee weep—the big bright tear
Came o'er that eye of blue,
And then methought it did appear
A violet dropping dew.'

'Their similes are very just and striking; that, for
instance, of the blue eyes of a woman bathed in
tears, to a violet dropping dew.'

Essay on the Poetry of the Arabians.

BYRON AND COLONEL TITUS.

'Shall we who struck the lion down,
  Pay the wolf homage ?'
> *Childe Harold*, c. iv.

'Shall we who would not suffer the lion to invade
us, tamely stand to be devoured by the wolf ?'
> *Killing no Murder.*

BYRON AND PROFESSOR WILSON.

'She walks the waters like a thing of life.'

'She sailed amidst the loveliness
  Like a thing of heart and mind.'
> WILSON.

BYRON AND WALLER.

'So the struck eagle stretched upon the plain,
No more through rolling clouds to soar again,
Viewed his own feather on the fatal dart,
And winged the shaft that quivered in his heart.'
> *English Bards.*

'That eagle's fate and mine are one,
  Who, on the shaft that made him die,
Espied a feather of his own,
  Wherewith he wont to fly so high.'
> *Poems*, vol. ii., p. 29.

BYRON AND YOUNG.

'We gaze and turn away, we know not where,
Dazzled and drunk with beauty.'
> *Childe Harold*, c. iv., 50.

> ' On which the dazzled eye can find no rest,
>   But drunk with beauty, wanders up and down.'
>   *Revenge*, Act v., s. 2.

Before dismissing these literary *curios*, I may refer to one of a different description published by my father in the *Literary Gazette*, 1820, and never by him reprinted. It was a copy of verses entitled 'The Siege of Belgrade,' written evidently as a vehicle for introducing some curious notes, accumulated in the course of his readings, on ' Alliteration in Poetry.' The lines were arranged alphabetically, from A to Z, and every word in each line began with the same letter thus :

> ' An Austrian army, artfully arrayed,
>   Boldly by battery besieged Belgrade ;
>   Cossack commanders cannonading come,
>   Dealing destruction's devastating doom.'

These verses having been published many years after, in a London magazine, with somebody else's inititals, I am induced now to claim them for their writer for the little they are worth.

CHAPTER XI.

WHETHER, at the time my father made to his friend's sister the handsome offer recorded in the eighth chapter of this narrative, he had formulated any definite idea how he was to maintain her if she were to accept it, I hardly like to inquire. He had relinquished his only certain source of income, the editorship of the *New Monthly Magazine*, from the commencement of that very month of June, 1819; though, except as respects the element of certainty, I do not know that he had made any serious sacrifice in so doing. He had, as before set forth, established, in lieu of it, an intimate connection with the rising literary weekly journal,—the *Literary Gazette*,—of Mr. Jerdan. He wrote also for the *Gentleman's Magazine* under the editorship of Mr. Bowyer Nichols, and possibly, I think, now and then for *Blackwood*. But such work was in its nature more or less intermittent and precarious. A casual income is not without a certain affinity with no income at all. As honest Gwyllym says : ' Acciduity is cousin-german to nothing.' In possibilities he may have been richer. He had, for example, a volume of poetry ready for the press. He had, moreover, projected a tragedy, and had, indeed, proceeded so far as to have written several poetical passages to be mortised into it. He had made some way with a ' Biography of the Living Poets,' accompanied by specimens and critical notes ; and he had made collections, and was carefully watching contemporary poetical literature for a volume or two of selections from the fugitive poetry of the day, after the example of 'Dodsley's Specimens' and Southey's ' Anthology.' From these works, when completed and happily disposed of to an enterprising publisher, some money might, sometime, possibly be expected.

But with all these resources, present and possible, qualified, perhaps, by a little debt, he was, it may be feared, not greatly removed in condition from that of the young engraver of whom he used to tell, in later days, who came once to confide to him that he was going to be married. 'Married, my good fellow!' said he ; 'why, what have you got to be married upon?' 'Well, sir, you know, (as who should say, 'surely you have not forgotten,') 'there is the plate for Mrs. Watts' book.' It was a vignette for which, when he had completed it, he was to receive fifteen guineas.

But Providence,—or Fors, if the reader so prefer,—and the prudence of the lady were, the one providing an opening for him, and the other a protection against his own impetuosity in the interim, as Providence, (or Fors aforesaid), will often be found to do, and permit the wisdom of others to do for us, where, though the will be impatient, the way along which it is directing us is substantially right.

On the 5th of this very month of June, 1819, 'the Nobility, Gentry, and Patrons of the Fine Arts in England, and the other countries of Europe and America,' were advised by notices in the leading journals, that 'Hurst,

Robinson and Company had succeeded the late Messrs. Boydell, and had entered into possession of their immense and valuable stock of engravings, at No. 90, Cheapside.'

Mr. Joseph Ogle Robinson, the junior but more active partner in the great house of Hurst, Robinson and Company, which, at one time, bade fair to the indiscriminating eye, by the magnitude of its enterprises and apparent extent of its resources, to compete on something like equal terms with the Murrays and Longmans of the day, had been a bookseller at Leeds. There, in partnership with his sister, he had carried on a prosperous business, kept the public library, had his newspaper, the great ambition of a country bookseller, and maintained a lively competition with Mr. Baines for the custom of that division of the county. Of a sanguine and ambitious spirit, and dissatisfied with the limited sphere for his activity afforded by a country town, he came to London, and, associating himself with Mr. Thomas Hurst, brother to one of the then partners in Longman's house, purchased, in the year 1819, as before set forth, the printselling business of the Boydells. This concern, by the taste and liberality of Mr. Alderman Boydell, the founder, about the middle of the last century, had acquired not only a European reputation in the trade, but an honourable place of its own in the history of the progress of the Fine Arts in this country. It is still represented at No. 6, Pall Mall, where Messrs. Hurst and Robinson, in 1821, established a West End branch, by Messrs. Henry Graves and Son, the surviving representatives of the house of Moon, Boys, and Graves, which succeeded, and was indeed founded on, the print-selling business of Hurst and Robinson.

The firm did not, however, confine themselves to the publication and sale of works of art. They speedily developed, through the enterprise of Mr. Robinson, a valuable connection as booksellers and publishers. A fair proportion of the successful books of that day were issued from No. 90, Cheapside. Among them, I remember some of the novels of Maturin, the early poems of L. E. L., the famous ' Cook's Oracle ' of Dr. Kitchener ; and more important than all, the Waverley Novels of Sir Walter Scott.

Mr. Robinson was a kind-hearted and liberal-spirited man, and of a gentlemanlike and handsome exterior. He retained, however, some Yorkshire peculiarities, and was no other than the silent person who astonished Coleridge, at a dinner of intellectuals, by opening his mouth for the first and only time in eulogy of a dish of potatoes with the pregnant utterance, ' Them's the jockies for me.'

With Mr. Robinson my father struck up an acquaintance, arising, probably, out of occasional visits in Cheapside when reviewing works of art for the *Literary Gazette,* which ripened into something approaching to friendship. The publisher soon acquired confidence in the sound judgment and quick instinct in matters of literature and art, of the young writer, and would sometimes consult him on works offered for publication to the firm, generally, I believe, with satisfactory results. In return for good offices of this nature, the worthy publisher would respond by gifts of books an engravings, and now and then some little literary work such as a bookselling firm can often throw in the way of a young author, and perhaps, occasionally, by a little friendly accommodation in the shape of money. There is a letter of the young man's extant requesting some friendly help of this kind, in relation to an overdue bill, in which he explains with much innocent periphrasis the nature of the transaction of renewing such a security, which must, I imagine, rather have tickled the worthy bookseller, who, as became more universally known later, was perfectly conversant with that operation.

Of one of these literary enterprises, prematurely cut off by adverse criticism, a word may here be said, if only as a warning to literary aspirants doing job-work. Mr. Robinson, who was rather partial to speculative investments, and made sometimes very wonderful purchases indeed, had bought the worn-out plates of a series of portraits by Kneller of the distinguished Whig statesmen and others who composed the Kit Kat Club, with collections for supplying literary notices of them from a printseller dealing in oddities, named Caulfield, for a very small sum. To have the plates touched, the letterpress arranged, and the work issued in imperial quarto at four guineas, was a happy and natural conception; and Mr. Robinson applied to his young friend to revise Mr. Caulfield's letterpress. This he readily did, giving more attention, it is to be feared, to the rectification of its style, than the verification of its dates and its details.

It was certainly not very easy to give an interest to the portraits of these 'round-faced peers, as like each other as eggs to eggs, looking out from the periwigs of Kneller,' as Macaulay somewhere describes them; and the young editor proposed, as a happy expedient, 'plenty of letterpress' between each, in order that the reader might have time to purge his eyes of their monotonous similarity. But Mr. Robinson knew his customers better. He knew that the book was one which nobody would dream of reading, but which everybody would agree that no gentleman's library would be complete without. An edition of four hundred copies was produced at a cost, including editor £70, of £1 18s. a copy, leaving a handsome margin for profit at the selling price of four guineas. The work was a signal success, gentlemen's libraries coming forth to acquire it in great force, and copies going off day by day, as the worthy publisher gleefully expressed it, 'like penny rolls.' The impression was well-nigh exhausted, when an untimely estop was put upon all this prosperity by an article in the *Quarterly* which, possessing naturally no sympathy with Whig statesmen and works devoted to their glorification, exposed its errors, which were probably not few, denounced it as a catchpenny, as it certainly was, and gentlemen's libraries sought it no more. The editor, anonymous though he was, felt somewhat discomfited at this reverse, but was reassured by his publisher, who bore it with entire equanimity. 'It may be gratifying to you to know,' he says in a letter written a little later, 'that by this K. K. Club the publishers have made a profit of £500.'

The confidence engendered by this acquaintance with the prosperous publisher, the success of the papers in the *Literary Gazette*, and an opportune engagement to succeed Mr. Alexander Stephens in the editorship of the 'Annual Biography,' a necrological work, though one might not from the title so imagine, and which, as some distinguished persons die every year, might be supposed to possess a certain element of permanence,—all combined to encourage his impatience to abridge the period of his courtship and take to himself his wife. It was very easy for him to persuade himself, and not, perhaps, very difficult to persuade her, that the anxiety and suspense of a protracted engagement was the only thing standing in the way of his various literary projects, which required only the peace and quiet of domestic life for their realization.

He had very early, as will have been seen, taken the two brothers into his confidence and counsels, and had received from their frank and ingenuous natures all the encouragement which he could reasonably have expected. Their good offices and discretion aided him greatly in removing the natural objections of their mother to her daughter's marriage ' out of the Society,' in Friends' eyes, a grievous *mésalliance*, and involving on all concerned, and not making due submission, the awful penalty of 'disownment.' She was, however, as will have been seen, a large-hearted woman. She knew well that there were needs in her youngest daughter's nature, intellectual, emotional, and imaginative, not very easily to be answered by the average 'young man Friend' of that day. That the result of the contemplated union would be a training and life-discipline of care and anxiety, the uncertain position and impetuous character, already sufficiently disclosed, of her proposed son-in-law could leave her in no doubt; but that character was wedded to an active and energetic nature, and a tender and generous heart. Her own life had been one of care, but, at the same time, of entire domestic harmony and felicity; and, on the whole, she was content, if not satisfied. Her instincts did not deceive her. Fifty years afterwards, her daughter, then in her turn a widow, speaking to a dear friend, expressed herself in the following words: They were accom-

'panied, says the friend, the late Miss Loaden, in the letter in which they were subsequently quite casually communicated to her family, ' by an expression of rapture on the countenance such as I cannot forget.'   ' My life,' she said, ' has not been a prosperous one,—far from it,—but it has been a banquet of love.'

My parents were married at the church of Woburn, by the Rev. John Parry, on the 16th September, 1821, and took up their residence at No. 4, Beaufort Terrace, Chelsea, where my father had lodgings, and had made the best arrangements at his command for the reception of his young bride.

A few final words respecting the circle at Woburn may be permitted before parting with it in this narrative.

The elder of the two brothers, Jeremiah Holmes Wiffen, continued to devote himself, as leisure served, to literature and literary studies.   In addition to some volumes of miscellaneous verse, he produced, from the Spanish, a translation of the poems of Garcilasso de la Vega, surnamed the ' Prince of Castilian verse,' and a version, in the Spenserian stanza, of the ' Jerusalem Delivered ' of Tasso, each with a well-digested biography.

In the year 1823, the attention of John, the sixth Duke of Bedford, having been directed by Mr. Rogers, the poet, to the young writer, he was led to seek him out, and soon after to offer, or rather create for him, the post of librarian at Woburn Abbey. In this congenial situation he passed a life of singular ease and tranquillity. He married Mary Whitehead, of Nottingham, a member of the Society of Friends, and left three daughters.

The younger brother, Benjamin Barron Wiffen, though not without his own literary tastes and aspirations, was of a shy and diffident nature. He was content, or from duty so compelled himself, to remain at home and assist his mother in the business she was carrying on at Woburn ; and it was largely owing to his sagacity and fidelity that she was enabled to pay her husband's debts and retire on a competency. On withdrawing from business he reverted to poetry, and a long poem, which he entitled ' The Quaker Squire,' bears testimony to his love of nature

and human nature, and his ability to delineate
both. He is, however, more particularly remembered in connection with the labours to
which he devoted, with unwearied assiduity,
acuteness, and enthusiasm, the later years of
his life, in the discovery and reproduction, in
concert with his friend Senor Don Luis de
Usoz y Rio, of the works of the Spanish Reformers of the sixteenth century. Any further
information desired respecting 'The Brothers
Wiffen' will be found in a work bearing that
title, by Mr. Samuel Rowles Pattison and
Miss Wiffen. It contains the poem, 'The
Quaker Squire,' to which I have referred.
'The Bibliotheca Wiffeniana' of Dr. Edward
Böhmer, of Strassburg University, may also
be referred to in this connection.

CHAPTER XII.

THE first communication that met my mother
on her arrival at her new home, was her 'bill
of divorcement' from the Society of Friends,
wherein it was signified to her, with all that
pretermission of superfluous civility of which
the Society has acquired the happy art by two
centuries of 'plainness of speech,' that she
stood disowned from further membership.
Her husband was highly incensed at this.
'Not,' he would say, 'at the thing itself, but
at the way in which it was done.' In this,
possibly, he deceived himself. The way in
which a thing is done never greatly disturbs
us, if the thing itself does not. The truth is,
perhaps, that it brought home to him prac-

tically, for the first time, the responsibility
he had assumed in introducing this young
Quakeress into a sphere of life so different in
many respects, and so inferior as regards the
best of them, from that in which she had been
brought up.   Nor was she wholly indifferent to
her excommunication ; but she had counted the
cost with more forethought than he had, and
knew that she had now to look forward, and
not back.   The immediate present, ' honey-
moon ' though it was, was not without some un-
foreseen perplexities,—sufficient, at all events,
to occupy the moment.   To say truth, she
found the little establishment over which she
was called upon to preside, more deficient in
many ways than, even with her simple habits
of life and desires, she had been prepared to
anticipate ; and I fear that her early experiences of married life, like the early experiences
of most women, if they will admit it to themselves, (they never will to others), were not
without their element of disappointment.   It
occurred to her more than once, at this season,
that some of the elegant utilities wasting their
usefulness on the desert air in the cottage at

the Thornery in Woburn Park, would be very welcome additions to her domestic properties. If, however, needful conveniences were sometimes found to be wanting, there was less lack of luxuries, or what she might be disposed so to regard. There were valuable books, for example, rare editions of the Jacobean and Carolean poets, with old engravings interleaved, and bound conformably. Costly engravings in russia-leather portfolios, the larger and more precious in tin cylinders, to preserve them from the dust ; and the silver, sometimes inconveniently deficient at the tea-table, present in the less utilitarian form of handsome mountings and fittings to costly flutes on the chimney-piece. These things, most of them not absolutely purchased with 'coinéd money,'— that he would probably have admitted to himself to be extravagant,—but taken 'on account' of job-work done for the publishers, the money itself to be replaced, at some future time, out of fresh work, if replaced ever. This inharmonious combination of absence of needful conveniences and superfluity of luxuries was something quite new to her, and a little startling.　But it was a marked characteristic of the life to which she had wedded herself, and an important factor in its future, and therefore not as insignificant as it might seem to this history.

Her husband was not in the least aware of these deficiencies.　He wanted no society; nor did it probably much occur to him that she might desire it, or the conveniences necessary to the enjoyment of it.

'She for him only ; he for only her,'

the ideal theory of young husbands, sufficed him.　He was sensible of no desire to share his wife's society with others.　He was almost avaricious in matters of feeling, loving to hoard up the delights of his emotions until they became sometimes like manna kept over the Sabbath, and he grew wayward and fitful. They lived, therefore, a retired life, he, working hard at reviewing and such work for the *Literary Gazette* and magazines, and completing for the press his volume of poems ;— nothing more heard of the tragedy, nipped in the bud, perhaps, by the ill success of 'Fredolpho' and other dramatic disillusionments.—She, gradually falling cheerfully into her new life, bringing a spirit of harmony and comfort more and more into his, and very willing and very capable of rendering him more practical literary assistance, if he had only comprehended, which he was, as yet, far from doing, the breadth and depth of instinctive judgment, experience, and reflection, of 'help meet' for him, which lay there at his disposal.

On the 23rd August, 1822, she presented him with a son, whom, however, they were so unfortunate as to lose after a few months of much suffering. The loss of a first child is often the earliest practical revelation afforded by the experiences of life of those mysterious laws which appear to involve something of cruelty and caprice in the rule and government of human existence; the inexplicable problem, rarely solved to the reason, wherefore innocence should suffer, precious gifts be given to be withdrawn, and life created apparently only to be destroyed. The young husband was completely unmanned by this calamity, and did not for a long time recover his equanimity. A year after, writing to his wife, then in the country, he says : 'I have intended, from day to day, to go to Chelsea and attend to the putting up a stone over the remains of our darling ; but I have found myself unequal to it, and have, with a sickening thrill whenever I have thought of it, deferred it. I must summon resolution to go to-morrow. It distresses me very much, but I will not leave town till it is done.'

The domestic instincts were intensely strong in him. They imparted a deep and distinct colour and quality to his whole being, and to all his work in it that was instinctive ; and they were, at all times, its comfort and protection in the conflicts and trials of life. To give them harmonious embodiment through the medium of verse was a comfort and means of restoration to him of the harmony of his own interior life. This is, indeed, the fountain and source of all genuine poetry.

Some verses written by him on this occasion were, as he was to enjoy the satisfaction of learning, from the repeated assurances of persons wholly unknown to him, a source of comfort to many a suffering human heart, gifted with the divine faculty to feel, but unaccompanied by the fuller endowment of being able to analyze its feelings, and compelled, in consequence, to have recourse to others for that definite expression of its experiences which may console it by displaying that it does not sorrow alone.

This poem, published in the year 1825, was entitled 'The Death of the First-born.' It will be found at the end of this volume.

My parents' friends and acquaintances at this time were Dr. Kitchener; Mr. and Mrs. Basil Montague; Mr. Procter; Miss Benger; Mr. Colton, the author of 'Lacon;' Mr. Shee, R.A.; Mr. Northcote, R.A.; Mr. Brockedon, the painter; Mr. and Mrs. Croly; Mr. William Read, author of 'Rouge et Noir;' Mr. Barry St. Leger, a young writer who had made a reputation by a single book, 'Confessions of Gilbert Earle;' and Mr. and Mrs. Jerdan.

'Mr. and Mrs. Alaric Watts,' writes the daughter of the last-named to a mutual friend some sixty years afterwards, 'were friends of my early years. I was a young girl when they married, and I remember her sweet face and rather grave Quaker manner as well as possible. He also was most agreeable, and very poetical-looking.'

But the most interesting of their acquaintances at this time was the Reverend W. Lisle Bowles, the poet, to whose friendship my father had been introduced by an article which he had written in the *Gentleman's Magazine*, in support of the poet's views on the ' invariable principles of poetry,' as expressed in his edition of ' Pope.' Of Lisle Bowles and his influence, as the founder of the poetical school of the second period of the Age of Sentiment, which I have ventured to characterize as the Poetry of Taste, I have spoken in the first chapter of this work. My father had indeed intended to write his life, and has left behind him copious collections with this view derived from Mr. Bowles's correspondence, to which access was permitted to him through the late Dr. Bowles, of Stanton Lacy ; but the project fell through.

It might have been said of Bowles, as Lord Thurlow said of Crabbe, ' He was as like Parson Adams as twelve to the dozen.' While of a tender and sensitive nature, and the parent, as

I have said, of the poetical school of tasteful sensibility, he was a man of vigorous and independent judgment, great critical discrimination, and upon questions of argument feared no man living, laying about him in controversial conflict, when it presented itself, with all the readiness and aptitude to the use of his weapons of the admirable athlete and sound divine with whom I have ventured to compare him.

The particular controversy now in question, into which my father had thrown himself with corresponding ardour and stomach for fight, and which is, I think, of general and permanent critical interest, arose in this wise :

Mr. Bowles had produced for the booksellers in the year 1806 an edition of the works of Pope, with *variorum* notes, in no less than ten volumes. He had concluded this work with some observations on the poetical character and status of Pope, in which he referred to the outcry which had attended Warton's essay on the life and genius of this writer, as though Warton had intended to deny to Pope his just measure of fame as a poet ; and he endeavoured to lay down some principles of poetical criticism as a basis for a judgment on the subject on his own part.

In doing so, he presumed that it would be readily granted 'that all images drawn from what is beautiful or sublime in the works of Nature are more beautiful and sublime than any images drawn from Art;' and that they are therefore *per se* more poetical. Ensuing on this proposition, he went on to the observation that, in like manner, ' those passions of the human heart which belong to Nature in general, are *per se* more adapted to the higher species of poetry than those which are derived from incidental and transient manners.'

Founding on this line of argument, and making allowance for the qualities displayed in the 'Epistle of Eloïsa,' which he declares his conviction to be infinitely superior to everything of the kind, ancient or modern, he proceeds to affirm that while one of the first poets that England and the polished literature of a polished era can boast, Pope does not stand pre-eminent in the highest sense of the definition of a poet.

To these propositions Mr. Campbell, the poet, in his essay on English Poetry, prefixed to his ' Specimens of the British Poets,' took serious exception, claiming that the faculty by which a poet luminously describes objects of Art is essentially the same faculty as that which enables him to be a faithful describer of simple Nature. In the second place, that Nature and Art are to a greater degree relative terms, in poetical description, than is generally recollected; and thirdly, that artificial objects and manners are of so much importance in fiction as to make the exquisite description of them no less characteristic of genius than the description of simple physical appearances.

To this criticism, which was supported by a variety of acute and interesting arguments, Mr. Bowles, in the year 1819, rejoined in a pamphlet on ' The Invariable Principles of Poetry,' written in the form of a letter to Mr. Campbell, in which, with much grace, good humour, and courtesy, he reviewed his original arguments and those of his brother bard, replying to the latter with great force,

both in principle and detail; and while dis-
claiming the smallest desire to underrate the
poetry of Pope, maintaining with firmness and
dignity the position already assumed.

For these opinions Bowles was attacked in
various quarters with much virulence, as was
the fashion of that day. It was as an answer
to this pamphlet that Lord Byron's well-
known letter to Bowles was written. It contributed fun and humour to the controversy,
but added, I think, little to the arguments.

The result of this controversy upon the
mind of the impartial reader will perhaps be
to recall and confirm the observation of Johnson, that it is much more easy to determine
what is not poetry than to define what is.

CHAPTER XIII.

A QUARTER of a century had passed since the introduction by Bowles, as sought to be shown in the first chapter of this narrative, of the poetry of sentiment purified by taste. The great masters of the poetical art of this period, Bowles and Coleridge, Southey and Wordsworth, Scott and Byron, Campbell and Moore, Shelley and Keats, had done their work. Some

'Home had gone and ta'en their wages ;'

the rest had said all that they had to say. Much there was in the writings of some,—nay, most of them,—for which the age was not prepared, and which, as yet, was in wait to

vitalize, if not to create, the spirit of a later
day. The psychological element in the poetry of
Coleridge, the philosophical in that of Wordsworth, the poetry of intellect and the free spirit
of Shelley, the poetry of passion and free
humanity of Keats, were, as yet, rather as wine
for the few than as bread for the many. It
was for the various aspects of sentiment displayed in the writings of these illustrious men
that they were valued in their own day and
generation ; for it may here be remarked, that
the qualities which give value to a poet in his
own day will rarely be those for which he
is esteemed on the morrow; and that it is in
the degree in which his genius anticipates the
future that his place on the sacred roll will by
men be ultimately defined.

At the period to which my narrative is now to
be taken up,—the year 1823,—the torch kindled
at the great fire-fountain of Imagination by the
distinguished men, and some others, of whom
I have spoken, had begun to be divided and
subdivided. Its divine light was now being
borne, and its genial warmth diffused, into
many a diverging valley, many a sequestered

region little known, and its needs and capabilities little suspected, of the human heart, by a race of writers more or less gifted in various ways, by the spirit of sentiment introduced into the age, by the greater spirits who had already passed, or were passing, from the scene.

It was the function and office of these writers, playing upon the spirit of the time, to combine rather than to create ; not by imitating one, but by more or less assimilating all the varied forms in which the spirit of sentiment had been manifested in their great predecessors, and to reproduce it in variations and shades of feeling of infinite delicacy and refinement. The ' singers had gone before,' the ' players on instruments ' were now following. Of such writers already favourably known to the public in greater or less degree, may be instanced,—without disrespect to others, for I am not making a catalogue,— Mrs. Hemans and Miss Landon, Milman and Procter, Wilson and Hogg, Allan Cunningham and David Moir, the Etonians Moultrie, Praed and Sidney Walker, Horace Smith and Love Peacock, Pringle and Croly ; writers of poetry of different degrees and distinctions of creative originality, but all with an individuality of sentiment of their own.

Among these, my father was now to seek a place, and to find his claims not disallowed. In the year 1823, being then in his twenty-sixth year, he collected into a little volume of some hundred and fifty pages, the poems which he had contributed to various periodicals during the preceding five years, under the modest title of 'Poetical Sketches.' An edition of five hundred copies was sold out before the end of the year.

'I shall most readily accept your proposal of dividing profits on a new edition of your poems,' writes his publisher, December 6th, 1823. 'Your notice of this edition would have been as well delayed one month, while the trade had sold their copies of the present edition. Simpkin and Co. had ten copies yesterday.' Again, a week or two later: 'Your "Poetical Sketches" are in the hands of the artist. They are much inquired after, and the new edition would sell well.' Again, February 14th, 1824: 'I have

received from Brockedon a beautiful drawing
for the title-page of your new volume. In a
few days I expect for it two drawings from
Stothard. I have great pleasure in saying that
this book is not only entirely out of print, but
that we have a great number of orders in the
house for the new edition.' Again, 31st July,
1824 : 'Spooner is going to Ireland, and will
push your poems. We are selling it hourly in
London. Four hundred of the second edition
are sold already, and I have no doubt a new one
will be required in the winter.' Again, August
10th, 1824 : ' Your poems are selling daily. I
am glad you have decided to give us some more.'

I do not know that the prevailing sentiment of that day can be better illustrated
than in the sale, in two years, of a thousand
copies of this unpretending little volume.
The truth is that, coarse and vulgar as the
age was, in many respects, there was within it
a very tender and guileless spirit of sentiment
rectified by taste, which enabled it to enjoy,
and to purify itself by enjoying, whatever
was genuinely tender and pathetic, if expressed with power and without exaggera-

tion. This youthfulness of spirit in that age is highly deserving attention by those whose vocation it may be to write its history. No writer of to-day, it may be affirmed, is qualified to write that history who is incapable of such rejuvenation as may enable him to perceive and feel sympathy with this spirit.

Animated by the general spirit of the poetry of its time, sensibility and taste, what, it may be asked, were the qualities which gave to this little book a distinctness and individuality of its own! They were, I think, a nicely delicate discrimination in the perception of tender shades of feeling, and an ingenuous frankness in displaying them, vitalized by an under-current of passion allowed to approach the surface, and yet always kept under and in reserve, which gave to the whole a glow and spirit as of subdued fire. In the former, it had affinity with the sonnets of Bowles; in the latter, if I may permit myself to say so, with the lyrics of Byron. It makes a strange impression upon the mind of a later day of combined youth and age,—maturity and innocence; and in this last respect, but in no other, recalls the peculiar spirit in which, I think, to many natures lies so much of the charm of the poetry of Shelley.

In its frank and manly disclosure of the feelings; of ingenuous youth and early manhood, it had certainly struck out something then new. Charles Lamb, in a kind and characteristic acknowledgment of the book offered for his acceptance through a mutual friend in the India House, notices the novelty of its boldness in the delineation of tender feeling, and expresses his fears whether the age may be of sufficiently advanced sensibility to receive them.

' East India House,
' 22nd December, 1822.

' DEAR SIR,

' I beg you to accept my thanks for a copy of your poems, which I have found very elegant and full of fancy. I had seen and admired one of them attributed to Lord Byron. The volume is externally handsome, and the poetry of a kind, I should judge, to have taken. But you have described feelings too inward, perhaps, to be exposed to odious criticism. I have inadvertently written this short acknowledgment sonnet fashion,—in fourteen lines,—but where is the poetry! When your occupations give you leave, I shall hope for the pleasure of seeing you.

'Your obliged
'C. LAMB.'

Coleridge, whose acquaintance, and I may say friendship, my father acquired in the interval between the publication of the second and third editions, strikes, I think, in the following letter, a truer note of criticism. While bearing, as will be seen, a very handsome testimony to the passion and eloquence, the glow and spirit displayed in these poems, he cautions the writer, not against the free and full display of genuine feeling, but rather against too great or too obvious a fastidiousness of taste,—a too definite delineation of the beautiful.

'Highgate.

'MY DEAR SIR,

'As some slight proof that you have been in my thoughts, I send you some observations and *criticunculæ* suggested by your volume of poems.

'"The Broken Heart" is a poem of great and powerful interest. The specks in it are therefore only not too trifling for notice that they are specks in a diamond.

' "I Think of Thee" is impassioned and eloquent with the eloquence of lyric poetry.

' "A Sketch from Real Life" reminds me of the best verses of the first James's and Charles's reigns. It is between Chapman and Cartwright, and partakes of both.

' "Ten Years Ago" cannot but be a favourite at every fireside where love and piety are seated.

' The poem "To Octavia" is a very sweet composition; but, oh, by the immortal Nine, the jealous guardians of the purity of language, let not the English ear be demoralized by hybrid participles equivocally generated of noun-substantives. Southey is a sad offender in this way—mirror'd—"fountain'd," etc.

' "Remember the Past." Some critic of the year 2828 will affix an asterisk to the fourth line of the second stanza of this poem, and swear by all the gods that Alaric Watts never wrote such a line. Like all your poems, these lines are full of glow and spirit; but this metre has always impressed me unpleasantly, and I believe I should be more pleased, at least less dissatisfied, with this poem, if the thoughts and imagery had been less interesting, because they overbalance the tintinnabulation of the verse.

' "A Waking Dream" is a noble poem! A genial half-hour employed on page 62, after you had been reading the second Psalm, and the first, eighth, and tenth chapters of Ezekiel, and had thus put the Apollo Belvidere, and the Arts, and

all the complacencies that arise from the con-
templation of the distinct and beautiful in figure
wholly out of the imagination, would leave nothing
to be wished in this grand " skyscape."

'I have no objection, be assured, to your spiritual
cranium containing both the taste exquisite, and
the faculty divine,—this in one hemisphere, and
that in another;—or like Light and Darkness in
Milton's apotheosis of a Dutch weather-glass; but
let the poet keep at a distance from the connoisseur.
Music and imagery he must have; but imagery
acting more as music than as painting.

'Altogether I have received great pleasure from
the volume; and I thank you for it sincerely. Remember me respectfully and affectionately to Mrs.
Watts. She will be pleased to hear that my ramble
on the Continent has benefited my health.

'Blessings on the little ones.

'Believe me very truly yours,
'S. T. COLERIDGE.'

CHAPTER XIV.

LEEDS.

My father was not long, I fear, in finding that a very inadequate livelihood for two persons was to be realized from the rather miscellaneous literary undertakings, upon the strength of which, if indeed he had reflected on the subject at all, he had cast the die of marriage.

Life, both to the artist and author, was in that day a perpetual struggle against penury. When Miss Martineau's publisher told her, a little later even, that an author, could not then realize more than £100 or £150 a year by that vocation, he was not greatly exaggerating the state of things. A writer who should, at the time now in question, secure, from purely literary avocations, double that income, must have been a person of considerable energy and power of work, as well as talent, some versatility, and a ready perception of the opportunities of the hour; and even then the income would be earned more or less casually, and received at irregular intervals.

One resource, alone, was open to secure an adequate income, even from the most moderate point of view, and that was the routine of the newspaper press. Strange as it may now appear, this was not, in that day, held in high esteem as an occupation, and was indeed, save in few and exceptional instances in which the political influence of the particular daily newspaper had secured a corresponding influential recognition of the writer for it, scarcely regarded as a literary occupation at all. Nevertheless, it possessed two important advantages; the income derived from it was certain and regular, and it provided, from day to day, its own materials. It was therefore accepted, not without some sacrifice of pride, as an occupation by literary men; and very few indeed there were who did not find occasion, much against the grain, to have recourse to it.

It was in such a condition of things, general

and particular, that, towards the close of the
year 1822, a proposal was made to my father,
by his good friend and well-wisher, the great
publisher, Mr. Joseph Ogle Robinson, of the
editorship of the *Leeds Intelligencer* newspaper,
of which he was a proprietor in partnership
with Mr. John Hernaman, and which, from un-
skilful editorship, or some other cause, was in
a moribund condition. The salary was to be
£300 a year, coupled with those indefinite
prospects of a share in profits which give a
glow to such enterprises in the eyes of the
literary adventurer, and never come to anything. This proposal he was wise enough to
accept.

The quality, in my father's mind, of taste,
and what was then called ' connoisseurship,'
against too great a preponderance of which
Mr. Coleridge had rather cautioned him as a
poet, led him to desire to give to his newspaper a more æsthetic and critical character
than was then common in the provincial press
He found at Leeds a public more advanced in
culture, at all events as respects the former,
than he had been prepared to anticipate, and

his efforts in this direction met with prompt and cordial appreciation.

Leeds was at that time quite in advance of the other large towns in the provinces in its capacity to enjoy and understand works of art, and organized, indeed, in the year 1823, a Public Loan Exhibition of Pictures, which must certainly have been one of the earliest, if not in fact the earliest, of such provincial enterprises in England.   This taste for art in Leeds was perhaps referable to the opportunities enjoyed of seeing what was good in art in the well-known collection, especially of Turner's works, of Mr. Fawkes of Farnley Hall, in the immediate vicinity.   It even enjoyed, favoured by such circumstances, an independent school of art of its own, if we may judge from the following anecdote.   Walking one afternoon through this Loan Exhibition, my father remarked, standing before one of the magnificent drawings of Turner, from Farnley Hall, a sturdy Yorkshireman, who from his appearance might have been a grazier or farmer, but who, it may be inferred from the result, was a landscape-painter.   Backing to get a better view, with his head a little on one side and his chin resting on his right hand, he thus apostrophized the work under review :

' I'm na stalled o' mysen.'

Although advanced in matters of art, the Inhabitants of Leeds in that day, at all events as represented by the subscribers to the *Leeds Intelligencer* newspaper, did not prove equally progressive in another direction. Some short time after my father's accession to its editorship, he was invited by the late Michael Thomas Sadler, M.P., one of the earliest of the Factory Reformers, to accompany him on a visit to the Infirmary. He was much shocked and surprised at the number of operatives, including women and children, under treatment for injuries, some of the most serious character, caused by the pertinacious neglect of the manufacturers to ' box their machinery,' or in other words to guard, by the very simple contrivances needful against risk from the machine wheels. Wholly unaccustomed to the sight of personal oppression, and with sympathies unseared by familiarity with such sights, he proceeded in his next week's newspaper to comment in strong language on the inhumanity of the mill-owners in perpetuating such a condition of things. On the following Monday,—the *Leeds Intelligencer* was a weekly paper,—he received as many letters discontinuing subscription to it as filled a breakfast-tray.

It is fair to bear in mind that many of the manufacturers in that day were men who had raised themselves by industry and enterprise from the position of operatives. Honest traders and just, doubtless, according to their lights and the traditions of their class ; frugal, hard-working, and unsparing of themselves, but capable of being tyrannical, if not cruel, to their inferiors, who, they might think, if they thought at all about it, could well bear to suffer the life which they had endured and from which they had raised themselves to opulence.

The following conversation, heard in a little tavern in a by-street in Leeds, may afford an illustration of the state and condition, at this time, of the particular class of manufacturer to which I am referring :

' Thy lad's leuking aater my wench !'

' Whaat then, Jaames ?'

'Whaat then, Joseph? Whaat do thee mean to gie'n?'

'Thee speak first, Jaames.'

'Well, I'll gie'n the little factory, if I'm content.'

'Well, I'll gie ten thoosand dawn and share with the rest.'

'It's a bargain, Joseph.'

'Well, then, let's have t'other pint on't.'

All the Leeds manufacturers of that day were not of course of this class. Many were cultivated gentlemen, according to the measure of the times, especially in art, and highly solicitous that their children should not only inherit money, but be liberally educated and well trained. Dining one day at the house of one of these gentlemen, the lady of the house happened to remark to my father upon the difficulty experienced in Yorkshire in obtaining governesses whose mode of speaking was free from the local *patois* and peculiarities. She had had to part with several ladies who had suited her in other respects, in consequence of this defect; but she had just succeeded in obtaining one so very highly recommended, that she hoped her troubles on this score were at an end. The lady in question had arrived that very day, and she had not indeed yet had an opportunity of seeing her. At that moment one of the gentlemen observed that a strange lady was crossing the lawn with the young people of the family; and opening the French window, proceeded to admit the new governess, whom, as being a paragon, everybody was naturally anxious to see. The lady made her acknowledgments gracefully enough, and took her seat and glass of wine with dignity and composure, when the host, in order to make things pleasant, observed to her :

'You must not allow the girls to take you too long walks. They are great walkers. I hope they will not have tired you already !'

To which the lady replied, with much good-humour :

'Na, na! I'm na tired! When a once gets agate, a pegs it awa' rarely !'

My father threw himself into this new life with his usual energy. In these newspaper labours he derived no unimportant assistance from his young wife, whose judgment and capacity he was now beginning more adequately to appreciate. During his absences in London, which important engagements with his publishers, to be described later, rendered more and more frequent, she was practically editor of the newspaper, with a faithful printer and reader named Townsend for aide-de-camp, revising and supervising all that went into it, except the leading articles, which he sent down by coach from London. I should judge from the following letters that it might not have been amiss if the latter had also undergone somewhat of the same wise supervision.

The suggestion of the worthy publisher that his young editor should be careful to refer in gentlemanly terms to everybody 'except Mr. Baines,' the proprietor and editor of the rival newspaper, has in it a spice of humour and human nature that renders its suppression impossible.

'London, Feb. 24, 1823.

' MY DEAR SIR,

'I duly received your kind favour, and it affords me great pleasure to find the paper so highly esteemed by all literary men. Your friend Croly was talking about it a few days ago, and expressed himself much pleased; but he remarked that he

11—2

thought sometimes you expressed yourself rather too strongly when speaking of individuals.

'I merely give you this hint, because it accords in some small degree with my own opinion. Not that I think you can express yourself too strongly when speaking of Baines. Nothing you can say is half bad enough for him; but all other individuals who in their private characters may be considered gentlemen, should in my opinion be always referred to in very gentlemanly terms.

'I offer my opinion from real friendship, and I hope you will receive it as a hint from a real friend, and not as the language of complaint.

'Yours very truly,
'J. O. Robinson.'

' London, Feb. 28.

'My dear Sir,

'Thanks for the newspapers. I like the vigour and direct application of your leading articles.

'The extracts and literary notices place your work above competition on the part of any country newspaper that I have seen. I can have no hesitation in my conviction of your success; but, I have some as to your directing that success to the best advantage for yourself. I wish to see your articles less calculated to involve you personally with the vagabonds about you. You have humour; humour is the best mode of disposing of an adversary, especially a political adversary. I wish to see your remarks and retorts made in a more laughing and

easy manner. Generally speaking, it is not worth
any honest man's while to involve himself in ill-
blood for the sake of either Tory or Whig. My
only fear for you is private quarrel.

'I know you will take these opinions as kindly
as they are intended. Kind compliments to Mrs.
Watts.

'Believe me,

'Very truly yours,

'G. CROLY.'*

His brother editors of the provincial press,
those at all events who, like himself, were
vowed to the cause of 'social order against the
anarchists,'—in other words, good Tories,—
were by no means scandalized by the warmth of
his philippics. Some of them, indeed, paid
him the compliment of adopting these compositions and standing *in loco parentis* to
them in their own newspapers; and one of
these gentlemen, (somewhere on the Welsh
border, I should surmise,) under the operation
of some qualms of conscience, was pleased to
send him a side of mutton, as a slight acknowledgment of the benefit which he very
candidly admitted he had derived from the

* The Rev. George (afterwards Dr.) Croly.

appropriation and adoption of his leading articles.

By his activity and enterprise he soon regained for his newspaper the subscribers which he had lost by his too enthusiastic efforts in the cause of factory reform, and many more ; and when this was accomplished, and the paper placed in a condition to hold its own, he began to weary of the work and perhaps of the place, and to wish to get away. Seeing an opening for a Tory organ at Manchester, where there was on the whole a fuller literary and intellectual, (though not artistic,) life than at Leeds, and where he had more intimate friends, he, in the year 1825, removed to that town, and established there the *Manchester Courier*, which survives as an influential organ of public opinion to this day. Before, however, this change of abode, his wife presented him on the 18th February, 1825, with a son.

CHAPTER XV.

AMONG the literary projects fermenting in his brain at the time of my father's marriage, was one suggested by a friend, of a literary and artistic miscellany, in which a variety of short tales, sketches and poems, by popular authors, should be associated with carefully executed line engravings from good pictures. He had even ventured to anticipate that such a volume might issue, every year, in competition, as a gift-book, with the 'Ladies' Polite Remembrancer,' and other pocket-books, published annually by the London booksellers in great variety, and which had a large sale for presents at Christmas and the New Year. He proposed this work to Hurst and Robinson, in the year 1823. The firm had, however, already in hand an

enterprise of somewhat similar character under
the editorship of his friend Mr. Croly, entitled
'The Graces, or Literary Souvenir;' the latter
the title of an old and popular pocket-book.
This work was avowedly suggested by the
German literary almanacs, 'an old and popular
species of publication,' as the editor claimed for
it, and as indeed it had been 'in Germany' from
the days of Schiller and Goethe. This book
was a 12mo., with two engraved title-pages and
two frontispieces; one an engraving from the
well-known picture of 'Titian's Daughter,' the
other an illustration by Smirke, R.A., from
Scott's poem of the 'Bridal of Triermain.' The
literary contents comprised—The Months, in
verse, with a calendar of the flowers; ruled
lines for a Diary; an Obituary for the year; a
selection of Jeux d'Esprit; Lists of Foreign
Ambassadors, Literary Institutions, Bankers of
the Metropolis, Theatres, and Tables of Foreign
Moneys. It was, in fact, a glorified pocket-book.

In the same year, 1823, Mr. Rudolph
Ackermann, a publisher of foreign prints and
illustrated works in the Strand, had produced
an annual publication of the same class, under

the title of 'The Forget-Me-Not.' It was embellished, like 'The Graces,' by the Months, in verse, from the pen of Mr. Combe, the author of 'Dr. Syntax's Tours,' illustrating twelve emblematical designs from drawings by Burney. It had somewhat less of the almanac and pocket-book character of publication than 'The Graces.' It, nevertheless, did not disclaim utility, which it sought to combine with fashion. The former characteristic it justified by copious Tables of the Population Returns 'from the last census,' and an Historical Chronicle of the events of the preceding year; the latter by Genealogies of the reigning Sovereigns, and Lists of their Diplomatic Agents. Arranged, sandwich fashion, between the two, were some tales or sketches, apparently of German origin. The work was a link between the 'Almanac de Gotha,' to which it avowed its obligations, and the 'Annual Register,' diversified by some of the more popular characteristics of the pocket-book. Its interest is that, with all its defects, it was the first of the 'Annuals' which enjoyed in their day so much popularity, and in the improved form given to them by my father, exercised so much influence in popularizing in that age a taste for art in this country.

A similar work was issued by Mr. Lupton Relfe, a bookseller in Cornhill, under the title of 'Friendship's Offering,' in 1824.

On the 23rd December, 1823, Mr. Robinson reverted to the idea of the 'Literary and Artistic Miscellany.' 'If,' he says, 'you keep to your plan of an "Annual Book," and will make it as unlike Croly's as possible, I shall be most happy to join you in it.' My father had no desire to enter into a rivalry of this description with the friend whom he had himself introduced to his publisher, and this proposal was not entertained by him. On the 31st July, 1824, Mr. Robinson writes : ' Croly has relinquished "The Graces ;" therefore · I hope you and we may make a good thing of it, though it is not very polite to ask you to take it up after Croly has abandoned it ; but I am aware that you are in a great measure ready for such a volume.'

The fact was, 'The Graces' had not been a success. The public could not be brought to favour the union of ‘Titian’s Daughter,’ ‘fair one with golden locks’ though she were, with the ‘Bankers of the Metropolis;’ and the connection, if any could be discovered, between ‘Gyneth starting from Sleep’ and the ‘Obituary’ for the year, was of too occult and mystical a nature to be apprehended by the general reader. ‘The Royal Red Book,’ illustrated by the Royal Academy and the ‘old masters,’ was not the sort of ‘Annual’ required.

Whether the similar publications of Mr. Ackermann and Mr. Relfe had up to that time met with better fortune, I have no means of knowing.

My father entered upon the undertaking, for which his plan had long been matured, heartily enough; and early in November, 1824, was published ‘The Literary Souvenir and Cabinet of Poetry and Romance, edited by Alaric A. Watts.’

Of this work were sold within the year more than six thousand copies.

It was a small octavo volume bound in pale green, pink, or violet boards, ornamented by an

engraved design by Corbould, the edges of the
leaves only gilt. It contained some twenty
original compositions by the principal writers of
the day, in prose and verse, and ten line engravings, with some fac-similes of autographs.
The price was twelve shillings. All element
of the pocket-book, almanac, diary, or red-book
was carefully eschewed ; all, in short, which
could make it less acceptable or give it less
value at one period of the year than another.
It was strictly a literary and artistic miscellany,
though for it, as respects the art, my father had
little responsibility, the embellishments having
been selected and put into the engraver's hands
before the work was committed to him.

The progress of this enterprise, from its
projection to this propitious conclusion, is very
graphically pourtrayed in the correspondence
between the editor and publisher, of which the
following extracts may afford a fair sample, and
carry on the drama in the words of the actors.

MR. WATTS TO MR. ROBINSON.

‘ July 5, 1824.

‘ As to “The Graces,” I accept your proposal with
pleasure, though the choice made of some of the

embellishments does not altogether accord with my taste. I have just forwarded to Mr. Ackermann, at his request, a poem, "Kirkstall Revisited," and two other papers. These I must recall.'

'August 12, 1824.

'As soon as I arrived at home, I set to work, *vi et armis*, at the book. I have for it an exquisite copy of verses by Thomas Campbell, also poetry and prose by James Montgomery, Lisle Bowles, Lacon Colton, Maturin, Mrs. Hemans, Miss Landon, Archdeacon Wrangham, Mrs. Opie, Thomas Dale, Allan Cunningham, James Hogg, Moir (of *Blackwood's Magazine*), Herbert Knowles, and William Read, the author of "Rouge et Noir." Of Wordsworth and Coleridge I have some hopes, but no certainty. If we can but manage to establish a large sale for the volume, it will become an annual property of importance. I am indifferent to profit this year, if we can but get the thing in a fair train for success in future. I shall fix on the title with all possible expedition. The design for the covers, instead of being naked women, should be something emblematic of the contents—Poetry, the Arts, etc.; in short, polite literature.'

'September 1.

'The mischief of asking people to furnish papers is that one is then compelled, as it were, to accept one from them whether it suits or not. Mr. Kendrick's MS. will not do; Dr. Kitchener's literary friends may generally be looked on with suspicion. What think you of the following lines from Sir

Walter for the motto on the title-page ?   The title
to be "Literary Souvenir":

> ' " I have song of war for knight,
>   Lay of love for lady bright ;
> Fairy tale to please the heir ;
>   Goblin grim the maids to scare."

The plate from Nash, of " Père la Chaise," I admire
very much.   It is beautiful.   I am afraid that as
Windsor Castle is about to undergo so much important alterations, the engraving from De Wint's
drawing may prove out of date.   I should like to
see the drawing of " The Decision of the Flower,"
after Retsch.

' September 2, 1824.

' You have no doubt heard of the success of your
Mr. Mann in subscribing the "Literary Souvenir.
Mr. Bankes, twenty-five copies; Sowler the same ;
Agnew the same; David Grant has given me an
order for ten copies for himself.   If I can have a
little aid in the production of the book this year, I
venture to predict that it will turn out a profitable
speculation for ever.   I am disposed to think you
may print two thousand with safety.'

The letters of Mr. Robinson continue the
narrative very happily :

Mr. Ogle Robinson to Mr. Watts.

' September 4, 1824.

' I have written to Mr. Constable for Sir Walter
Scott's answer to our request for a contribution to

the work, and shall hear next week. I really think
we shall sell three or four thousand copies. Indeed,
one bookseller offered the other day to take one
thousand, if we would give him a little advantage.
L. E. L. will be ready for you on Monday with some
beautiful verses, but don't give us more poetry than
prose. Poetry is beyond many of the purchasers
of this description of book. Sale to the trade
should be in October.'

' November 16, 1824.

' We shall not be able to publish before Monday;
but on Saturday we intend to forward our most
important country orders, such as Leeds, Halifax,
Manchester. All our Irish orders on Thursday.
H. Mann is now out subscribing the book. Orders
from the country increase constantly. Bentley
could not print a second edition in less than fourteen days. I have no doubt we shall sell the whole
five thousand copies, and have therefore taken upon
ourselves to print two thousand more copies; and
go to press this day.'

' November 30, 1824.

' We are going on gloriously with the " Literary
Souvenir ;" and altogether living above the malice
of our enemies ; and enjoy in our own breasts
nobler feelings, pursuing the direct course of business, disregarding all tricks, and selling more books
than they ! You may rely upon it, next year we
will sell ten thousand copies.'

'December 14, 1824.

'I have much pleasure in handing you the enclosed order in part of what will be due to you on the "Literary Souvenir," and I trust this is but a small portion of what will appear on the face of the account to your credit. I am highly delighted with our progress with the "Souvenir." Longmans are buying them daily at what we call "scrip" and no odd book. This gives a relish to business every day. As for next year—Leslie's "Rivals" you shall have. What would you like from Sir Thomas? and what from Wilkie? And we must have some beautiful landscape from that giant Turner.'

'April 6, 1825.

'Of the "Souvenir" we sold about sixty copies at our last trade sale, whilst all our rivals are as dead as though they had never existed.'

Of the contents of the 'Literary Souvenir,' a sufficient idea may be gained from the preceding narrative. The writers were all among the most popular of that day. Sir Walter Scott's contributions, which duly arrived, added no more value to the book than might be afforded by his illustrious name in the table of contents. Campbell's poem, 'Lines on quitting a Scene in Bavaria,' were, however, of a very different quality. Byron, in a letter to Murray, given in Moore's 'Life,' says of this poem, 'Campbell has an unpublished poem on a scene in Germany, Bavaria, I think, which I saw last year, that is perfectly magnificent, and equal to himself. I wonder he don't publish it.' Three contributions, by three young writers of Manchester, may be worthy a passing record; some lines bearing the initials W. H. A., one of the earliest literary compositions of that popular writer Mr. Harrison Ainsworth; a poem entitled 'The Convict Ship,' a very noble effusion, by a young gentleman of Manchester, Mr. T. K. Hervey, best remembered now by his editorship in later years of the *Athenæum;* and a prose sketch, full of humour, signed with the initials M. J. J.

The editor's contributions were two poems, 'Kirkstall Abbey Revisited,' and 'The Death of the First-born.'

Of the embellishments I must not omit to note one by Brockedon, which greatly seized upon the imagination of Mrs. Hemans, in which a child, playing close to the edge of a dangerous cliff, is being wiled back, in the most natural way in the world, to the bosom of its mother.

CHAPTER XVI.

MARIA JANE JEWSBURY.

In the foregoing notice of the contents of the first volume of the 'Literary Souvenir,' I have mentioned amongst the contributions a sketch published under the initials 'M. J. J.' The name of this lady, Maria Jane Jewsbury, like the names of more than one of the literary personages to whom I may have to refer in this narrative, is little more than an echo in the age to which I am addressing myself, and might, indeed, scarcely be even that if it had not been kept somewhat in mind by the writings of a younger sister. She died in the prime of life, and she produced in quantity but little; but she became, nevertheless, a very distinct, because truly original personality, in the history of the literature of that period, and is remembered as such with respect by those who are familiar with it.

Of her, Wordsworth, in a note to a poem addressed to her, published in his collected works, has placed upon record that, apart from other high qualities, in one, quickness in the motions of the mind, she had, within the range of his acquaintance, no equal.

Mrs. Hemans, to whose acquaintance my father introduced her, writing of her after her early death in 1833, speaks of her in words of much tenderness. 'How much deeper power seemed to lie, coiled up as it were, in the recesses of her mind than was ever manifested to the world in her writings! Strange and sad does it seem that only the broken music of such a spirit should have been given to the earth; the full and finished harmony never drawn forth.'

Miss Landon said of her: 'I never met with any woman who possessed her powers of conversation. If her language had a fault, it was its extreme perfection. It was like reading an eloquent book full of thought and poetry.'

Such was the person of whose introduction to the public, as a writer, I am now to speak.

In a biographical work entitled 'The Literary Women of England,' by Jane Williams, there is a careful sketch of the life of Miss Jewsbury, from which I extract the following notice pertinent to this narrative :

'Mr. Aston, the editor of the *Manchester Gazette*, being acquainted with her father, had the honour of first printing and publishing a little poem of hers; and being impressed with a high opinion of her talents, he introduced her to Mr. Alaric A. Watts, who, from the latter part of the year 1822, edited the *Leeds Intelligencer*, and three years afterwards resigned that paper, removed his residence to Manchester, and became editor of the *Manchester Courier*. Mr. Watts was less than two years older than Miss Jewsbury, and, with generous zeal, aided her in the work of mental culture, gave publicity to her occasional poems, urged the completion of her first book, and found a publisher for it.'

This account, derived, I conclude, either from Mr. Aston or Miss Jewsbury's family, for it was seen for the first time by my father in print, epitomizes substantially the actual facts, and leaves little for his biographer to add in detail; but he may perhaps be allowed to tell the story in his own way.

In the course of the year 1823, while keeping a watchful eye upon contemporary verse in the newspapers and periodicals for the collection he was forming of miscellaneous fugitive poetry, subsequently published under the title of the 'Poetical Album,' his attention was attracted by some verses in the *Manchester Gazette* of unusual maturity of thought and perfection of form, bearing the initials M. J. J. Having occasion shortly after to visit Manchester, he took the opportunity to inquire of the editor of the *Gazette*, Mr. Aston, an early friend, who was this mysterious M. J. J. He learnt that she was the eldest daughter of a gentleman, carrying on business as a manufacturer at Manchester, of the name of Jewsbury; that these, with other compositions, as yet unpublished in prose and verse, were written in intervals of leisure from domestic occupations, the death of her mother having devolved upon her, at an early age, the charge of her father's household and the care of a young family of six younger brothers and sisters, to whom she was at once mother, nurse, and governess.

This information could not fail to increase my father's interest in the young writer; an introduction was arranged, and the favourable opinion already formed of her talent and originality was more than confirmed by her conversation and the perusal of her unpublished MSS. These displayed not only much poetical power and feeling, as he had anticipated, but a vein of humour, observation and instinctive knowledge of human character, the first a rare quality in women's writings at that day, for which he was wholly unprepared. He introduced her to his wife, who liked her, and was equally impressed by her freshness of spirit and powers of mind.

It happened, at this time, that a quarterly magazine, published by Andrews of New Bond Street, under the title of *The Album*, had fallen into the editorship of a friend, Robert Sulivan, (best remembered now as a dramatist), a young writer of taste and possessing a peculiarly delicate vein of wit and humour, a man of all men qualified to do justice to the similar qualities of this young writer. An opening was readily made for her, and, in the numbers for January, 1824, and April, 1825, appeared two prose sketches full of humour and nice observation of character, entitled ' Boarding School Reminiscences,' and ' The Complaint of the Schoolmistress,' the first of her prose writings ever printed.

Nor did my father's good offices rest here. On one of his now frequent visits to London for the purpose of conferring with his publishers respecting the ' Literary Souvenir,' he took the opportunity of introducing Miss Jewsbury's name to the notice of Mr. Robinson, and threw himself into the cause with so much ardour as to succeed in awakening some corresponding enthusiasm in the mind of the worthy publisher, who, as may be judged from his correspondence, was both enterprising and of a generous spirit. The result was that he took back with him to Leeds an agreement from Hurst and Robinson to purchase from the young authoress a work, unseen, and for the most part un- written, to consist of miscellaneous sketches

and essays, for the, to her, magnificent sum of
£100.

This work, under the title of 'Phantasmagoria,' was published in the year 1825, the
writer being in her twenty-fifth year. It
displays a ready grasp of the limited experiences of a young woman, considerable perception of human nature, and a vein of
humour in character and quality greatly in
advance of its age, at all events in the writings
of women. In this respect it may be affirmed
to have preceded its day by at least thirty
years. The titles of some of the sketches
afford the only idea which the space at disposal enables me to give of this highly promising literary *essai*. Here are some of
them : 'The Age of Books,' 'Human Sorrow
and Human Sympathy,' 'Religious Novels,'
'On the Habit of Analyzing One's Emotions,'
'Why is the Spirit of Poetry Anticheerful?'
'The Comfortable Woman,' 'First Efforts in
Criticism.'

In the last-mentioned paper, she parodies
the Reviewers of that day, weekly and
quarterly, with considerable humour, and even

ventures on a joke at the expense of Mr. Southey, rather hinting that certain influential reviews, in whatever subject originating, were sometimes apt to land the reader, without any very definite connection of subject, in the Brazils, the Peninsular War, or Church History. To appreciate the audacity of this suggestion, it is necessary to bear in mind that the 'great and good' Mr. Southey, as it was the fashion with a large section of the community to designate him,—I am far from insinuating unjustly,—enjoyed in Tory circles somewhat of the moral pre-eminence over the rest of the world so universally, in the opposite camp, assigned at the present day to Mr. Gladstone, and that to laugh at him involved a daring only to be paralleled by that of Sydney Smith's man who had been heard to speak disrespectfully of the Equator. The matter was not mended when Mr. Wordsworth, desirous of serving his young friend, in the innocency of his heart, sent the book to Southey and asked him to review it in the *Quarterly!* The Laureate, who, like many eminent men, preferred his own jokes to other

people's, responded to this overture with some
austerity ; and signified, no doubt truly
enough, that, in all the circumstances, the best
service he could render to this misguided young
person was to leave her wholly unnoticed. Mr.
Wordsworth, whose interest in the young lady
had possibly not gone so far as to lead him to
read her book, unless, perhaps, the dedicatory
poem to himself, must have wondered what it
all meant.

In 1827, Miss Jewsbury published ' Letters
to the Young,' which went into a second edition
in 1829, in which year she collected her poems
into a volume which she entitled ' Lays of
Leisure Hours.'　Her final and most sustained
work, ' The Three Histories,' which contains a
sketch of the character of Mrs. Hemans under
the name of Egeria, appeared in 1830.　In
1832 she married the Rev. Kew Fletcher, a
clergyman of the Church of England, employed
in missionary labours in India, where she died
of cholera in the following year.　There is a
portrait of her in the ' Christian Keepsake,' an
annual published in the year 1838.

The following letter relates to the episode in

the literary career of Miss Jewsbury with which this narrative is more immediately concerned:

' 13, Brooke Street, Chorlton Road,
' Manchester, 6th March, 1824.

' MY DEAR FRIEND.

'What shall I say to you for your letter? Pleased, and gratified, and surprised, are all cold and insufficient terms, indeed I cannot find terms that will adequately express my feelings; and you must not, therefore, because I say little, suppose I do not feel much. I am quite sure that your warm and undeserved exertions gratify me more than even the success itself; and whilst, as a child, I rejoice in the prospect of contributing to the comfort of my father; and, as a woman, exult in the prospect of winning a little attention, the feeling of respectful gratitude to yourself forms, just now, my predominant feeling. The results which you communicate surpass my expectations, if, indeed, I had formed any, and ought to satisfy the most sceptical of my friends. I have, I confess, a real horror of second volumes, unless they are good; but perhaps, like many other young ladies, I am turning timid in the wrong place. I will, therefore, undertake to make the work two volumes, and shall not rest till I have finished them,—and finished them, I hope, to your satisfaction. How often before then shall I wish that Leeds were nearer to Manchester,—or Manchester to Leeds! When you have leisure, on your return I shall be highly gratified by hearing

from you.   Will not Mrs. Watts also gratify me
by a line? It would give me great pleasure. My
father I shall not see till the evening, so that he
cannot unite with me in thanks on the present
occasion ; but, rest assured that you will have made
happy one of the kindest and worthiest of men.
Ever believe me, with a deep feeling of your
kindness,

'Your obliged friend,
'MARIA JANE JEWSBURY.'

CHAPTER XVII.

THE REV. CHARLES R. MATURIN.

'Dublin, April 17, 1819.

'MY INESTIMABLE FRIEND,

'I never deplored my want of *l'eloquence de billet* before; but if I possessed all the eloquence I do not possess, it must fail under the task of expressing my obligations to you. How much do I owe you, and how much am I proud to owe you! I have implicitly followed your advice, and written to Young. Your suggestions relative to curtailment I adopt unhesitatingly; reject and retain what you like. Present, I beg you, my best acknowledgments to Mr. Young for his friendly zeal for a part but little worthy of his great abilities; and, in your kindness, apologize to Mr. Charles Kemble, Mr. Macready, and the other gentlemen, for my not having had the pleasure of witnessing their talents, and thus of qualifying myself for writing parts more worthy of their acceptance than the wild and crude sketches of Adelmar and Wallenburg.

' But, my dearest friend, remember how much is
at stake on Miss O'Neil's approbation of the female
character, and try to propitiate her *for her country-
man.* Pray assure her of my entire dependence on
her for the effect of the tragedy, female distress
being the soul of the drama, and she can embody
that soul if she pleases. Your observations on the
fourth act, on the obscurity of the cause of Fredolpho's domestic calamity, are eminently judicious;
but I dare not more explicitly describe what you
justly conceive to be the cause of his misfortune
and crime. The modern stage is so puritanically
delicate, that any strong allusion to such a circumstance would damn the play as effectually as the
crime of Imogen destroyed the short-lived popularity of " Bertram." The contrast to which you draw
my attention between Fredolpho's boast of his
wealth in the first act and confession of his poverty
in the second, is outrageously absurd. Do, my dear
friend, attend to this ; inconsistency always leads to
ridicule. I must revert to the part of Berthold,
which is sufficiently eccentric and extravagant.
Don't let him, on any account, appear a ludicrous
figure. Perhaps his deformity may be best expressed by a certain savage picturesqueness of
costume, which I could sketch were I upon the
spot, but which I readily submit to your taste in
my absence ; but don't let him be ludicrous, that
must be the ruin of the play. No one could bear
a *Kitchen-Richard.* Much depends on Berthold.
He should not be tall, he must not be well-looking,

yet he must not be like a clown in a pantomime. All this I commit to you, with the most perfect confidence in your judgment and friendship. Of the latter, I must now require the strongest proof I have yet ventured to demand. I am in despair for an epilogue! I was promised one by Sir Charles Morgan, and,—disappointed. My dearest friend, let me call on you in that confidence which your kindness has taught me to indulge for this last, but not least, of favours. Let me hear from you as soon as possible.

'Your most grateful
'CHARLES R. MATURIN.'

THE REV. W. LISLE BOWLES.

'Bremhill, Dec. 25, 1823.

'MY DEAR SIR,

'It has given me much pleasure to hear from you, and still more to hear that you are so well established at Leeds. I thought that as an editor there was great facility and power in your pen.

'I assure you that whenever I have read your poems, which I am delighted to find have been so successful, I have felt as though I had scarcely done them justice. No one can be more sensible than I am of the melody, pathos, and purity of your poetry. I hardly know anything in the English language so affecting as the lines on first hearing the voice of the infant. Your "Ten Years Ago" also is truly exquisite. In your next edition, pray do not forget, in the beautiful lines entitled "The Profession," to reconsider the imagery respecting "words" streaming. We may say a stream of eloquence flows, for then the metaphor is entire; but the one which you use in "The Profession" is too abrupt. You will excuse these observations; I do not think I should object to another expression in the whole volume. I beg my best regards, and those of Mrs. Bowles, to Mrs. Watts, and am, my dear sir,

'Most faithfully yours,
'W. L. Bowles.'

The Rev. W. Lisle Bowles.

'Bremhill, Sept. 18, 1824.

'My dear Sir,

'As to the proposed volume of selections from my poetry, Moore thinks it probable that there was an assignment to the publishers of the copyright of the two first volumes. There would be no difficulty with Crutwell, but there might, he thinks, be some with Mawman and Cadell. The bargain was a gross imposition; for my poems, though I did not know it at the time, were the most saleable and popular productions of the day, in defiance of critics who did not spare them. The booksellers were proprietors, and published almost in successive years six, eight, nine, ten, and eleven editions. With little knowledge of the world, without a single literary adviser, and ignorant, above all things, of such transactions, and the market value of such commodities, I received from them altogether only sixty pounds.

'Moore thinks that if they offer an opposition to the selection, the whole circumstances should be brought before the public for the good of poor authors; and as I am not a poor author, it should be '*marte meo*.' Before I take any step, let me know your opinion.

'Believe me, ever most sincerely yours,

'W. L. Bowles.

'P.S. Whatever I have said about the sale of my poems, the cause of their success was that they had something of nature, and nothing in common with Hayley and Seward, the objects of my early scorn.'

Joseph Ogle Robinson.

'London, Nov. 28, 1824.

'My dear Sir,

'We have not fifty copies of your poems left. It is selling daily. I wish you would authorise me to print a new edition in London agreeably to my own taste, and you shall have a beautiful book. I will make it answer all your wishes, and produce you a good profit. I shall not want to divide profits with you; I will only charge you the usual commission. With best regards to Mrs. Watts.

'I am, my dear sir,

'Yours very truly,

'J. O. Robinson.'

SAMUEL TAYLOR COLERIDGE.

' December 21, 1823.

' DEAR SIR,

'A very severe cold caught by me, as the Irishman caught the Tartar, "struck in," as the wise women say, on my chest; and till it " struck out" again, it so confused my head and depressed my spirits that I was both morally and intellectually unfit to return such an answer to your letter as such a letter deserved. Nothing but your great kindness, and my very strong wish to pass a few days under your roof,—very strong, I say, since I perused your volume of poems,—could have induced me to hesitate in declining the flattering proposal of the Literary and Philosophical Society at Leeds. I received the proposal with lively feelings of respect for the Society, and of regard for yourself. In one instance only has the Lecture scheme repaid me in any proportion to the time and effort. Your letter, for a short time, staggered me, not indeed the advantages, but the wishes it excited. However, illness confined me to my room; and Mr. Gillman, both as my dearest friend and as the medical adviser to whom I owe under God my life and power of being useful, negatived the undertaking, and other friends coincided. I shall write again in a few days.

' Yours cordially,
'S. T. COLERIDGE.'

Miss Jewsbury.
'13, Brooke Street, Manchester,
'May 18, 1824.

'My dear Mrs. Watts,

'The indisposition of one of my children, and the dearest, if it be true that

"The bird that we nurse is the bird that we love,"

has prevented our setting out for Halifax; but I confidently anticipate reaching Leeds sometime next Monday. Though I come almost a stranger, I hope to leave, a friend. * * * How inexpressibly sad is the death of Lord Byron! Had he been, as Friar Tuck says of Rebecca, "but the least bit of a Christian," I should have thought his death the ideal of poetry. I would not have great men die in their autumn, or linger on to their winter, to see themselves "overtopped" by younger and greener growths. They should be

"Extinguished—not decay."

I would not have them tread the downward steps of life like other men; but,

"In the full meridian of their greatness,
Haste to their setting."

They are the flowers of our earth, and I would have them plucked, not left to wither. I would, however, make some exceptions to this my rule of cutting off genius; and Mr. Watts, though a poet, should be allowed to enjoy in peace his three score years and ten.

'Believe me, my dear Mr. Watts,
'Yours very sincerely,
'M. J. Jewsbury.'

13—2

MISS JEWSBURY.

'August 30, 1824.

'MY DEAR FRIEND,

'I was gratified by your approval of my two last papers. I am always gratified by Mr. Watts's approbation; but I do not know whether I am not more pleased with yours. I mean no offence to the higher powers, or special compliment to you. It is merely that one suspects a little of a gentleman's approval may spring from his gallantry. I have not the least hope of the accompanying paper gaining the approbation of either of you. A love-tale I never shall write. The moment I begin to cogitate over the proper materials I feel an irresistible inclination to laugh. With one or two exceptions, I never have read a love-tale without seeing its ludicrous side; and, sure am I, that not even from the Rosabella Annes shall I ever extract a tear. If you had any compassion you might make me a present of a love-tale; I would be very grateful, and honest too, and acknowledge in a note that I was indebted for it to a married friend of great experience. But I know how it is; you are now on your sofa in a state of enviable serenity of body and mind, and from that sofa and that serenity no elocution of mine will stir you. How different is my condition at this present! Three dear children are catechizing me at the rate of ten questions in every five minutes. I am within hearing of one servant stoning a kitchen floor; and of another practising a hymn; and of a very turbulent

child and unsympathetic nurse next door. I think
I could make a decent paper descriptive of the
miseries of combining literary tastes with domestic
duties.

> " Oh, why is this world made so coarse,
>   Or a Poet made so fine ?
> The kick which scarce would move a horse,
>   May kill at once ' the Nine.' "

' I have been reading " St. Leon." Maturin seems
indebted to it for some of his best things in
" Melmoth," especially in the " Tale of Walberg."
Godwin is more of the philosopher than Maturin,
and goes to deeper sources for his horrors. They
are less physical. Now farewell.

' Yours very sincerely,
' M. J. JEWSBURY.'

ROBERT SOUTHEY (POET LAUREATE).

' Keswick, August 29, 1824.

' SIR,

' I have only this evening received your
letter of July 24th, and the little volume which
accompanied it ; I should otherwise most certainly
have written to you long since to thank you for it,
and also have sought an opportunity of expressing
my thanks in person when I passed through Leeds.
With your name I have long been acquainted ; but
one piece which I saw in a provincial newspaper,
" Ten Years Ago," convinced me that you had not
been praised without highly deserving it ; and in
merely cutting open the leaves of this little volume
I see much to admire. Should you visit this

beautiful part of England at any time, it would
give me much pleasure to have an opportunity of
shaking you by the hand.

'Believe me, dear sir,

'Your obliged and obedient servant,

'ROBERT SOUTHEY.'

SIR WALTER SCOTT.

'Abbotsford, Melrose,
'October 12, 1824.

'SIR,

'I have to make you many apologies for
not more early acknowledging your very obliging
and acceptable present of your poetical volume. I
was very long of receiving it, as it was lying at my
house in Edinburgh, with which I have little communication when residing at this place.

'The acknowledgment of your kindness, to speak
truth, I had procrastinated till my thanks could have
had no longer a graceful appearance, and I really
became ashamed of intruding them on you so long
after they were due. Your continued attention has
given me an opportunity of thanking you with a
better grace than I deserve, and at the same time
of expressing the pleasure I have received from
your poems. I am not accustomed to lay weight
on my own judgment in poetical matters; but I
cannot help saying, that in my opinion the elegance
both of expression and conception in your poetry
entitles it to rank very highly. I am glad to see
that the taste of the public has called for a second
edition. This is no small tribute to the merits of

an author at a period when good poetry has become
so general, that whatever is not peculiarly marked
by excellence is sure to fall into neglect. I have,
therefore, to wish you joy of having obtained the
attention which is not always conferred upon merit.
Begging you once more to excuse my irregularities
as a correspondent.

    ' I am, very much,

        ' Your most obedient, obliged servant,

                ' WALTER SCOTT.'

WILLIAM WORDSWORTH.

                ' Rydal Mount, Ambleside,
                ' November 16, 1824.

' DEAR SIR,

    ' On my return home, after a prolonged
absence, I found upon my table your little volume
and accompanying letter, for both of which I return
you sincere thanks. The letter written by my
sister upon their arrival does not leave it less in-
cumbent on me to notice these marks of your
attention. Of the poems I had accidentally a hasty
glance before; I have now perused them at leisure,
and, notwithstanding the modest manner in which
you speak of their merits, I must be allowed to say
that I think the volume one of no common promise,
and that some of the pieces are valuable, independent of such consideration. My sister tells
me she named the " Ten Years Ago." It is one of
this kind; and I agree with her in rating it more
highly than any other of the collection. Let me

point out the thirteenth stanza of the first poem*
—with the exception of the last line but one,
as exactly to my taste, both in sentiment and
language. Should I name other poems that particularly pleased me I might select the "Sketch
from real Life," and the lyrical pieces, the "Sere-
nade," and "Dost Thou love the Lyre." The fifth
stanza of the latter would be better omitted, slightly
altering the commencement of the preceding one.
In lyric poetry the subject and simile should be as
much as possible lost in each other.

'It cannot but be gratifying to me to learn from
your letter that my productions have proved so
interesting, and as you are induced to say bene-
ficial, to a writer whose pieces bear such undeniable
marks of sensibility as appear in yours. I hope
there may not be so much in my writings to mislead
a young poet as is by many roundly asserted ; but
I am not the less disposed strenuously to recommend
to your habitual perusal the great poets of our own
country, who have stood the test of ages. Shakespeare I need not name, nor Milton ; but Chaucer
and Spenser are apt to be overlooked. It is almost
painful to think how far these surpass all others.

'I have to thank you, as I presume, for a *Leeds
Intelligencer*, containing a critique on my poetical
character, which, but for your attention, I probably
should not have seen. Some will say, "Did you ever
know a poet who would agree with his critic when
he was finding fault, especially if on the whole he

* 'The Profession.'

was inclined to praise?" I will ask, did you ever know a critic who suspected it to be possible that he himself might be in the wrong?—in other words, who did not regard his own impressions as the test of excellence? The author of these candid strictures accounts with some pains for the disgust or indifference with which the world received a large portion of my verse, yet without thinking the worse of this portion himself; but wherever the string of his own sympathies is not touched the blame is mine. "Goody Blake and Harry Gill" is apparently no favourite with the person who has transferred the article into the Leeds paper; yet Mr. Crabbe in my hearing said that "Everybody must be delighted with that poem." The "Idiot Boy" was a special favourite with the late Mr. Fox, and with the present Mr. Canning. The South American critic quarrels with the "Celandine," and no doubt would with the "Daffodils," etc.; yet on this last the other day I heard of a most ardent panegyric from a high authority. But these matters are to be decided by principles; and I only mention the above facts to show that there are reasons upon the surface of things for a critic to suspect his own judgment.

'You will excuse the length of this letter, and the more readily if you attribute it to the respect I entertain for your sensibility and genius.

'Believe me, very truly,

'Your obedient servant,

'WM. WORDSWORTH.'

James Montgomery.

'Sheffield,
'December 28, 1824.

'Dear Sir,

'I have been too long in your debt for the first copy of your "Literary Souvenir;" but as it was accompanied by a promise of another, my politic indolence immediately calculated on killing two birds with one stone; for though they were birds of paradise in plumage, and nightingales in song, my stones, methought, were too precious to be thrown away unnecessarily. The truth is, I could write ten letters in the time that I lose in hesitating to write one.

'Think what you may of my remarks on your "Kirkstall Abbey" verses, they came warm from my heart as well as pure from my head; and, of the two, the former is always the best critic in cases where its genuine sympathies are interested, as they were indeed in the very subject of these stanzas. I have spent many of the most poetic hours of my life among those ruins, when I was a boy at Fulneck School. There was the rich skeleton of a window in the tower, which we used to call the Giant's Window; and the winding staircases, now closed up, that led to the roofless walls and broken arches, on which, in all the joy of terror, we schoolboys loved to clamber and risk our lives for the pleasure of escaping with them. There is a couplet in your lines which I dare say you wrote almost unconsciously, and yet you will perhaps acknowledge to be worth all that ever came by mere elaboration from your pen—

> " The steps in youth I loved to tread,
>   Have sunk beneath the foot of Time."

Write always so; and Time will, in vain, attempt to wear out the everlasting flint of those steps by which you shall have ascended as high in the Temple of Fame as you ever climbed up Kirkstall Abbey. I was glad to see Campbell's noble Ode reclaimed by you from neglect. How could the parent of such an offspring have abandoned it? I would thank you for a copy of Archdeacon Wrangham's verses. We had much talk about you at Hunmanby last October; and, in spite of your Toryism, allowed you credit for as much talent as you would be disposed to lay claim to.

' Your friend,

' JAMES MONTGOMERY.'

CHAPTER XVIII.

THE BLUES.

'I AM going,' my father says in a letter to his wife on one of his visits to London about this time, 'to dine with Miss Benger, to meet Miss Jane Porter, Miss Spence, and some other blues.'

If Miss Jewsbury, by the keenness of her intellect and the virility of her humour, may be taken, as I think she may, and in this, perhaps, lies her chief interest to-day, as a prophecy of the female writer of some forty years later, these ladies, and in this, I think, lies their interest, may perhaps be regarded as in a greater or less degree representative of the authoress of a preceding day.

My mother made their acquaintance later. They liked her and her husband, of whom, by the way, they always spoke as her *caro sposo*, thus avoiding, as the refinement and propriety of their age so obviously dictated, the indelicacy of referring in direct terms to the conjugal relations !

Miss Benger was a writer who enjoyed a reputation in that day in a walk of literature represented later by the historical biographies of Agnes Strickland and Caroline Halsted. She was, I believe, the daughter of a purser in the Navy, and mainly self-educated. She once told my mother that, in her youth, books were so difficult of attainment to persons in her station, that she had often, when a child, stopped at the bookseller's shop in the town in which she was brought up, to read the two pages of a new book exposed open in the window; and had gone round to the same shop-window, the following morning, to see if, by good luck, the opened pages had been changed.

The 'Blues' of that day expressed themselves, it may be believed, in a simpler style in their serious compositions than in their familiar correspondence ; at least I would so assume

from two specimens of the latter, for which
as relating to this period, if not to the very
symposium in question, and as illustrating a
phase of manners, I must reserve a place.
Miss Anna Seward, that learned lady of Lichfield, (from some of whose letters to the Bath
coterie I strongly suspect Sheridan derived
the idea of his Mrs. Malaprop,) would seem to
have been the model followed by ladies of a
certain age making claim to culture and refinement in that day in their correspondence.   It
is only fair, however, to say that their modest
euphuisms, as compared with the flowers of
style of the Lichfield lady, are but as a *pot-
pourri,* fragrant but faded, to

> ' The roses by Bendameer's stream.'

MISS BENGER.

> ' Warren Street, Fitzroy Square,
> ' July 31, 1826.

' DEAR SIR,

  ' If I was tantalized to discover, by your last,
that you were in London when I believed you far
distant, still more was I mortified to miss the visit
you had kindly destined for me.   I shall be happy
to transmit you a contribution from an accomplished
friend, who is at once Paintress, Poetess and Tourist,
and will, I flatter myself, prove an acquisition.   For

myself, I dare not present verses, and fear I have not, in my desk, any prose congenial to the elegant "Souvenir." Next year I dare hope to be admitted to your delicious *parterre*, unless I should be banished from life and consequently consigned to oblivion. I entreat you not to allow Mrs. Watts to approach our capital without giving me an opportunity to welcome her steps. My excellent friend, Mr. H. Crabb Robinson, the distinguished friend of Wordsworth, is very anxious to see you. May I bespeak for him the privilege of being admitted by Mrs. Watts to the *sanctum sanctorum* of your domestic fireside ?

' Your truly obliged,
' E. BENGER.'

I may perhaps be permitted to adorn my ' parterre ' with another letter, seeming to possess a certain appositeness of time and place, and suggesting somewhat of the same odour of faded rose-leaves, from a more distinguished and popular writer, whose romance of ' The Scottish Chiefs ' anticipated the Scotch romances of Walter Scott, and whose novel, ' Thaddeus of Warsaw,' will be remembered by sexagenarians as quickening in · a lively degree the sensibilities of its day over the wrongs of Poland,—Miss Jane Porter.

It would have been a sight to see the face

of the recipient of this letter justly gratified, but surely with a modest blush thereupon, after perusing it.

Miss Jane Porter.

> 'Esher, Surrey,
> 'June 26, 1826.

'My dear Sir,

'I shall be happy to do my best to furnish you with a little story for your beautiful work, in the course of the time you propose. I regret that my leaving town, when I did, prevented the kind intentions of my friends Miss Benger and Miss Spence. contriving a little party at one of their houses, where they hoped to give me the gratification of being personally introduced to you ; but when I do revisit London I shall yet anticipate that pleasure,— a real one,—in being made known to a poet and an author, who has, indeed, ever "taught the Muse to move at the command of the Virtues." With much respect,

> 'I remain, dear sir,
> Your obliged and sincere,
> 'Jane Porter.'

Of the third of these literary Graces whom he had been invited to meet at this memorable dinner, I possess no letters ; but some characteristic anecdotes I have preserved, which I am unwilling should, as Mrs. Benger says, be 'consigned to oblivion.'

Miss Elizabeth Spence was a niece of Dr. Fordyce, author of 'Sermons for Young Ladies,' and a friend of Richardson, Mrs. Chapone, and other literary celebrities of the didactic school of that day. Miss Spence made some claims to be included among the celebrities of her day, and must be held to have had her claims allowed then, whatever may have become of them since, as there is a portrait of her, with memoir, in *La Belle Assemblée* for March, 1824, dressed in a gown without any waist, and *coiffée d'un Madras*, after the fashion of Madame de Staël. She enjoyed a small independence, which it was her pleasure to supplement by an occasional novel or other piece of *belles lettres*. She possessed a large acquaintance in the literary world, and among aristocratic ladies, some of whom, in those days, liked to 'sport a bit of blue,' and thus was enabled to attain a degree of notice, and even a sale for her literary productions, which it is possible their intrinsic merits might not have so readily secured for them. She is indeed believed to have been the originator of an artless contrivance for stimulating the circulation, which was apt to become languid, of her works of fiction.

'That is all very well,' she would say out of the window of Lady Caroline Lamb's carriage, in reply to the enumeration, by the bookseller who kept the circulating library at the watering-place, of the new books at the disposal of his customers, 'but have you got " Dame Rebecca Berry, a Tale of the Time of Charles II.," which is creating the greatest sensation in town ? No ! Well, I *am* surprised ! Only imagine, my dear Lady Caroline, they have not got " Dame Rebecca Berry " !'

We can picture Lady Caroline composing her features into a look of as much surprise as might be compatible with their not broadening into a smile on their way back to their usual aspect of graceful serenity, and the bookseller retiring, covered with confusion as with a garment, to order this remarkable work down by the next coach.

Miss Spence did not, however, confine herself to the composition of fiction. She had visited the Highlands at a time when such an enterprise was rare with single ladies, and had published her experiences simultaneously, as the malice of circumstance would have it, with a work on the same subject, by a commercial traveller. *Blackwood's Magazine* reviewed these works together; and made rather merry with ' Miss Spence and the Bagman,' who it irreverently suggested had better make a match of it.

Miss Spence was much discomposed at such unseemly jesting :

' Do you not think, dear Mr. Watts, that it was most unmannerly? I, who never had any connection with trade, unless I may except my cousin Orme,' (a partner in Longman's house of that day); ' and that reminds me that I do think it very remiss of my cousin Orme, that he will not put my book through a second edition.'

This amiable lady saw a good deal of literary and even aristocratic society, in her apartments on the second-floor in Quebec Street, Portman Square; and with an incident connected with these hospitalities I will close this notice of her. Calling upon her later than usual one afternoon, my father found her somewhat ruffled.

'Yes, my dear friend, I am put out. To-night, you know, is one of my evenings,—you never come to my evenings,—and my little maid had prepared my refreshments, and cut my sandwiches, and decanted my wine, when who should call but that horrid Mr. K——!'

Mr. K—— was a literary gentleman, connected with the press, with whom Miss Spence considered it desirable to be on good terms, and who, indeed, up to this time had been rather a favourite with her, having written in her album the following neat distich, of which she was naturally proud ;

> ' A cheerful friend, replete with sense,
>   Is known to all who know Miss Spence.'

These festive preparations arranged on the sideboard, Miss Spence's sense of hospitality had led her to offer refreshment to her unwelcome guest.

'And would you believe it, my dear friend, he sat and sat, and talked and talked, until he had drunk all my wine and eaten all my sandwiches ! And he is only just gone ; and we have to begin all over again. It is so very

inconvenient, and so inconsiderate of Mr.
K——.'

We will hope that public opinion, in the
degree in which it was in Mr. K——'s power
to influence it, was long propitious to Miss
Spence after this incident, and that that gentleman himself sustained no ill effects from it !

As, when looking over a collection of old
miniatures, we make innocently merry over the
strange and, to us, ridiculous fashions of the
day, the cossack trousers, the coalscuttle
bonnet, the high stock, the *gigot* sleeve,
without loving and appreciating any the less
the worth or beauty of the excellent people
so strangely attired,—though congratulating
ourselves naturally on our own superior taste
and discrimination ;—so will we now, with
all affection and respect, notwithstanding the
eccentricities, regarded by us as unbecoming,
in which they costumed their minds, take a
respectful leave of these estimable ladies,
upon whose retirement it will not be needful
again to intrude in this narrative.

CHAPTER XIX.

So successful had been the enterprise of the
'Literary Souvenir,' that its editor was enabled
to introduce the second volume, that of the
year 1826, with the announcement that the
sale of the preceding volume had reached, as
I have said, six thousand copies.

With more time, more resources, and the
energizing stimulus of achieved success, he was
now to produce, in all respects, a much better
book. 'I should be disingenuous,' he says in his
preface, 'were I to lead my readers to expect
any material improvement hereafter.' It included contributions from Coleridge, Southey,
and Campbell; from Milman, Montgomery,

and Lisle Bowles; amongst the female writers were Mrs. Hemans, Miss Mitford, Miss Landon, Miss Jewsbury, as well as ' one of the authors of " The Forest Minstrel," ' Mrs. Mary Howitt. This was, I believe, Mary Howitt's first independent appearance in print as a poet. The poem was entitled ' Surrey in Captivity.'

But the great charm of the book, no doubt, was in its embellishments. The frontispiece was engraved by Charles Rolls from a picture by Stewart Newton; a work which Leslie, in his ' Autobiography,' characterizes as Stewart Newton's best picture—' The Lovers' Quarrel.' Two lovers of the days of Sir Peter Lely are re-exchanging miniatures. The gallant, erect, with face averted, and an air of dignity, coxcombical, but not comical, for he is not intended to be made ridiculous, though exquisitely serious, is removing the lady's portrait from beneath his laced cravat; the lady, also, with averted face and an air of pettish displeasure, the fan working actively in one hand, has withdrawn its counterpart from its place of tender concealment, and is handing it, ribbon and all, in exchange, with well-assumed indifference. Clever are all the accessories, animate and inanimate, which help to carry on the story. The arch waiting-maid, who makes no great secret of her merriment behind her mistress's chair; the pictured happy shepherd and shepherdess upon the tapestry of the chamber, emblematic of the lovers' past, and, who would doubt, also, future paradise of contentment: even the Japanese screen with its gilt border and hinges; the gold-fish in the glass bowl; the reels of silk for the lady's embroidery lying in careless disorder upon the table, mingled with the scattered letters of the lover just withdrawn from the open dressing-case. Such details are a matter of course now; but the time was, when a picture of this character, filled with such carefully wrought-out detail, afforded a stimulus to imagination, and was a source of enjoyment in many a middle-class home, not now to be conceived.

Take another of the embellishments to this volume,—'The Rivals,' one of Leslie's earliest and happiest *genre* pictures, engraved by Finden. Here, as in the 'Lovers' Quarrel,' the age is of Charles II., or it might be a little earlier, the presiding spirit being here rather of Vandyke than Lely. A young and capricious beauty, attired in the conventional white satin dress, followed by her black page bearing a guitar. Two young cavaliers, full of suppressed merriment, accompany her, lagging slightly behind on the left hand, as personages for the moment of secondary importance. One appears to be whispering in her ear, while she drops from her hand, as though by accident, her fan of peacock's feathers, which has rolled down a step of the terrace-walk. She drops it, laughing the while merrily, as, keeping the younger gallant in the background, she allows a very corpulent and rather elderly cavalier, sumptuously attired, to stoop at her feet, and, with much evident discomfort and difficulty, pick up the fan. Very heavy and very stiff is this elderly admirer of the wicked girl, as, bowing low, he leans upon his walking-cane, which bends beneath his weight. The scene is a broad and stately marble terrace in a grand old pleasaunce garden; and you have a very vivid sense of afternoon sun, and a long walk under

it along the hot marble flags for the tired
gentleman before reaching the house ;—

'First through the length of yon hot terrace sweat.'

These works, then engraved for the first
time, became so popular that larger engravings
were subsequently made from them, as was the
case with other subjects first introduced to the
public in this work. As an illustration of the
technical beauty of the engravings in this
volume, I may mention that another subject
by Stewart Newton, entitled 'The Forsaken,'
engraved by Charles Heath, was so highly
valued by *connoisseurs* for the engraver's
work,—it possessed, I think, little other value,
—that proofs of it, before letters, were purchased in this very year by Messrs. Colnaghi,
the print-sellers, at a public sale, at an uniform
price of 19s. each.

The plates in this volume, of 'Richmond Hill,'
engraved by Goodall, and of 'Bolton Abbey,
Wharfdale,' by Finden, after the well-known
drawings by Turner, are too well remembered
for their beauty and brilliancy to call for more
than a passing reference. The latter drawing
was lent, for the purpose of this work, by Mr.

Lister Parker; the former was made by Mr. Turner expressly for it.

Its editor had produced perhaps the most beautiful Christmas book that had, at that time, ever been presented to the public; but what was the Christmas to which it was to address itself! Certainly one of the gloomiest that any undertaking, publishing or otherwise, had ever had to face in England, was the Christmas of 1825. It heralded the year of the Great Panic, with which there has been nothing since, in the way of commercial distress, to compare. In the very month of November in which the ' Literary Souvenir' for 1826 was published, the number of bankruptcies in England had doubled those of the preceding January; and these were again to be doubled in the following month. These failures in November and December, 1825, included between seventy and eighty banks, of which six were London banks,—nay, it was afterwards confessed by Mr. Huskisson, in Parliament, that the Bank of England itself was on the verge of stoppage. As may well be believed, the consternation was universal.

Here is an experience of the Panic graphically portrayed by one who was both a bookseller and a writer.

'On the 6th December,' says Charles Knight, in his 'Passages of a Working Life,' 'I learned that the banking house of Williams and Co. had stopped payment. They were the bankers who transacted the business of our Windsor bank, the partners in which were my friends. Late at night they arrived at my house in Pall Mall. One of the partners and I set out, west and east, to seek the assistance of friends. In the Albany we found the partners of one firm, Messrs. Everett, deliberating by lamp-light. A few words showed how unavailing was the hope of help from them. "We shall ourselves stop at nine o'clock."

'The dark December morning gradually dawned; the lamps died out in the streets; but long before it was perfect day we found Lombard Street blocked up by eager crowds, each man struggling to be foremost at the bank where he kept his account, if its doors should be opened.'

Such being the condition of affairs with the

Banks, it may be imagined that matters did not wear a smiling aspect with the Book-sellers.

'The meeting,' continues Mr. Knight, 'of our Publishers' Club was dismal. How well do I remember the anxious face of Mr. James Duncan, most prudent and sagacious of publishers! Duncan would have told us, if he dared, that half the Row was shaky. The panic had come, passing over all our tribe like the simoom, bringing with it feebleness and terror, if not death.'

This distressful condition of affairs was, of course, not confined to England. At this moment it was sadly exercising in Scotland one who, of all men, might be supposed to be sheltered from such storms; for had he not been the most successful and popular writer of the day, counting the profits of his every work by thousands, and his readers by hundreds of thousands? The great Wizard of the North, who could conjure up at will such exquisite and powerful creations, had no conjuration valid to lay the terrible spectre of Bankruptcy, and was awaiting with manly fortitude the hour which should disclose, whether it was by his Edinburgh publisher, Constable, ' The Crafty,' or their London agents and publishers, that the stroke, which was to include all, was to be delivered.

On the 14th January, 1826, it became known in the City, that a bill drawn by Constable and Co., the Edinbugh publishers, on their London agents, Hurst, Robinson and Company, had been dishonoured ; and, with a great crash, Sir Walter Scott and his two publishers came to the ground together.

Such events have many ramifications. On the same evening,—the circumstance was mentioned to my father by a gentleman who was present,—Mr. Secretary Peel and Mrs. Peel entertained a select circle at dinner at their residence in Privy Gardens, Whitehall. A gentleman arriving late from the City brought the intelligence that Hurst and Robinson had stopped payment. Another guest was observed to exhibit marks of agitation, so much so as to drop his knife and fork. It was Sir Thomas Lawrence, to whom, with reckless liberality, the firm had been in the habit of paying

£3,000 a year for the privilege, which did not belong to him, of engraving his portraits.

But authors probably were among the greatest sufferers. ' The booksellers here,' writes to my father a friend from Edinburgh, Mr. John Malcolm, a writer of much pure and tender verse, ' are very timid now,—January, 1827,—in bringing out any new book. A friend of mine, Mr. Carlyle, author of a " Life of Schiller," disposed of the copyright of certain translations from the German to the Taits, booksellers here, and they have had them ready these four months, always expecting the times would mend. They have at last published them; but, I understand, are terrified lest they should not take.'

To my father, the failure of Hurst and Robinson was a serious blow, the more discouraging, coming as it did at a time when he might fairly have hoped that his struggles were over, and that an assured position in the walk of life which he had chosen as congenial to him, had been definitively secured.

His success with the works already published with the firm had established a mutual confidence, and other literary projects were under arrangement between them. Moreover, he felt for Mr. Robinson, who had been to him a kind and considerate friend, a regard which he knew to be reciprocated; and to a person of his temperament, in which the element of feeling entered strongly, if it did not predominate, these were conditions important, if not indispensable, to satisfactory business relations. These relations were not readily or rapidly to be established with another.

There was, moreover, another element of embarrassment,—which, however, had its aspect of consolation,—in the fact that the balance of his account with the firm proved to be against him, at which he seems to have been surprised, a surprise not on the whole shared by this biographer. He had, I think, much the same dislike to accounts that Dr. Johnson admitted himself to entertain of 'clean linen,' perhaps for something of the same reason, their cold, unaccommodating character. He had possibly discovered,—at all events, he was so to find on more than one occasion,—that an 'account,' whether of a publisher or any other 'man of business,' is justly to be regarded with apprehension by persons not skilled in the manufacture and use of such engines; and, under all such, when sought to be therein emmeshed, he writhed like Samson under the withes of Dalilah, though not always with the same success. No doubt his peace and comfort were more or less disquieted for years by the presentation from time to time of copies of this document, with interest carefully computed to date. Certainly the 'Assignees of Hurst and Robinson' are remembered by this biographer as representing to his youthful imagination some mysteriously powerful and perpetually present malefic influence.

Of Mr. Joseph Ogle Robinson a few kind words may here be justly added. He was one of those men whom the world calls enterprising when they succeed, and culpably rash when they fail; and both with a certain reason. He possessed some sterling virtues. He was a kind friend, a fair and liberal man of business, and I have been informed by his faithful clerk, the late Mr. William Spooner, of the Strand, a considerate master. He made some attempt to carry on affairs after his bankruptcy, in the Poultry and in Red Lion Square, but with no great success. He published at this season an edition of 'Johnson's Dictionary,' the very able preface to which, I may mention as a literary curiosity, was, Mr. Spooner informed me, written by Dr. Maginn.

In the meantime the 'Literary Souvenir' for the year 1826 had been published; and, notwithstanding the badness of the times, met with even greater success than its predecessor, a prosperity which, in view of the adverse 'account' in question, did not, I fear, very greatly advantage its editor.

CHAPTER XX.

To Joseph Ogle Robinson, Esq.

> '4, Beaufort Terrace, Chelsea,
> 'August 26, 1822.

'My dear Sir,

'I have finished one, and am concluding the second number of the tales. It will perhaps be a sufficient excuse for my not calling with them in Cheapside, that I have been recently attending to the publication of a work, which has been some time in the types, of much more interest to me than any of my former productions. This is no other than a very fine boy,—"musical" just now, though not altogether "as is, Apollo's lute,"—who is a "perfect copy," and, unlike most of my other works, entirely free from "errata of the press." It is not my intention to "subscribe" him, so I shall conclude by subscribing myself,

> 'Yours obliged and faithfully,
> 'Alaric A. Watts.'

15—2

TO HIS WIFE.

'Pall Mall,
'June 14, 1823.

MY DEAREST LOVE,

'Mr. Robinson sees our repugnance to Leeds, and wishes to make our residence there as profitable as possible. We have various matters in train together. Sir Richard Phillips will make my volume the subject of his "News from Parnassus" next month in the *Monthly Magazine*. Jerdan will notice it directly; so will the *Morning Chronicle*. The last *Leeds Intelligencer* was quite as I could wish, and my dear editress has fulfilled her duty to the utmost of my expectations. . . . I have intended, from day to day, to go to Chelsea and put up a stone over the remains of our darling; but I find myself unequal to it, and have with a sickening thrill, whenever I have thought of it, deferred it. I must summon resolution to go to-morrow. It distresses me very much; but I will not leave town on any account without doing so. Oh, when I think of the death of that little angel, my anguish knows no bounds! I do not intend to go to any useless expense, but simply a very small stone, with the name and age. Had the dear child been spared us, how happy we should have been! It seems but yesterday that I pressed him to my heart. Never, never, shall I possess such another. I wish we were both with him, free from the bitter struggles to which we are exposed in this cold-hearted world. I see that I shall never be at rest till this shall be.

Forgive me these complainings, my dearest love, and believe me,

' Your ever affectionate husband,

' ALARIC.'

TO JOSEPH OGLE ROBINSON, ESQ.

' Leeds, July 31, 1824.

' MY DEAR SIR,

'The manuscript of " Reine Canziani " I have perused as you request. I like what there is so well, that I am desirous of seeing the whole. It will make, as I judge, one handsome volume, of the size of " Adam Blair." The preface is not very judicious. Candour is all very well; but it will never do to inform the public that the book has lost much of its interest, because more than one popular writer has described the same scenes since it was written ! Novels combining with narrative, descriptions of interesting places and things actual, are always valuable,—witness the success of Mr. Hope's " Anastasius."

'" Histoire de la Domination des Arabes et des Maures en Espagne." The publication of this work in English would, I fear, prove unprofitable. The subject is of limited interest, and the class of persons who might feel disposed to give it a place in a library would prefer it in the original. Not the less so, as I perceive the three volumes will be sold in Paris at much less than it could be produced for in England. I should advice its rejection at once.

' Spooner has sent me a syllabus of some travels

in Greece and the Ionian Isles by a Mr. Lee. It is
impossible to form an estimate of the value of a
book from an analysis of its contents. One could
form a very inadequate idea of the merits of a
Yorkshire pudding from a statement of its compo-
nent parts, without some reference to the qualifications of the cook. Books, like puddings, are often
made of excellent materials, and,—marred in the
making. The author says he has some drawings
" which might be lithographed." Lithography is
damnation to any respectable book. If found worth
engraving, they should be slightly etched.

' I am, my dear sir,

' Yours very faithfully,

' ALARIC A. WATTS.'

To Mr. WILLIAM SPOONER.

' Leeds, Saturday.

' DEAR SPOONER,

 ' The design is exquisite, full of grace and
beauty. " Mnemosyne " would be a very good title
for the book if it were only meant to circulate
among persons of fine taste; but to the greater
part of the buyers of such books it would be wholly
unintelligible. Indeed, many ladies, from the fear
of mispronouncing it, would order a book with a
simpler name. I have given the matter much consideration, and am finally of opinion that the best
title will be " The Literary Souvenir and Cabinet of
Poetry and Romance."

' I think I recognise in the handwriting of the

poem of " The Convict Ship " the autograph of my quondam friend, T. K. Hervey. Be this as it may, the poem is one of infinite beauty, and would, in my humble opinion, do honour to the pen of any living poet. I shall be very happy to insert it. I received two copies of L. E. L.'s poems, one for a friend, who has paid me for it, the other for a present. Be pleased to direct that both be charged to me, as I could not consent to receive a second copy gratis. I will cavil with you any day about sixpence if you overcharge me ; but I have nothing mercenary in my composition, I am sure. I am very desirous to send a copy of my book to W. Read, author of " Rouge et Noir." Can you tell me his address ?

' Mrs. Watts is at Manchester. Never mind the kerchief; I am sorry she has given you so much trouble, but she is a tiresome girl !

' Yours very truly,
' ALARIC A. WATTS.'

To His Wife.

' 10, Howard Street, Strand,
' November 20, 1825.

' MY DEAREST LOVE,

' I write a hasty line with my leading article. Indeed, my best beloved, I do thank you very much for the great attention you must, I am sure, have paid to the paper, as all has been quite as I could wish. You will be pleased to hear that exquisite plate of Finden's, " The Rivals," after Leslie, and that of Rolls of Stewart Newton's "Lovers' Quarrel," are said by many artists to be the finest engravings

ever executed in England of that size. We have
received upwards of seventy retail orders for large-
paper copies already in consequence of these plates.
Mr. Sheepshanks has taken eight proofs of Finden's
plate before the letters. The picture has created
quite a sensation in London, artists having looked
in at Waterloo Place, again and again, to inspect the
proofs. . . . I am going to dine with Miss Benger,
to meet Miss Spence, Miss Porter, and some other
blues.

'Mr. Robinson is about to publish a post-octavo
Shakespeare, and wishes me to edit it. He has also
offered me £200 for a novel or set of tales with my
name. Please send my thick walking-shoes and a
pair of my gaiters; also my common yellow flute.
Brockedon has taken my portrait for himself.

'I am, my dearest love,

'Your ever affectionate

'ALARIC.'

To His Wife.

'Manchester, April 18, 1826.

'MY DEAREST LOVE,

'I saw John Murray before leaving town,
and there is, I think, a great probability of coming
to' terms with him for the publication of the
"Literary Souvenir." Andrews, of Bond Street,
offers liberally for a third share, I shall do something with one or other. Murray was extremely
polite, and mentioned a circumstance which he said
he was sure would gratify me, as it certainly has

done.   A few days ago, Mr. Peel, Canning, Giffard, and Rogers were at his house, when Mr. Peel, taking up my "Poetical Sketches," observed that "Ten Years Ago" was one of the most beautiful poems in the English language.   Murray added that he should like to publish my "Lyrics."

'The Papists have subscribed to prosecute us for the paragraph furnished by Mr. Gilpin, of Stockport, respecting the drunken priest there.   It is a trumpery affair, and Sowler treats it with the same contempt that I do.

'Taylor has published a most outrageous personal attack on me!   It is worth a thousand a year to be mixed up with such cattle.   Hanshall is here, doing all he can to be helpful.   God bless you, my dearest girl!

'Ever thy most affectionate husband,
'ALARIC A. WATTS.'

To His Wife.

'Manchester, April 24, 1826.

'My dearest Love,

'I write a hasty line, to say that I have sold my half copyright of the *Manchester Courier* for £500, and considering all things, and the imperious necessity with reference to the "Literary Souvenir," for my speedy removal to London, I am quite satisfied. As one of the stipulations of my agreement with Mr. Sowler is that he shall release me in a month at furthest, there is nothing to prevent our move, so soon as we can fix upon a residence.   I hope for your approval of what I have done. It was all settled in half an hour, and very amicably. As we can obtain no house *in* town at a reasonable rate, I would suggest a small one on the western suburb; or we might take furnished rooms and look about us. I can rely confidently on from six to seven hundred a year from the " Literary Souvenir," and our habits are very inexpensive. I feel as one just to be released from a dreary dungeon into a pure and enlivening atmosphere.

'I have got Hurst and Robinson's accounts, and by the most monstrous charges and omissions of credits in my favour, they make me *their* debtor. I fear I shall have some trouble in getting these matters adjusted; but it will be my first business.

'Believe me, my dearest love,

'Ever your most affectionate husband,

'ALARIC A. WATTS.'

CHAPTER XXI.

THE success of my father's negotiations on behalf of Miss Jewsbury, as detailed in a former chapter, was naturally communicated by her to her kind friend and well-wisher, Mr. Wordsworth, whose acquaintance my parents made at this time through her introduction. This circumstance, coupled with some expressions into which my father had rather unguardedly been betrayed of his readiness to be of any service in his power to the poet in relation to literary matters in London, led to his being favoured with another commission of a similar nature, which it was not his good fortune to bring to so successful an issue. This was to find for Mr. Wordsworth an enter-

prising and liberal publisher for a new edition
of his poetical works, the edition of the
miscellaneous ' Poems,' published in four
volumes in 1820, being now out of print, or
nearly so, and the publishers not being, as it
would seem, very sanguine about adventuring,
at all events on such terms as would content
the poet, on another edition.

The correspondence on this subject is interesting, as showing the degree of progress which
the poetry of Wordsworth had attained up to
that date in the estimation of the general
public, tested by the irrefragable evidence of
demand and supply.　From Mr. Wordsworth's
letters it appears that this edition of the
' Poems ' (which did not include the ' Excursion,') consisted of five hundred copies.
That nearly three hundred of these, by
which the first expenses of printing, publishing, and advertising had been covered,
were disposed of immediately.　That about
one hundred and fifty more had been got
rid of up to 1824, but that this had been
effected only by so considerable an expenditure
for advertisements, as left the author little

profit; and that when no cost was incurred on this head, the profit would be about £50 on every hundred copies sold without it.

Mr. Wordsworth's wish was to obtain £300 for the right of printing one thousand copies of a new edition, including the ' Excursion ;' but no publisher had been found willing to give such a sum.

My father had opened negotiations with Hurst and Robinson, and was endeavouring to extract a liberal proposal from them, when some circumstances which came to his knowledge led him to suspect that all might not be quite safe in that quarter; and after some correspondence and interviews with Mr. Robinson on the subject, he had deemed it prudent to hold his hand. He was thus placed in a position of some embarrassment between the two, as he did not feel himself at liberty to disclose what it was that occasioned the delay, and Mr. Wordsworth was urging him for a definite answer, which he was not in a position to give. Mrs. Wordsworth, indeed, in her anxiety to see the matter settled, pressed him hard on her own account. The reason she gives

for being so urgent is worth a passing notice.
'Nothing short,' she says, after expressing
her regrets at having to be so persistent, 'of
the peculiar injury which the delay occasions
to Mr. Wordsworth, by giving him time to
tease, and exhaust himself by attempting needless corrections, or, at least, what we presume
to consider such, could justify my having
expressed myself so strongly.'

My father,—whose position in the matter
was certainly not an enviable one,—declined,
however, to be drawn even by the lady, but
kept his own counsel, until the crash of
January, 1826, revealed the mystery.

Of my parents' intercourse with Wordsworth
my mother has left the following notes, made
at my request in later life :

'We made the acquaintance of Mr. Wordsworth on the occasion of a visit to Miss
Jewsbury at Manchester, in the year 1824 or
1825.   Of the various portraits which have
been published of him, one painted by Mr.
Carruthers, and engraved for Galignani's edition
of his poems, issued in Paris in 1828, reminds

me more of the poet, as I remember him, than
any other. I recall an evening passed in his
society on this occasion in which we discussed
poetry, and he repeated to me, at my request,
some of his sonnets. I happened to quote
some lines from Coleridge's "Christabel." He
did not dissent from my expressions of admiration of this poem, but rather discomposed me
by observing that it was an indelicate poem,
a defect which it had never suggested itself to
me to associate with it. I was, perhaps, the
less prepared for a censure of such a description on his friend Coleridge, as he had just
before been talking of Burns, to some of whose
writings it might certainly have applied, in
terms of cordial admiration. From this, and
some other characteristics of his criticism, I
could not forbear the impression that his sympathies were rather with his predecessors than
his contemporaries in the gentle art. I
observed that he rarely left a commendation
of the latter wholly unqualified ; so that the
effect of his criticism seemed to be rather to
qualify mercy with justice than, as I should
rather have preferred, to temper justice with

mercy.   I could have imagined him born, like
Charles Lamb's Hester,

> " Of those who held the Quaker rule,
>   That doth the human feelings cool,
>   Though he was trained in Nature's school,
>   And Nature blessed him,"

for he reminded me not infrequently of some
of the older male members of the Society of
Friends whom I had known in my youth.

'Of his own poems he expressed himself with
a confidence not unlikely to be misunderstood
by strangers, whom he might not have had
the opportunity of impressing, (as a very short
conversation would ensure his doing,) with the
entire singleness and sincerity of his nature.
He asked me what I thought the finest elegiac
composition in the language ; and, when I
diffidently suggested " Lycidas," he replied,
" You are not far wrong.   It may, I think, be
affirmed that Milton's ' Lycidas,' and my
' Laodamia,' are twin Immortals."   I admired
" Laodamia," and was quite willing that so
it should be.

' Indeed, it was difficult to differ from him
on any question of poetical criticism.   He
delivered judgment on such matters as one

having authority, reasoning, as it seemed to me, from some clearly defined principle in his mind, with which the opinion was in accord, so as to be beyond question ; and as though it were his duty to lay down the law as he found it, without fear, favour, or affection. I was much struck by the spirit of rectitude which seemed to animate the expression of every opinion he uttered. He spoke always as though he were upon oath.

' He was a patient and courteous listener, paying the most scrupulous attention to every word, never interrupting, and with a certain fixedness of his clear grey eyes which made one feel that, whatever one's opinion might be, one must be prepared to give a substantial reason for it, and, in doing so, to discard all that might appear fanciful, and not to be readily explained.

' We had the pleasure, at a later period, of receiving Mr. Wordsworth at our residence in London ; and we also visited him at the house of his son-in-law, Mr. Quillinan, to whom he had given some time before a letter of intro-duction to us, and whom we liked extremely.

'The poet at that time had just received a visit from a young American lady, who claimed to be a great admirer of his; but who had profited, nevertheless, so imperfectly by his philosophy, as to have announced to him, that she was one of the richest girls in the States, and didn't intend to marry anybody lower in rank than a Duke. He raised a smile from us all by characterizing his admirer as " rather a tumultuous young woman."

'We made the personal acquaintance of Mr. Coleridge at a somewhat later period, soon after we came to London from Manchester, though some correspondence had, I think, passed between him and my husband when we resided at Leeds. He visited us frequently at our residence at North Bank, Regent's Park, and in Torrington Square, an easy walk to him from Highgate, where he was at that time residing with the Gillmans. The bond of union with my husband had its origin, I think, less in his metaphysical opinions and conversations, than in a certain harmony of critical taste in poetry, and a substantial agreement of opinion in politics. To the former was, I think, to be attributed the desire he once expressed to associate my husband with him in the editorship of an edition of Shakespeare ; while the latter led to contributions from him to the new evening journal, the *Standard,* with which my husband was at that time associated in connection with his friend, Dr. Stanley Lees Giffard.   There should be amongst my husband's papers a characteristic letter addressed to me by the poet about this time, which would give a good idea of him and our intercourse with him.   We named after him a son, Francis Coleridge Watts, born to us in 1827 ; and I perfectly remember being not displeased, when informed by some good-natured mutual friend, that Mrs. Gillman had been good enough to say she was rather jealous of me.'

Here is the letter :—

To MRS. ALARIC WATTS.

' Grove, Highgate,

' Monday afternoon.

' MY DEAR MADAM,

'You do me but justice in believing that the part of your note respecting Mr. Watts's health would give me pain, though having had some

16—2

experience of a newspaper office in my own person,
I was almost as much surprised with what you told
me on Saturday as I am grieved with the information of this morning.   Oh, dear madam ! the world
is a stern and sour goddess, that will not be con-
ciliated without costly sacrifices ; and life, and the
duties of life, yea, even the very affections that
give it zest and value, are pressed into the service !
Were it in Mr. Watts's power to set up a paper, of
which he would be the master *will* as well as the
master *mind*, and a co-proprietor and controlling
editor, though, even so, I should think it a costly
sacrifice, I could more easily reconcile myself to
the thought.   An early competence is so great a
blessing for a man ; I mean of his powers and his
activity of mind.   In this case, it would be a benefit
to society, no less than to himself.   Never was there
a time when a paper of this kind, which should
bring the aims, avowals, and professions of both
parties, measure by measure, and day after day, to
the test of a pre-established code of principles, more
needed than at the present moment, or more certain
of success, supposing that means existed for securing it a fair trial. But these, the knowers of the world
will say are *pia somnia.*   Visions which the seers
must shut their eyes to have ; and alas ! by holding
them for pious dreams, we make them so.

‘ On Thursdays I make a point of remaining at
home, as, on my account, and to prevent my mornings from being at the mercy of visitors, Mr. and
Mrs. Gillman have given a general invitation to

my London and suburban acquaintances for Thursday evenings, a humble sort of conversazione. I will, however, soon take my chance of finding Mr. Watts at home, and beg my tea of you.

'One subject I wished to talk over with him, namely, an edition of Shakespeare's works, with notes that should *bonâ fide* explain what to the general reader needs explanation as briefly as possible, and with the expulsion of all mere antiquarian rubbish. After all the labours of the numerous editors, much remains to be done, even for the text of Shakespeare, and this not consisting of trifles. The prominent feature, however, would be the properly critical notes, prefaces, and analyses, comprising the results of five-and-twenty years' study; the object being to ascertain and distinguish what Shakespeare possessed in common with other great men of his age, or differing only in degree, and what was his, peculiar to himself. I should prefer undertaking the work in concert with some other person, could there be found a man of letters who had confidence in me, and in whom I could have confidence. Should Mr. Watts think the scheme both desirable and feasible, and an opportunity should present itself, he would perhaps sound a publisher on the subject.

'I saw an old epigram of mine in the *Standard.* If it were of any service, beyond the mere filling a gap, I would send him a sheetful; only I would not have my name subscribed to things which, if they afford amusement for the moment, have answered all the purpose they were intended for.'

'Hoping that I shall soon hear better tidings of my friend's health, I remain, dear madam, with affectionate respect,

'Your and his sincere friend,
'S. T. COLERIDGE.'

With the following letter to my father, (written some years later), by Professor Anster, of Dublin, the distinguished translator of 'Faust,' containing an anecdote which in the person of sweet 'Dolly' Wordsworth, tenderly unites Coleridge and the Wordsworths, I will close these imperfect reminiscences of them.

'12, N. Frederick Street, Dublin,
'October 3, 1835.

'MY DEAR SIR,

'I need not say I felt greatly gratified by your affectionate letter. I have lately promised the Gillmans, Coleridge's friends, whom of course you know, and knowing, must love, to pass some days with them, when I am next able to go to London. It will then give me real pleasure to renew and cultivate a friendship I so greatly value. Coleridge, when I last saw him, spoke to me of you with affection. I scarcely heard him ever speak with more affection of anyone than of you. You were at Leeds, and, though I do not think he had any settled intention of going to Leeds to lecture, yet he often talked of it, and this led him first to speak of you. * * * * I am almost unwilling to tell you how strongly he shared the feeling which you express as to the London *literatuli.*

'I will conclude this dull letter by telling you an anecdote of Coleridge. He told me, that when he first thought of literature as a means of support, he formed some connection with one of the Reviews, I think the *Critical:* he was at the time living somewhere in the Lake country, together with Wordsworth. A parcel of books were sent down to be reviewed; among the rest, a volume of poems, he did not tell me the name, and I believe he had forgotten it. He wrote a smart review of the work; every sentence of his article was, he said, an epigram. When he had concluded, he read his review aloud to the ladies of the family. One of them, Wordsworth's sister, burst into tears, and asked him how he could write it? "I was thinking," said she, "how I must feel if I were to read such a review of a poem of yours or William's. And has not this poor man some sister or wife to feel for him?" Coleridge described himself as so affected that he never afterwards wrote a review, and he appeared to me to have even a morbid feeling on the subject.

'Is not the circumstance a striking and characteristic one?

'With sincere regards to Mrs. Watts, in which Mrs. Anster joins.

'I am, yours faithfully and affectionately,
'J. ANSTER.'

CHAPTER XXII.

'LITERARY SOUVENIR,' 1827.—THE EDITOR'S DIARY.

THE 'Literary Souvenir' for the year 1827, notwithstanding the failure of the original publishers, and much adverse vaticination on the part of the editors of rival publications, came up to time, or nearly so, and proved not less successful than its predecessors. It was 'subscribed,'—that is, presented to the trade for their orders,—on the 1st November, 1826, and the 'subscription book' has been preserved. It may, perhaps, be a curiosity, it will certainly be a novelty, to most readers, who are not accustomed to be admitted to the mysteries of the Publishers' *atelier*, and the first page is herewith presented for their information. The names of the various publishers and the number of copies taken by each firm are 'subscribed' by the senior partner.

Nov. 1, 1826.

LITERARY SOUVENIR;

OR,

CABINET OF POETRY AND ROMANCE FOR 1827.

EDITED BY

ALARIC A. WATTS., ESQ.

Sells 12s., subs. 9s., now offered 8s. 6d. ; 25 as 24.

LARGE PAPER COPIES,

With proof impressions of plates on India paper.
Sells 24s., subs. 18s., now offered 17s. ; 25 as 24.

	SMALL.	LARGE.
Longmans, Rees, and Co.	3,500	100
Baldwin, Cradock, and Joy	600	12
Simpkin and Marshall	200	6
George B. Whittaker	150	
Sherwood and Co.	150	4
James Duncan	50	
Rivingtons	25	
Smith, Elder, and Co.	50	
T. M. Richardson	80	
Lupton Relfe	75	
Harrison and Co.	25	
J. A. Hessey	25	3
Charles Tilt	25	2
R. Ackermann	50	2
Thomas Tegg	25	
Robert Jennings	25	4
F. G. Moon	25	6
Sampson Low	25	
W. Pickering	6	
Hatchard and Son	25	

and about a hundred other booksellers. The
total number subscribed, on the day of publication, was 6,433 small-paper copies and
201 large-paper. From memoranda in a diary
I find that the number actually printed of
small-paper copies was 10,169. Of these
335 were presentation copies ; 700 were sent
for sale, and, I conclude, sold there, to
America; and 7,712 were sold in England
between the . date of publication, November 1, 1826, and the month of April, 1827.
In addition to these, 528 large-paper copies
were sold in the same interval, out of 750
printed. There was, furthermore, a considerable sale of the engravings, published sepa-
rately, without the letterpress, in portfolios.
As there was a certain demand for these books
throughout the year for birthday presents,
and every year brought some demand for back
volumes, it may, I think, be assumed that the
whole impression was sooner or later exhausted.

In a further account in the same book, the
cost of production is set out roughly at
£2,620.

I have ventured to enter into these details, as they afford a certain basis upon which something approaching an estimate may be formed of the amount of money spent, and consequent encouragement to Art given, by these publications.

The 'Literary Souvenir' for 1827 was on the whole, I think, more interesting from the quality and variety of its literature than for its art. It, however, contained the engraving by Robert Wallis of 'Buckfastleigh Abbey,' after Turner, (numbered on the list of Turner's engraved works appended to Mr. Ruskin's notes on the Exhibition of 1878, 122, and inadvertently assigned to the year 1828 instead of 1827) ; also the last portrait of Lord Byron, painted in the year 1822 by W. E. West, a clever American portrait-painter, of which Lord Byron had thought so highly as to desire to have an engraving made from it for himself by Raphael Morghen. This portrait will perhaps be recalled to recollection by the following description. The poet is seated against a dark sky background, enveloped. in a cloak which, thrown over the shoulder, he is drawing

round with his right hand. The collar of the
shirt, thrown well back, displays the neck
in half-profile; the face looking full over
the left shoulder. It is, whether as regards composition or resemblance, a powerful
work.

The literature of this volume is certainly
striking, and a list of the contributories would
prove practically a list of all the distinguished
writers of that day, with one exception. Mr.
Wordsworth excused himself from associating
his valued name with the volume, on the plea
of a general rule which he had laid down to
himself, not to contribute to these annual
publications. But Southey, Coleridge, Bowles,
Campbell, and Montgomery all favoured him
with contributions. Amongst the contributors,
in addition to these, were Washington Irving
—an admirable sketch in the style of Jouy—
entitled 'The Contented Man;' Galt; Horace
Smith of the 'Rejected Addresses;' Praed;
Francis Hodgson (Byron's friend, afterwards
Provost of Eton); Shee (afterwards President
of the Royal Academy); James Emerson,
(better remembered by this generation as Sir

Emerson Tennent); and one of the authors of 'Odes and Addresses to Great People,'— Thomas Hood.

Among the ladies were Mrs. Hemans, Miss Mitford, Miss Landon, Miss Jewsbury, and Mrs. Gore, afterwards to be so popular as a novelist of society (this being almost her first appearance in print). In this volume were published for the first time, 'The Better Land' of Mrs. Hemans, and Thomas Hood's 'Retrospective Review.'

As I have said, more than eight thousand copies were sold between the date of publication in November, 1826, and the month of April in the following year.

No sooner were the labours of one year completed than those of the next began. Suitable works of art for engraving, to be bought or borrowed, which became more difficult every year; good copies of the picture to be made for the engraver, where the work, though allowed by the owner to be engraved, could not be spared from the walls for the purpose; the engraver to be set to work and very carefully looked after, for these were golden

days for the line-engravers, and those who
were of any eminence had almost more work
than they could fairly do justice to, and much
stirring up was needed. Then the literature
was to be looked after. To get together one
hundred contributions in prose and verse from
popular authors, and return with thanks the
five hundred at least that were offered and
were not suitable, required both labour and
diplomacy. Then the plates to be distributed
for illustrations, like parts in private theatricals,
every player dissatisfied and wanting somebody else's.

Of the difficulty of obtaining subjects for
engraving, the following autobiographical notes
afford some idea.

Extract from Diary, February, 1827.

'Accompanied Mr. Leslie to Sir Willoughby
Gordon's for the purpose of requesting the loan of
his "Slender and Anne Page." The female face
most beautiful: Anne is pulling a rose to pieces as
Slender is talking to her. Saw also several beautiful sketches by Wilkie; a finished copy in small

of the "Chelsea Pensioners receiving the News of the Battle of Waterloo." My prejudice against Leslie entirely removed on this occasion : he is not only one of the most delightful artists, but also a most agreeable person. Sir Willoughby, however, declines to lend his picture. Early last year I applied to Pickersgill for permission to engrave his "Oriental Loveletter," to which he acceded, but before the picture could be placed in the engraver's hands he sold it to Miss Sheepshanks. Mr. Thompson, R.A., assured me, that much as his pictures have been admired, he has never been able to make £300 a year by his brush; he added, that there was not an R.A. of the present day, Sir Thomas Lawrence always excepted, who could realize £1000 a year by his art. The most eminent artists of the day the most moderate in their charges. He voted for Stewart Newton at the last election of the R.A., and thinks it far from creditable to the Academy that Wilkins should have been elected. Mr. Green informed me that he purchased the copyright of Colton's "Lacon," stereotyped plates included, for £46. If a copy could be procured for the "L. S." of that picture of a "Woman," by Giorgione, which Lord Byron in "Beppo" says is the most beautiful creation in the world, it would be an acquisition.

'Went to Brixton to call on Mr. Prout in consequence of a proposition I had received from him to make a drawing for the next "L. S." Fixed upon a view of the Rialto, which he promised to complete

for me in a month.   His sketches for the most part
admirable.   Note from Leslie, expressing his regret
at Sir Willoughby Gordon's refusal to lend the
"Anne Page and Slender," and promising, if a
suitable picture of his cannot be borrowed, to paint
me something expressly for the purpose.   Concluded
finally to take the house, 58, Torrington Square, at
£110 a year, to enter at the March quarter.   Lent
£10 on account to Messrs. Bradbury and Co., the
printers, making £50 in all.   Servant lad, Thomas,
comes this evening.   Called on Mr. Thompson, R.A.,
and arranged with him finally respecting his "Juliet."
He mentioned that since my application, Charles
Heath had requested permission to engrave it for
the "Keepsake."   Mr. Thompson walked with me
to the house of Mr. Seward, the gentleman who
possesses the small duplicate of the "Juliet," who
readily consented to allow me the use of the picture.
Called on Mr. Robson, and looked over the beautiful
series of drawings intended for Mrs. Haldimand's
album.   Wrote Allan, of Edinburgh, on the
subject of a picture.   Called on Mr. Westall, R.A.,
to look at some drawings which Mr. Pickersgill had
suggested would afford subjects : the most beautiful specimens of Westall that I had seen.   One of
them, "Sunday Evening," well adapted to my
purpose.   Wrote Theodore Hook.   Gave my first
sitting to W. E. West for my portrait.   Visited the
British Institution ; nothing likely, save a picture
by Briggs from "The two Gentlemen of Verona,"
price eighty guineas.   Gave Bradbury a cheque for

£12, making £62. Called on Mr. Stothard, R.A., and purchased his drawing of the "Shakespeare Characters" for twenty guineas. Price of Stothard's large and beautiful picture of "Una surrounded by Satyrs," £60. Called on Mr. Cooper, R.A., and gave him a commission to paint me a subject for next year. Called upon Mr. Howard, R.A., who has undertaken to paint me a small picture of Oberon squeezing the juice of the flower into the eyes of Titania. Bought a beautiful drawing of the "Virgin and Child" in a handsome frame in Weymouth Street for four guineas. Called on Mr. Hilton, R.A., in regard to the engraving of one of his pictures. He suggested "Love taught by the Graces," in the possession of Mr. Phillips, M.P. He told me he had declined four similar propositions from the editors of other annuals—Hall, Ackermann, Heath, and Balmanno— so that I suppose I must regard his willingness to suggest a picture of his for my purposes as a compliment. Receive the Duke of Bedford's permission to engrave for the " L. S." the painting upon which Mr. Leslie is engaged, provided Leslie makes the drawing. Went to Richmond for the purpose of seeing the copy of the Cenci, in Lady Sulivan's possession. It disappointed me; but saw a Guido —a Magdalen—of exquisite beauty. Dined with Andrews, Allan Cunningham, Rovedino, Barry St. Leger, Poole, Tom Hill, Jerdan, D'Egville, etc. Andrews proposes a toast, "Authors and Publishers," observing that their interests were indivisible. " I quite agree with our friend," said Hood, "for I can

testify to having published more than once on the
half-profit system, and to this day I have never
come to any division."   A note from Lady Stafford,
offering any modern pictures in the Marquis's possession either at West Hill or elsewhere; also from
Mrs. Peel, offering the loan of the Wilkie or any
other picture in the Secretary's Gallery.   Mr.
Wadmore having lent me William Allan's picture
of "Stealing a Kiss," put it into the engraver's
hands to be delivered in July.   Mr. Phillips com-
plies with my request to be allowed to copy Hilton's
" Love taught by the Graces " for engraving for
" L. S."   Wrote Mr. Jennings, the print-seller, about
the piracy of my engraving of Stewart Newton's
picture of the "Lovers' Quarrel."   A letter from
Mr. Hilton, inquiring what I mean to give him for
the liberty of copying Mr. Phillips's picture for engraving.   As the picture was sold without reserve,
this claim appears scarcely tenable.   Wrote Mr.
Hilton, informing him that on no previous occasion
had I paid, or been asked to pay, for the loan of
paintings even when borrowed from the artists
themselves, still less when lent by the proprietors;
but expressing myself desirous to meet his wishes if
his expectations did not exceed the sum which
could be afforded for a single subject for such a
work.   The drawing will cost from ten to twelve
guineas.   Called on Mr. Stothard, and saw the drawing entitled " A Conversation," which he has been
making for the "L. S."   Much pleased with the effect,
but thought it wanted finish.—Gave Mr. West a

second sitting for my portrait.—Put Chalon's
" Thief Detected," from *Figaro*, into the hands of the
engraver.—Mr. Freeling lends me Chalon's " Jewel
of the Philippine Isles," from Gil Blas.—Arranged
with Mr. Wood to engrave his picture of " Psyche
borne by Zephyrs to the Island of Pleasure." '

CHAPTER XXIII.

In the year 1827 my father was invited by Messrs. Baldwin, the proprietors of the *St. James's Chronicle* newspaper, to associate himself with a new evening journal, which was established by them in that year in support of 'The Throne and the Altar'—the latter more especially, since it was set on foot in opposition to the Roman Catholic claims, under the now familiar title of the *Standard*. The editorship in chief was entrusted to Dr. Stanley Lees Giffard, one of the most learned and powerful writers of that day, with whom my father established and maintained during life a firm and uninterrupted friendship. Finding, however, that the duties of this situation interfered

with his work on the 'Literary Souvenir,' he
soon relinquished this post, returning to it at
a later period. He was succeeded on this
occasion by Dr. Maginn.

The following letters have an interest in this
connection. It will be perceived that both
Wordsworth and Southey, as also Coleridge,
were adverse to concessions to the Catholics.
They were all, indeed, supporters of Conserva-
tive policy, for which, especially Southey, they
have been subjected in later days to much
illiberal and irrational criticism. Their Con-
servatism did not proceed from want of
liberality, but from apprehension of change.
In judging them, as politicians, it is to be
borne in mind that they had seen the French
Revolution, from which such immediate and
glorious results had been anticipated by ardent
lovers of liberty, culminate in the subjection
of the nations to the despotism of Bonaparte;
and they had further lived to witness even a
more surprising phenomenon, this despotism
justified and supported, and all attempts to
subvert it discouraged and discountenanced,
by politicians who claimed to be the sustainers

of the liberties of the world. This spectacle
had transferred many thoughtful and liberal
minds, these amongst the number, from the
class of those who hope to that of those who
fear from political change. In one respect,
however, not less essential to practical progress
than political foresight, these poets were
greatly in advance of politicians of both classes
in that day, and that was in political moderation,—both Southey and Wordsworth concur-
ring to deprecate the violence of party-spirit
and party-language of the time.

May the hopes of the future, entertained by
the great poets of our time, nurtured in happier
days, prove better founded than were the fears
which agitated the later years of their great
predecessors !

FROM WILLIAM WORDSWORTH.

'May 21, 1827.

'MY DEAR SIR,

'Along with a copy of my new edition I
directed that two should be enclosed to you to be
forwarded, the one to Miss Jewsbury, the other to
Mrs. Hemans, believing that you are in communication with those ladies. Certainly any paper has my
good wishes that promises to be judiciously con-

ducted with a view to support the Protestant cause. I am not a friend to further concessions to the Catholics, being convinced that, as those restrictions are not the cause of the misery and discontent of Ireland, so the removal of them neither will, nor can, tranquilize that unhappy country. The present aspect of public affairs is to me anything but encouraging. You will not, however, be surprised when I say that I participate in little of the heat which the late changes appear to have called forth in London.

' With respect to the seceders, my opinion is that they have acted most injudiciously. It must have been galling, I own, to act under Mr. Canning, or any other concessionist Minister; but surely it would have been much wiser to stomach that, and make the best of a bad state of things, than to leave their places empty to their adversaries. I have no doubt that numbers of the party are heartily sorry for having decided so hastily; and this brings me to a part of the case which bears upon your engagements with the *St. James's Chronicle* and the *Standard.* Undoubtedly there exists at present a strong feeling to support the principles which those papers undertake to defend, but I am inclined to think that it will not be long before much of that feeling abates. If it be true that many seceders regret the course they have taken, it is to be expected that they will fall back into the ranks as soon as they decently and conveniently can; but in what a sad condition will they find the cause which they have conscientiously supported, compared with the state it would have been in, however far short of their and our wishes, provided they had never retired. It grieves me to speak in this manner of men to whom the country has such reason to be grateful for their public services; and who, in the steps they have taken, have, I sincerely believe, been as much guided by a sense of duty as we have a right to expect any party of men to be. I am sorry on their account; and when I look on the other side, what consolation can be found? If I grieve for Mr. Canning's position, it is not more so than he must grieve for it himself. He can have no comfort, knowing what the opinions of the King are on the Catholic question; and feeling what compromises and sacrifices must be reciprocally made to keep him and his new friends together for an hour.

' Mr. Canning is a man to whom I am personally attached. His attentions to me have been beyond what I had the least right to expect. I had occasion to ask a favour of him, not as a member of Parliament, some time ago, and he met my wishes with the most obliging readiness. It is far less on this account that I regret Mr. Canning's present embarrassment than because I shall ever feel grateful to him for the services he rendered the country and the world during the long protracted struggle against the domination of Bonaparte. He was no doubt one of the principal agents in keeping the British army in the Peninsula, at a time when his new friends were clamouring for its recall, and doing all in their power to discourage our noble exertions, and animate our deadly enemy. For this I never can forgive the Whigs, or cease to deplore that a man like Canning should have been brought to unite with such heartless politicians, Englishmen so unworthy of their name and their country.

'Ever sincerely, your obliged friend,

'W. WORDSWORTH.'

FROM ROBERT SOUTHEY (POET LAUREATE).

'Harrogate, June 21, 1827.

'MY DEAR SIR,

'I trouble you with this hasty note to request that the *Standard* may henceforth be directed to Keswick, for which place we set out on our return to-morrow. As soon as I am settled there, which will be in the course of some ten or twelve days, you will hear from me, and I shall commence what I hope may be a useful correspondence. The story of George Fox looking on while his house was burning, which is noticed in the *Standard* to show the ignorance of the biographer, is indeed proof enough of that ignorance. The fact itself is related in the first or second of Espriella's Letters, and belongs to an old acquaintance of mine, Charles Fox by name, who was in all respects a very remarkable person. Your paper has started well. I thought it unguarded in its language concerning Huskisson, imputing to him a wish to subvert the institutions of the country. That there are many of the Whigs who have the wish, I do not question; but it may be doubted whether any of them have confessed to themselves the design. But I do not think Huskisson aims at anything worse than his own advancement. Be that as it may, it is perhaps better to show what must be the natural consequence of their schemes of policy than to charge them with having those consequences as an end in view. I will soon send you some observations on the state of Portugal, and enter upon other subjects of importance.

'Meantime, believe me, dear sir,

'Sincerely yours,

'ROBERT SOUTHEY.'

FROM ROBERT SOUTHEY (POET LAUREATE).

'Keswick, September 11, 1827.

'MY DEAR SIR,

'On my return last night from a visit to Wordsworth I found your letter. One reason why you have not heard from me during the last two months, you have divined. That, however, would not have kept me silent, had the hurry and worry which this season brings with it, left me leisure for composition. I should indeed be altogether unwilling to enter into the warfare of parties; and while Canning lived would never have sought occasion of speaking with severity of one towards whom my personal feelings were kindly. But if time had permitted, I hoped, and still hope, to send you some letters in which great questions will be treated, with the intention of showing that class of the people who are already the fearful majority that it is their interest to support the existing institutions of the country, not to overthrow them, —this in a way that shall rather tend to conciliate and persuade than to provoke a contradictious spirit. You give a sad account of public affairs; and you have sad proof of the disadvantage under which an advocate pleads, when there are certain points which he must not touch, though they are material to the strength of his case. In opinion I have generally gone with the *Standard*, not always in temper; but it is ably conducted, and makes itself felt.

'I have nothing in the way of prose that would suit your "Souvenir," and what I have of verse is, as you see on the opposite page, of little worth; but it will answer the purpose of adding a name to your advertisement, and perhaps next year I may finish for you a long ballad, the story of which is good, and the commencement promises well. Pray send me the proof leaf of these lines, for the chance of improving them; it shall not be detained beyond the next post.

'Believe me, dear sir,

'Yours very truly,

'ROBERT SOUTHEY.'

CHAPTER XXIV.

IT was not to be supposed that an enterprise
so successful as the 'Literary Souvenir' should
be permitted to hold command of the book-
market. Mr. Ackermann, as he was well entitled to do, lost no time in indemnifying
himself for the original idea of naturalizing
the *Taschenbuch*, for which the proprietors of
the 'Literary Souvenir' had been indebted to
him, by adopting, for his 'Forget-Me-Not,' the
improved form which my father's taste and
judgment had given to that idea. 'The Illu-
minated Pocket-Book and Friendship's Offering,' under the editorship of Mr. T. K. Hervey,
and afterwards of Thomas Pringle, had ceased

to be a pocket-book at all, and in its new and improved form had become a formidable rival. It was always ably conducted, and survived to receive in later days contributions from Mr. Tennyson and Mr. Ruskin.   But the most dangerous competitor of this time was the ' Keepsake,' established in 1827 by Mr. Charles Heath, the eminent engraver, under the editorship, at first, of Mr. Harrison Ainsworth, and afterwards, for some years, of Mr. Frederic Mansel Reynolds, son of Frederic Reynolds, a well-known dramatist of that day.   Early in 1828 Mr. Reynolds and Mr. Heath made a pilgrimage into Scotland and the Lake districts, buying up with much gallantry and enterprise, if not always with equal discrimination, contributions from the great masters of the day, blowing their trumpet with no uncertain sound, and killing their contemporaries in anticipation without scruple or remorse.   ' Charles Heath the engraver,' says Southey in a letter to his daughter, written in February, 1828, ' who *is* the " Keepsake," was here last week. He sold fifteen thousand copies last year, and has bespoken four thousand yards of red

watered silk, at three shillings a yard, for bind-
ing the next volume. Four of the existing
annuals will drop this year.'   To another
correspondent he writes : 'Heath has been
here, and offered me fifty guineas for something for the "Keepsake."   I sold him " a pig
in the poke " at that price.'   Sir Walter Scott
responded to a similar appeal, by accommo-
dating Mr. Heath likewise with " a pig in the
poke :' Mr. Heath receiving, in consideration
of no less a sum than £500, Mr. Lockhart
tells us, ' the liberty of printing in his " Keepsake " the long-forgotten juvenile drama of the
" House of Aspen," with " My Aunt Margaret's
Mirror," and two other little tales which had
been omitted, at Ballantyne's entreaty, from
the second part of the " Chronicles of Croft-
angry." '   Wordsworth, even, who had felt
that his years rendered it unsuitable for him
to enter into competition with younger writers
in these annual publications, allowed himself
to be carried away in this auriferous stream,
seeking the sustainment, under these wholly
unlooked - for circumstances, of his friend
Coleridge. ' Some weeks before my late tour,'

writes the latter to the subject of this memoir, September 14, 1828, 'Mr. Frederic Reynolds called on me with a letter of introduction from Wordsworth, in which he (Wordsworth) informed me he had been induced to furnish some poems to Mr. Heath's work; that the un usually handsome terms would scarcely have overcome his reluctance had he not entertained the hope that I might be persuaded to give my name—in short, he hoped I would write.'

It was Pactolus overflowing Parnassus.

The immoderate and injudicious expenditure of these considerable sums for productions, some of which, at all events, could not fail to be disappointing, associated with great names, was unsuccessful in securing in any commensurate degree the success of Mr. Heath's speculation; and the work passed out of his hands into those, I believe, of his publishers. He, however, continued to superintend the engravings of this and other similar enterprises. Conducted with more prudence and moderation, the 'Keepsake' continued to maintain for many years an important position among the annuals, and was, I believe, the last survivor of them.

As the discriminating physician will perceive the seeds of a mortal disorder long before it shall have pronounced itself, or become in the smallest degree apparent to less experienced eyes, so might the prophetic eye of the judicious critic have discovered in Mr. Heath's four thousand yards of red silk at three shillings a yard, and these 'pigs in pokes,' purchased, regardless of expense, to secure great names in a table of contents, symptoms of an alarming character as affecting the health and duration of life of the class of publications beginning to have recourse to such stimulants. In the meantime they seemed to flourish on competition.

The 'Literary Souvenir' for the year 1828 was, I think, less interesting on the whole than had been its immediate predecessors. I notice a copy of verses by Coleridge, 'Youth and Age,' and a powerful tale, a Talmudic legend, perhaps, popularized, by Dr. Maginn. Lord John Russell, too, was a contributor with a 'fable' addressed to Lady Spencer. The popular writers of the day were fully and fairly represented.

The embellishments were perhaps less varied and interesting than those of the two previous volumes; but they included 'The Duke and Duchess reading Don Quixote,'—afterwards engraved in a larger size in mezzotint,—by Leslie; a scene from 'The Marriage of Figaro' (the page detected with his mistress's ribbon on his breast), and the 'Ruby of the Philippine Isles,' from 'Gil Blas,'—kindly lent by Sir Francis Freeling,—both by Chalon.

The editor refers in his preface to the rising competition in these annual works, and, while yielding ungrudgingly to Mr. Ackermann the praise of having introduced books of this class into this country, vindicates to himself his claim to the merit of having, as he modestly phrases it, contributed to render them what they had then become; and as having been the first to set the example of engraving modern pictures in a style worthy their excellence, and at a price which has placed them within the reach of nearly all classes of persons. He concludes with a reference to a proposed

introduction of the 'Annual' class of publication into France, by a French 'Souvenir,' to
be published in anticipation of the year 1829.

In 1828 he published 'The Poetical Album
and Register of Modern Fugitive Poetry,' for
which he had been making collections before
he went to Leeds, but the production of which
had been deferred by the failure of Hurst and
Robinson.

It is in the fugitive poetry of an age that
the poetical spirit and characteristics of that
age are to be read. The great masters of
this divine art and mystery possess, or they
would not be such, too much of the spirit
of the age to follow, of which they are,
indeed, the creators or 'makers,' to enable
those, who come after, readily to discriminate
in their writings what was of and for the
day, and what, belonging to the spirit of
later time, was the delivery rather of the
prophet than the seer. This it is, that to
genuine students of poetry gives a charm to
such collections as those of Dodsley and
Peach, to Southey's 'Annual Anthology,' and
to the collection now in question. It was ex-

tremely popular, and had a large sale, which led to the production of a second series in 1829. It was followed later by two similar selections, under the title of 'The Lyre' and 'The Laurel,' which were also very popular. They have been reprinted in late years by Messrs. Warne and Co.

Among my father's literary *collaborateurs* in the 'Literary Souvenir,' who associate themselves in my memory with this period, was Mr. T. K. Hervey, best remembered now, perhaps, from his having held in later years the editorship of the *Athenæum*, but a noticeable man among the writers of that age on other grounds.

Mr. Hervey was the son of a drysalter at Manchester,—

> 'Foredoomed his sire's soul to cross,
> By penning stanzas when he should engross,'

and other youthful indiscretions. He quitted Trinity College, Cambridge, after a brief career, eventuating in a poem, if not in a degree, and finding the study of the law irksome and uninteresting to him, he came to London, and adopted the profession of literature. The late

Mr. Spooner, of the Strand, an ever-kind and faithful friend to Hervey, informed me that the attention of the public was first seriously attracted to him by the poem, of great beauty assuredly, published in the 'Literary Souvenir' for 1825, entitled 'The Convict Ship.' However this may be, his poems, 'Australia and other Poems,' went into a second edition in that year ; a third, with additions, under the title of 'The Poetical Sketch Book,' was published in 1829.

In 1827 Mr. Hervey migrated for a season to Paris ; but as it is easier for an Englishman to spend money than to earn it in Paris, he soon found himself in some perplexity, and wrote to my father, explaining his position, and seeking his friendly intervention. The means for his extrication were without difficulty obtained from his family ; and his friend wrote urging his immediate return to England, where literary occupation awaited his acceptance, and inviting him to make his house a home till his affairs should become more settled. A reply, from Boulogne, announced his progress so far, and the necessity for a further remittance.   It was forthcoming, and he was again urged to make his way, at once, to London, and to come, on his arrival, to his friend's house in Torrington Square, where all was arranged for his reception.   After some days' delay, which inspired solicitude lest he should have fallen into the hands of the Philistines, my father received a note from him from Hatchett's Hotel, Piccadilly, where he had the satisfaction of finding him in the liveliest health and spirits, closing an excellent dinner in the coffee-room, with a bottle of Mr. Hatchett's best claret.   He had been sojourning there indeed for several days, being naturally desirous, after so long an absence, of enjoying some of the diversions of the town before submitting himself to the tedium of domestic life.   A little difficulty with Mr. Hatchett arising out of these circumstances, and but for which possibly he might not have been heard of even then, having been happily surmounted, the friends drove to Torrington Square, where Hervey sojourned, at times, I fear, a little bored, for some months, comporting himself with great good-humour and amiability, and conforming generally, by means of a little judicious management, to the simple and orderly habits of the house.

One forenoon his hostess, having some little commission with which to entrust him, desired the servant to ask Mr. Hervey to be so kind as to come to her. The servant replied that he was 'in bed.' 'In bed!' she said. 'Why, Mr. Hervey was at breakfast!' 'Oh yes, ma'am!' was the reply; 'Mr. Hervey comes down to breakfast, but he always goes back to bed again.'

Under habits thus erratic was hidden away a temperament of exquisite sensibility to all that was beautiful in nature and art, in life and letters, every phase of which possessed to him its delight, and perhaps also its temptation. His intellect was admirably balanced, assimilating itself readily with whatever was of predominating good quality in the mental attributes of his associates for the moment, and drawing forth instinctively, in every companion, the best of whatever was in him, yet never seeking itself to dominate. Equally at home, equally agreeable, and to all appearance equally well contented in a circle of schoolboys as in a circle of *savants*, he was indeed a charming companion, and had his will been as well balanced and under control as his intellect, he had been a rare creature.

He occupied himself, intermittently, in miscellaneous literary pursuits ; but he was all his life a martyr to asthma, and was often, for lengthened periods, incapable of sustained labour. He contributed to the 'annuals,' editing for a time two of them, the 'Friendship's Offering,' and later the 'Amaranth.' He wrote also in its early days for the *Dublin Review*. The qualities of his mind, which fitted him peculiarly for criticism, introduced him to the acquaintance of Mr. Dilke, the proprietor of the *Athenæum*, which he edited with conspicuous ability and discrimination for some years. He married Miss Eleanora Louisa Montagu, herself an accomplished writer.

In the 'Book of Christmas,' a work which he wrote for his friend Mr. Spooner, then a publisher in Regent Street, there is included among some of the best illustrations of that admirable designer, Seymour, one entitled

'Seeing in the New Year,' which contains a portrait of Hervey in the person of a gentleman sustaining with one hand a candelabrum, and elevating in the other the glass with which he is setting the example to a congenial coterie of inaugurating the happy moment.

A notice *in extenso* of his life and works, written by my father, will be found in the *Art Journal* for the year 1859, page 123.

CHAPTER XXV.

FROM WILLIAM WORDSWORTH.

'Kent's Bank, August 5, 1825.

'DEAR SIR,

'The interest which you kindly take in the publication of my poems, as expressed by Miss Jewsbury, encourages me to trouble you with a letter upon the subject. A proposal was made to Mr. John Murray the publisher, by Mr. Rogers, to print seven hundred and fifty copies of six volumes, including the " Excursion," the author incurring two-thirds of the expense, and receiving two-thirds of the profits. Upon Mr. Murray agreeing to this, I wrote him to inform me what would be the expense; but to this letter, written three months ago, I have received no answer; and therefore cannot but think that I am at liberty, giving due notice to Mr. Murray, to make an arrangement elsewhere. Could a bookseller of spirit and integrity be found, I should have no objection to allow him to print seven hundred and fifty or a thousand copies, for an adequate remuneration, of which you would be a judge on whom I could rely.

'My daughter will have thanked Miss Jewsbury in my name for her two interesting volumes, "Phantasmagoria." Knowing the friendship which exists between you and that lady, it would gratify me to enlarge upon the pleasure which my family and I have derived from her society, and to express our high opinion of her head and heart. It is impossible to foretell how the powers of such a mind may develop themselves, but my judgment inclines to pronounce her natural bent to be more decidedly for life and manners than poetic nature. Yet it would not in the least surprise me if, with favourable opportunities for cultivating feelings more peculiarly poetical, Miss Jewsbury should give proof of capabilities for productions of imaginative enthusiasm.

'If I have ever the pleasure of seeing you at Rydal Mount, I should be happy to converse with you upon certain principles of style, taking for my text any one of your own animated poems, say the last in your "Souvenir,"* which along with your other pieces in the same work† I read with no little admiration. With many thanks and high esteem,

'I remain,

'Your obliged servant,

'WM. WORDSWORTH.'

* 'The Sleeping Cupid.'
† 'The Death of the First-born ;' 'Kirkstall Abbey.'

FROM WILLIAM WORDSWORTH.

'Lowther Castle, Penrith,
'August 13, 1825.

'MY DEAR SIR,

'Your very kind letter has been forwarded to me. I return you sincere thanks for the trouble you have taken on my account. I do not wish to dispose of the copyright of my works. The value of works of imagination it is impossible to predict; and it would be more mortifying to dispose of the copyright for less than might prove its value, than it would gratify me to sell it at a price beyond its worth. I would therefore wish to dispose of the right of printing an edition at a given sum. I therefore authorise you to treat with Messrs. Hurst and Robinson for a new edition of my poems, including the " Excursion," in six volumes.

'I remain, with great respect,

. 'Your faithful and obliged servant,

'WM. WORDSWORTH.'

FROM WILLIAM WORDSWORTH.

'September 5, 1825.

'MY DEAR SIR,

'The offer of Hurst and Robinson is anything but liberal, and, sharing your opinion, I decline it. Mr. Longman, on his recent visit, opened the conversation by observing that Messrs. Hurst and Robinson were about to publish my poems. I answered no,—that, through a friend, I had opened negotiations with them, but that their offer had not satisfied me. He asked me to name a sum; and I told him I could not incur the trouble of carrying the work through the press for less than £300 for an edition of a thousand copies, twenty to be placed at my own disposal. He made no objection, and proposed to lay my offer before his partners. Mr. Longman behaved perfectly like a gentleman, and had I to deal with him alone there would be no obstacle.

'It is now high time to thank you again for all the trouble you have taken. I wish I could make you an adequate or any return; and particularly regret that I am under general restrictions which prevent me contributing a small poem to your own next publication.

'I am, dear sir,

'Your obliged friend and servant,

'WM. WORDSWORTH.'

FROM WILLIAM WORDSWORTH.

'Rydal, September 5, 1825.

'MY DEAR SIR,

'Allow me to introduce to you Mr. Quillinan, a particular friend of ours, who is just leaving us. He is merely passing through Manchester, but I think you will be pleased with each other, however short the interview. I forgot to thank you for the favourable notice you took of the intended edition of my poems in your journal. I have this moment received my annual account from Longman. The "Excursion" has been more than a year out of print, and none of the "Poems" are left. I find that for

forty-nine copies of the four volumes I have received
£25 14s. 6d. net profit, great part of which would
have been swallowed up in advertisements if I had
not forbad them a year ago.

> ' Ever most faithfully,
>> ' Your obliged friend and servant,
>>> ' WM. WORDSWORTH.'

FROM WILLIAM WORDSWORTH.

> 'Coleorton Hall, Ashby-de-la-Zouch,
>> ' October 18, 1825.

' MY DEAR SIR,

' Messrs. Longman and Co., declining my
proposition, offer £100 on publication, £50 when an
edition of five hundred copies shall have been sold,
and the printing of five hundred more to be optional
on the same terms. This I have declined; but
have proposed to allow them to print an edition of
five hundred copies, they paying me on publication
£150, and placing twenty copies at my disposal.
Mr. Longman acknowledges that there is no doubt
of a thousand copies being ultimately sold, but he
says that the last edition of five hundred copies
took five years to go off. This is not quite accurate.
The " Poems " and " Excursion " were both ready for
publication in the autumn of 1820, and, if I am not
grossly mistaken, they cleared the expense of printing in less than a year; and in June, 1824, there
were none of the " Excursion " on hand, and only
twenty-five copies of the " Miscellaneous Poems "
remaining. Mr. Longman says that six volumes
cannot be sold for less than £2 8s.

'I am desirous to hear something of your " Souvenir." I should be very insensible not to be wishful for its success, and sincerely regret that the restrictions under which I am, do not allow me to make an exception in its behalf, without incurring a charge of disingenuousness.

'I remain, my dear sir, very sincerely,
'Your obliged friend and servant,
'WM. WORDSWORTH.'

FROM MRS. WORDSWORTH.

'Rydal Mount,
'December 27, 1825.

'DEAR SIR,

'From your continued silence, we cannot but be apprehensive that some demur, which is causing you trouble on the part of Messrs. Hurst and Robinson, has taken place. At the same time Mr. Wordsworth feels it his duty to request that he may be informed how the matter stands, it being both disagreeable and *very* inconvenient to remain in this state of uncertainty. I feel the more sorry thus to trouble you, having heard through Miss Jewsbury how very much you had been harassed; and nothing short of the peculiar injury which this delay occasions to Mr. W., giving him time to exhaust himself by attempting *needless* corrections, at least what we presume to consider such, could justify my having expressed myself so strongly.

'I need not tell you how much the enjoyment of the very pleasant day we passed with Mrs. Watts would have been heightened had we been so fortunate as to have found you at home.

      ' I remain, dear sir, with high respect,

          ' Your obliged servant,

              ' M. WORDSWORTH.'

FROM WILLIAM WORDSWORTH.

               ' January 23, 1826.

' MY DEAR SIR,

    ' Accept my cordial thanks for the care you have taken of my interests, and the prudent precautions your good sense and regard for me have led you to employ. Be assured that I never imputed remissness or negligence to you, and I cannot but admire the delicacy of your reserve in regard to persons of whose insolvency you had no proof. Truly do I sympathize with your probable losses upon this occasion. I will not detain you longer than to express a hope that the day may arrive when I shall be able to show, by something more substantial than words, in what degree

    ' I am your sincere and obliged friend,

             ' WM. WORDSWORTH..

' P.S.—Pray give our best regards to Mrs. Watts.'

FROM WILLIAM WORDSWORTH.

           ' Lowther Castle,

            ' June 18, 1826.

' MY DEAR SIR,

    ' I was from home when your last obliging letter arrived. Truly am I grieved to hear of your losses through Hurst and Robinson, and thankful for the prudent care you took of my interests. I will with pleasure speak to Mr. De Quincey of your wish to have him among the contributors to your "Souvenir;" but, whatever hopes he may hold out, do not be tempted to depend upon him. He is strangely irresolute. A son of Mr. Coleridge lives in the neighbourhood of Ambleside, and is a very able writer; but he also, like most men of genius, is little to be depended upon. Your having taken the "Souvenir" into your own hands makes me still more regret that the general rule I have laid down precludes my endeavouring to render you any service in that way.

'The state of Miss Jewsbury's health gives me and all her friends very great concern. She is a most interesting person, and would be a great loss should she not recover.

'I remain, my dear sir,
'Your much obliged friend,
'WM. WORDSWORTH.'

FROM SAMUEL TAYLOR COLERIDGE.

'Highgate (1827).

'MY DEAR SIR,

'You must indeed have thought that something strange had happened. It would be wasting strength to enter into a detail of the afflicting incidents and accidents which have thrown in their several successive weights to aggravate the languor of volition, which is but too effectually palliated by an inwardly felt, though in my face scarcely perceptible, decay of life and almost constant pain. Sleep is to me distemper's worst calamity. The truth is, I have for the last three or four months been under a depression of spirits, which I cannot easily characterize. If there be an insanity of the muscular life and voluntary powers, compatible with an orderly and even unweakened state of the intellectual faculties, I have been *non compos voluntatis.* I go on studying the Scriptures, writing notes, and even chapters of my philosophical works, and I can converse at times with a literary friend with unabated vigour; but all must be continuous. Meantime, never detected schoolgirl was more fluttered, or played prettier tricks of cowardice, at the sight of a letter, if from anyone to whom I am attached, or for whom I entertain a high respect. I literally am afraid to open it; and though I am at this time somewhat roused, yet I will communicate a little secret *to you,* which one or two of my friends have found out, viz., that if you would be sure of my reading and answering a letter in my worst of times, you should enclose it under cover to Mrs. Gillman, (Mr. Gillman is so much out he is not so certain), who is an outward conscience to me, just saying that you are anxious to have an answer. I would not on any account that you should suppose any want of respect or regard for you. If I had a sort of spiritual *camera obscura* that could reflect the constructions of my brain and fix them, you would have in your possession a full volume of letters addressed to you. I have so many things to speak of that I must try to see you ; and were I sure of finding you at home this evening I would start off for Torrington Square. There is another thing about the edition of my poems, by Pickering, which I have given over to my dear friend Gillman ; but I must reserve this for your private ear. Of the new poems I will select for you the best, especially the "Youth and Age." I will now go and take a lonely walk, and discover what else I can do, and you shall see or hear from me before the third day is over. God bless you !

'S. T. COLERIDGE.'

SAMUEL TAYLOR COLERIDGE.

' January 1, 1828.

' MY DEAR SIR,

'Under no imaginable circumstances that I can think of should I have suspected you of discourtesy, much less ingratitude, even if the latter were less inapplicable to the relation in which I stand, and have long stood, to you as the obliged party. You have decided wisely, as well as prudently, in omitting the lampoon on Butler. Not that I should so much have disliked its publication, as the publication without my name, and at my own request. I had hastily repeated, rather than deliberately adopted, a friend's advice, " Were I you I would not put my name to it." Now a lampoon is but of equivocal morality perhaps at the best ; but unequivocally bad when anonymous. He who thinks it his duty to give pain to another, and to excite his resentment, is bound at least to give this proof that he is indeed actuated by a sense of duty, that he does it openly, and faces the consequences.

'Mrs. Gillman begs me to add how much she and Mr. Gillman will be gratified by seeing you and Mrs. Watts at our house.

'Accept, my dear sir, for yourself and Mrs. Watts, my very sincere wish, A happy New Year, and a succession of them; for, believe me, that with a lively interest, both in your success circumstantial and in the genial evolution of your own strong intellectual powers,

'I remain, your obliged and sincere friend,

'S. T. COLERIDGE.'

SAMUEL TAYLOR COLERIDGE.

'Grove, Highgate,
'September 14, 1828.

'My DEAR SIR,

'I suspect that you have not received two letter-sheets of verse which, to the best of my recollection, I left at your house. The first a pretended fragment of Lee, the tragic poet, containing a description of Limbo; and, according to my own fancy, including some of the most forcible lines my niggard Muse ever made me a present of. For to compare one's self with one's self is, I trust, no offence against humility, and may stand absolved from the operation of the adage that "comparisons

are odious." Now, my dear sir, if you have not the
poems, or deem them inapplicable, I will send you
a short poem,—the best I have of the two or three
unpublished, though far from what I could wish,—
and I am glad it is in my power to do so without
breach of engagement.

'Some weeks before my late tour up and down
the Rhine, and through Holland and the Nether-
lands, Mr. Frederic Reynolds called on me with a
letter of introduction from Wordsworth, in which
Wordsworth informed me that he had been induced,
as likewise Southey and Sir Walter Scott, to furnish
some poems to a work undertaken by Mr. Heath,
with Mr. Reynolds as his editor; that the unusually
handsome terms would scarcely have overcome his
reluctance had he not entertained the hope that I
might be persuaded to give my name; and that,
besides Sir Walter Scott, Southey, Wordsworth, and
myself, Lord Normanby, and, as Reynolds believed,
Mr. Moore, were to be the only, or all but the only
contributors. In short, he hoped I would write. Mr.
Reynolds offered me £50,—more, by the way, than
all my literary labours, if I may except my salary
from the *Morning Post and Courier*, had procured
me;—but the condition was, that I was to contribute
to no other annual. I caught at the opportunity
thus afforded me for declining; for, in spite of the
£50, and Wordsworth's advice, and an unwilling-
ness to risk being misinterpreted at Keswick, I was
averse to it. My answer was : " The matter is settled
at once, for I have already promised the very poem

in question, with some other verses, to Mr. Alaric Watts for the 'Souvenir,' if he thinks them worthy; and it is not, therefore, in my power to accede to this condition." "Well," replied Reynolds, "what is done, is done. The condition, therefore, shall be understood, 'with the exception of any contribution to the "Souvenir."'"* So the contract was concluded. To-morrow I am engaged to pay my long-delayed first visit to my dear friends Charles and Mary Lamb, at Enfield, or I would come to town; or, if you write to-morrow, directing "Charles Lamb, Esq., Enfield Chase, next house to the Phœnix Fire Office, for S. T. C.," I shall receive it; or I should be happy to see you here on my return.

'Believe me, my dear sir,

'Very truly yours,

'S. T. Coleridge.'

---

* One of these poems was, in fact, printed in both works, with the tacit consent, possibly, of both editors.

CHAPTER XXVI.

IT will be perceived that my father had entertained the idea of introducing the 'annual' class of publications, so successful in England, into France ; but there were influences at work in France at this time, of which he, in common with more experienced observers, had failed to realize the importance, which were little favourable to the introduction into that country of the art and literature of sentiment and taste.

This condition of things is happily summarized in a letter addressed to Miss Caroline Bowles, afterwards Mrs. Southey, by the Duchess de Narbonne, to whom she had introduced him on the occasion of a visit which he paid to Paris about this time with the above object : '.J'aurais voulu,' she says, 'lui être bonne à quelque chose, mais il avait des lettres de recommandation que valaient toutes les connaissances que j'aurais pu lui procurer. Je crains cependant qu'il n'obtienne pas tout le succès qu'il s'est promis de son voyage. Notre esprit du moment est plus tourné vers la politique que livré au culte des Muses. Nous avons tant de mépris pour le gros bon sens de nos ancêtres que ne pouvant pas refuser quelque génie aux Corneilles, Racines, etc. ; nous prenons le parti de proscrire la poésie pour ne pas entendre parler des poètes. *Tout ce qui n'est que grace d'esprit, a peu de vogue !'*

It was, indeed, a time unsympathetic, not to say of ill augury, to the circles of society in which the introductions of the Duchess de Narbonne would have been so valuable ; and the fame of the Corneilles, etc., was, it must be admitted, as must happen to all fame at some seasons, undergoing a temporary eclipse. But the age was not so deficient in capacity for poetic feeling as the lady supposed. 'He who would understand me,' says Jacob Behmen, 'must have the hammer that will strike my bell ;' and so said France at this interesting time.   Nor was the hammer lacking.

It was the dawn of that great revolution in art and letters, which was to precede and indeed prefigure and prepare the political revolution of 1830, and the dethronement of Legitimacy in the person of Charles X.   That day of battle which has since become so famous, in which some dozen young men of genius, with Victor Hugo at their head, animated by an entirely new and vivifying intellectual and emotional spirit, were to succeed in reversing all the traditions of the elders, and in converting France from a formal adhesion to a frigid and artificial classicism to a zealous faith in a new *régime*, in literature and art, of force, truth, and picturesqueness.

Madame de Narbonne was evidently a classicist ; my father's taste or happy star threw him into the opposite camp.   It was a Rabelaisian time and coterie,—Rabelais was surely the first Romanticist,—into which my father found himself dropped from the sober sentiment of England.   It was, to say the truth, rather an inebriated age, and society was teeming in France with incongruous originalities, clothed in forms often grotesque and *bizarre*, through the strange masks of which was formulating a new spirit of exquisite force and beauty. It was not ashamed to be indebted,—originality never is ;—it borrowed freely alike from the art and literature, even from the forms and fashions of life if they suited it, of England, of Germany, of Spain, and of the East. It borrowed from all, it assimilated all, and, out of all, it gave to art and letters in France,—a new Renaissance.

Apart from his introductions, which, from Madame de Narbonne's letter, I gather to have been good, my father possessed, as the friend of that 'triste et terrible Maturin' (of whom the Romanticists freely avowed their admiration, and to whose writings Charles Nodier referred as having influenced those of Victor Hugo himself), a passport to Romantic circles. Moreover, he spoke good French, which was not very common in that day. There was indeed, as I have said, something French in his appearance ; and if he could only have prevailed on himself to obtemperate to Romantic fashions by substituting a beard for a shirt-collar, he might have passed muster readily enough for a member. of the *Cénacle.* It was also not unfavourable to his reception in art circles that he knew what was good, was catholic in his tastes, and made considerable purchases.

The centre of the new Romantic School in Art was the studio in the Rue de l'Est, occupied later by Regnault, and the family circle in the Rue Notre Dame des Champs, of the brothers Deveria. They used to say in that day, Théophile Gautier tells us, ' *Le Romantisme est chez lui, chez les Deveria.*' With this family, consisting of Achille Deveria and his wife, Eugene Deveria, and their sister Laure, my father formed an acquaintance that became intimate, and here he was introduced to many of the most interesting members of the new school. He met here Victor Hugo, made known to him as ' *l'auteur de Cromwell;*' Alexandre Dumas, who presented him with his portrait, *en médaillon,* in bronzed plaster, one of the famous series, possibly, now invaluable, of which he took care to possess himself of the rest, of Jehan du Seigneur ; M. Thiers, to whom he was introduced in the printing-office of the *National,* then just established, where the provident young journalist was correcting his proofs, with his arms carefully encased in black calico sleeves to preserve them from contact with the printer's ink ; Madame Tastu, the poetess of the Romanticists, author of ' La Chambre de la Châtelaine '—' imitation de Maturin.'

Much of his time and not a little of his money he spent in buying drawings, bronzes, etc., at the well-known house, then in the Rue du Coq St. Honoré, of Alphonse Giroux et Compagnie, where, at that particular time, he might, had he known it, have made the acquaintance of a writer who was at a later period to combine, so as to form almost a new school, the power and picturesqueness of Romanticism with the grace and purity of style of the best Classicism ; but who, at that moment, feeling like a blind person for a door into daylight, was gaining her livelihood by painting fans, tea-chests, coffrets, and cigar-cases for that firm, conscious of being ' *artiste,*' but not having as yet discovered in what direction,—Madame Dudevant.

Among the painters, in addition to his hosts, he made the acquaintance in this circle of Fragonard, whose picture forming the *plafond* to the sixth gallery of the Louvre, 'Francis I. receiving Knighthood at the hands of the Chevalier Bayard,' — the political bearing worthy of note,—he engraved in the 'Literary Souvenir' for 1833; Ary Scheffer, at whose studio he was a frequent visitor, and whom, I believe, he first made known to the English public by a picture engraved in the 'New Year's Gift,' a work of which I shall have to speak, in the same year; Decamps, of whom he also introduced a work into his 'Souvenir;' Boulanger, the painter of the famous picture of 'Mazeppa on the wild Horse,' who shared the studio of the Deverias; Aurèle Robert, the brother of Leopold; Couder, afterwards portrait-painter to King Louis Philippe, who, with his agreeable wife, visited my parents in London, and painted his portrait and many others.

Of the brothers Deveria a family group was introduced by him into the 'Literary Souvenir' for 1832. It represented the brothers and sisters descending a staircase in costume for a carnival ball; Eugene as Rubens; their sister in the high headdress and short petticoats, with a sash fastened by a large buckle of gold and steel, which was the ball-dress of the time, the whole *un peu carnivalisé;* Achille as a Venetian senator; and Madame Deveria as Madame de Sévigné.

At that time Eugene Deveria was the pride and hope of the Romantic School in art, having just then produced, in his twenty-second year, his remarkable picture of the 'Birth of Henry IV.,' purchased then, or a little later, by the government for the modest price of four thousand francs. 'On peut croire,' says Théophile Gautier, 'quand fut exposé la Naissance de Henri Quatre, que la France allait avoir son Paul Veronese, et qu'un grand coloriste nous était venu.' Of this interesting person, representing as he did the *Romantiste* painter of that day, I will venture to add the following portrait, full of character and *vraisemblance,* from the pen of Théophile Gautier:

'Eugene Deveria was then, (the time of which I am writing), a handsome young man, of hardy mien, large in figure, and of a certain robust delicacy. He wore his hair closely cropped, moustaches twisted at the ends *en croc*, and a long pointed beard,—the horror of the *bourgeois*. The beard, so common now, was regarded then as brutal, barbarous, monstrous; but Romantic artists were not solicitous to realize the ideal of perfection of the notary,—they cherished, on the contrary, whatever might distinguish them from the Philistines. Eugene had a taste for luxurious appointments of all kinds, like a Venetian senator of the sixteenth century. He was partial to satin, damask, jewellery, and would have liked nothing better than to go out to pay visits in a dress of gold brocade, like a magnifico of Titian or Bonifazio. Not finding it convenient to adopt the costume of his genius, he applied himself to modifying the hideous dress of his time. His open frock-coats were thrown back on the shoulders, exhibiting the glories of broad velvet facings, displaying the manly breast protuberated by waistcoats fashioned like a doublet. Heavy rings, studded with engraved stones and signets, glittered on his fingers. His hat recalled the low crown, wide brim, and curling sweep of that of Rubens; and when he walked the streets an ample Spanish cloak completed these elegant picturesque eccentricities.'

Such was the Romanticist artist of the years 1828-30.

Those who remember the fashions of the D'Orsay day in England, and recall the low wide-brimmed hat curved at the edge, the broad lapels thrown well back of the open frock-coat, the waistcoat following the same lines, displaying the chest, and padded where needful to assume the shape of a cuirass; and, above all, the large whiskers and stock, *without any shirt-collar*, will recognise how in costume as in other things the heresy of one age becomes the high religion of the next; and the dandy of to-day displays no linen because the Bohemian artist of yesterday, who set his fashion, had no linen to display.

I may add that Eugene Deveria's picture of the 'Birth of Henry IV.' will be found in the Gallery of Modern Art of the Louvre.

Speaking of the Bohemian artist, one cannot

but remember how many there were in that little army of Romanticists who, so to speak, never obtained any promotion at all ; the mere rank and file who won the battle. 'Dans l'armée de Romantisme,' says Théophile Gautier, 'comme dans l'armée d'Italie, tout le monde était jeune.' Like the army of Italy, too, it was poor,—feasting, when it could, which was seldom, joyously ; fasting, when it must, which was usual, cheerfully ; for it lived, as only an age or a human being who has tasted this divine food knows that men can live,—on its enthusiasm, on new truth and sympathy. 'When I was a student,' said one of the most distinguished of this coterie later to my mother, 'I lived on four hundred francs a year.' 'But on what did you live ?' she naturally inquired. 'Chiefly on bread and grapes.' 'But how did you clothe yourself ?' 'A large cloak,'—these cloaks *à l'Espagnol* were greatly affected by the Romantistes,—' covered all deficiencies when I went abroad in daylight, which was seldom.' His lodging he explained to the lady, with entire *naïveté* and simplicity, and without any periphrasis, was provided by the hospitality of—a friend.

CHAPTER XXVII.

THE year 1829 opened with a pretty lively competition among these annual books. There were already in the field, as I have said, in addition to the 'Literary Souvenir,' the 'Forget-Me-Not,' edited by Mr. Shoberl; the 'Friendship's Offering,' by Mr. Thomas Pringle; the 'Keepsake,' by Mr. Mansel Reynolds; also the 'Amulet,' by Mr. S. C. Hall. To these were to be added, this year, the 'Bijou,' edited by Mr. (afterwards Sir) Harris Nicolas; the 'Winter's Wreath,' by Mr. William B. Chorley; the 'Anniversary,' by Allan Cunningham; and the 'Gem' (in which was first published the 'Dream of Eugene Aram'), by Thomas Hood.

Nor were these all. The idea that among the Christmas and New Year's gifts of this description, provision should be made for the tastes and requirements of the young, who take an especial interest in such seasons, seems to have developed itself simultaneously, like the origin of man, according to the physicists, in a variety of directions at the same time. This year, 1829, witnessed the birth of the 'Juvenile Forget-Me-Not,' edited by Mrs. S. C. Hall; the 'Juvenile Keepsake,' by Thomas Roscoe; the 'Christmas Box,' by Crofton Croker; and, more important to this narrative, the 'New Year's Gift,' by Mrs. Alaric Watts.

The 'Literary Souvenir' for 1829, though it included amongst the names of its contributors, for the first time, that of 'the author of "Pelham,"' was, I think, more interesting from its engravings than from its letterpress. Of these embellishments may be noticed an engraving by Charles Rolls, from a picture by Leslie, full of elegant comedy. It bore the title of 'The Proposal,' and was, in fact, a *replica* painted on a commission, for my father, of the two principal figures of the artist's larger picture of ' May Day in the Time of Queen Elizabeth.'

In the foreground of a long pleached alley, with a fountain in the distance, the Euphuist is bowing over the hand of the Queen of the May, his ' fair Condescension,' with an air of serious, yet comical, deference and devotion. She, a comely and gracious maiden, not of the Court perhaps, but not of the village either, is listening with not displeased surprise to the pearls and diamonds of speech, which she does not in the least comprehend, proceeding from between the well-trimmed moustache and beard of her courtly admirer. His high-crowned hat and feather, his earrings and exquisitely plaited ruff, his gloves purfled, to correspond with his richly-guarded panes ; his cloak half off the shoulder ;

' The Switzer's knot
On his French garters,'

with

' The easie flexure of his supple hams,'

proclaim him a gallant worthy to contend for fair lady with Sir Fastidious Brisk himself.

20—2

And yet not so arrant a coxcomb either ; but a soldier and a gentleman, in Lily, no doubt,

> 'Exceedingly well read,
> And profited in strange concealments.'

Leslie asked Washington Irving for a sketch to illustrate this engraving. 'Sketches of the kind,' he replied, 'that are to stand by themselves in these collections of *jeux d'esprit*, require some lucky thought, or something striking, either in conception or execution. If I can think of anything in time, I will send it you.'

It was not, however, forthcoming ; and the plate was illustrated cleverly and appropriately enough by Mrs. Gore.

The volume also contained 'Cleopatra embarking on the Cydnus,' engraved by Goodall, after Danby; and 'Ehrenbreitstein,' engraved by John Pye, after Turner.

But the most interesting embellishment in the volume at that time was, perhaps, Leslie's portrait of Sir Walter Scott. The following extract from the 'Noctes Ambrosianæ' of *Blackwood's Magazine* (December, 1828) may have an interest in this connection.

' SHEPHERD. "What for didna ye send me out a' the anuwals o' the year, as you promised? I hate folks that promises, and ne'er performs."

' NORTH. "The reason, James, was that I had them not to send. But I have Mr. Alaric Watts' 'Souvenir' in my pocket; there. Ay! you may well turn up your eyes in admiration. Of all the engravings I ever beheld, these are the most exquisitely beautiful."

' SHEPHERD. "Sir Walter? Ma faith! The thing's dune at last! The verra man himsel', as if you were looking at him through the wrang end o' a telescope. Only see his hauns!—the big, fat, roun' firm back o' his hauns! I should ha'e said in an instant, 'That's Sir Walter,' had I seen nae mair than just by themsel's, the hauns! Hoo are ye, Sir Walter? Hoo are ye, sir? I'm glad to see ye looking sae weel! Na—am na I a fule, Mr. North, to be speakin' till an eemage, as it were, Lord bless him, the vera leevin' glory o' Scotland."

' NORTH. "I request Posterity to be informed that Leslie's is the best likeness of Sir Walter Scott ever achieved, face, figure, air, manner, all characteristically complete."

' SHEPHERD. "And is the writin' in the 'Souvenir' gude, sir?"

' NORTH. "Excellent."

' SHEPHERD. "If the 'Keepsake' beats the beauty of the 'Souvenir,' she may change her name into the 'Phœnix,' or the 'Bird o' Paradise.'"

NORTH. "Pocket the affront, James."

'SHEPHERD. "Hae ye made me a present o' 't, sir, ootricht? Ye hae? Then allow me to treat ye wi' the eisters at my ain expense."'

The following letters of Mr. Lockhart's refer to the engraving of Leslie's portrait of Sir Walter Scott:

FROM J. G. LOCKHART.

'September 22, 1828.

' DEAR SIR,

'My wife and her brother, Charles Scott, agree with me in thinking the print you have sent me, *as it is*, by far the best engraving of Sir Walter Scott's likeness that has yet appeared. I fancy that a little more of definition in the main line of the mouth might possibly make the likeness more perfect; but of this Mr. Leslie is the best, the only judge. I beg two proofs, as both my wife and her brother wish to have them framed for the ornature of their own rooms.

'Yours truly,
'J. G. LOCKHART.'

' DEAR SIR,

'I am still more delighted with the print as I now see it; and shall be much obliged at having the proofs half on India, and half on French paper.

'Yours truly,
'J. G. LOCKHART'

In the 'List of Portraits of Sir Walter Scott,' given by Mr. Lockhart in the concluding chapter of his 'Life,' published in 1836, this print is referred to in the following terms:

'A half-length, painted by C. R. Leslie, R.A., in 1824, for Mr. Ticknor, of Boston, New England. It has not been engraved, in this country I mean, but a reduced copy of it furnished an indifferent print for one of the annuals.'

I am not able to explain,—nor am I concerned to do so,—the discrepancy between Mr. Lockhart's opinion of this engraving in 1828, and his estimate of it in 1836. The engraver was Mr. Danforth, who was employed on it at the instance of Mr. Leslie.

The advertisements on the fly-leaf to the 'Literary Souvenir' for 1829, announced as preparing for publication, 'with eight highly-finished line engravings, " Lyrics of the Heart, and other poems," by Alaric A. Watts.'

My mother's annual, 'The New Year's Gift,' commenced in this year, and continued, annually, until the year 1836, to divide pretty equally, I think, with the 'Juvenile Forget-

Mc-Not' of Mrs. S. C. Hall, the suffrages of the rising generation of that day.

There is an interest, worthy perhaps a passing remark, in the difference between the spirit in which it was sought,—at all events by my mother,—to address and interest young people in that day, and the modes and methods of addressing youth now. Each, of course, has had its origin in the nature of the material to be dealt with, which was very different then in quality and character from that under treatment by parents and guardians fifty years later. Young people were much younger people then than they are now ; they believed more readily, and they reasoned less. It was needful, therefore, in them, to cultivate the reason, and, as my mother thought,—though such was not then the general opinion,— morality and Christian principles, through the reason. Religion, purely doctrinal, she left to other agencies. We should, perhaps, now deem it desirable to reverse the process ; to cultivate, in the first instance, the imagination, which is the faculty of belief, rather than the reason, which has become intuitive, needing no stimulant ; and to arrive at Christian principles and practice through the imagination. She excluded, therefore, from the subjects of her little book all apocryphal personages, giants and fairies, in all of which children of that age were quite capable of believing to their prejudice, and not to their profit. Stories of giants and fairies may now be told to children with impunity, for they will not believe them ; nay, greatly to their advantage, for, from them, they will formulate to themselves innocent and beautiful phantasies wherein to repose their poor work-worn brains, and gently stimulate their too infrequently exercised imaginations.

CHAPTER XXVIII.

WILLIAM SIDNEY WALKER, AND WINTHROP MACKWORTH PRAED.

ONE day, towards the close of the year 1829, Mr. Winthrop Praed, the poet, who was a frequent visitor in Torrington Square, called with a copy of verses, for which he was desirous of finding a market, on behalf of a friend. They were accepted as soon as read, and appeared in the 'Literary Souvenir' for 1830, under the title of 'Hymn to Liberty.' The writer was Mr. William Sidney Walker, of Trinity College, Cambridge, an old schoolfellow of Praed's at Eton. Of this gentleman, of whom as a poet too little is known, and who became intimate, or as intimate as his peculiarities admitted, in our circle, it had been my father's wish, in his autobiography, to give some account. He was anticipated in this desire by their mutual friend Mr. Moultrie, the rector of Rugby, himself distinguished as a poet, and a friend of Walker's from the Eton days, who in the year 1852 edited his ' Remains,' accompanying them with a touching biography and extracts from his correspondence.

Sidney Walker had been a member of the famous little coterie of the *Etonian Magazine,* of which Macaulay, Praed, and Moultrie were perhaps the most distinguished members, and some of his early poems were, I believe, first published in it. If the reminiscences of Walker's friends are to be trusted, not even Macaulay had, at the same age, given such extraordinary promise of future excellence. ' His precocity as a child,' says Moultrie, ' is almost incredible. At eighteen months old he could repeat most of the nursery poems of those days ; and such was his desire to read, that at that age he was permitted, against the better judgment of his mother, to learn his letters. It was only necessary to repeat them once to him ; he never required a lesson after-

wards, but asked a question if in difficulty.'
After statements so startling, for which it is
just and necessary to say his biographer's
authority seems to have been direct and
reliable, it will excite little surprise to learn,
upon testimony of a gentleman then surviving
who had heard him, that 'at two years of age
he should have been able to read aloud in the
"History of England."   At five years old he
had read history extensively, and poetry still
more devotedly.   In his seventh year, when
the tailor came to measure him for his first
suit, he found his little customer busied with
his book. " I am reading," he said, "and I
wish you would tell me about this line; I
cannot quite make out what Milton means
here."   The tailor,—who had never taken
Milton's measure,—was obliged to confess his
inability. " I am so sorry," the child rejoined
sweetly, " that you do not know about such
books; they would make you so happy."   He
was ten years of age,' says his biographer,
' when his uncle, observing one day his pockets
very much filled out, found the contents to be
translations which the boy had been making

of the Odes of Anacreon ; and ably done,' Mr. Moultrie adds.

The youth distinguished himself at Eton, gaining many prizes. Having been invited one day by Lady Howe, whose son was his form-fellow, to dine with them at the Christopher, he asked Dr. Keate, who had just before, as ill-luck would have it, given him an imposition of two hundred lines of Homer to learn by heart, whether he might repeat them, then and there ? 'Why,' said the Doctor, 'you have not had time to look at them.' 'Oh, sir,' replied the lad artlessly, 'I can repeat all the book to the end.' After this incident, Moultrie says, Dr. Keate's impositions took another form, that of composing Greek verse instead of repeating it. In this he would seem to have been not less ready, if the feat be genuine,—and not also an 'imposition'—with which his biographer credits him, of having, as an exercise, given him by Sir James Mackintosh, who had been told he could do anything in this line, turned into Greek verse a page out of the 'Court Guide'!

While at Eton, in 1813, was published by

subscription an epic poem in several books, which he had commenced in his eleventh year, entitled 'Gustavus Vasa.'

'Those who are acquainted with the subsequent writings of Sidney Walker,' my father has observed in some notes on his copy of this work, 'will discover in these pages but slight indication of the powers of mind which he had even then displayed, and which were manifested in his later poetical effusions. The excessive encouragement given to this early production, as evidenced by the unusually lengthy and influential subscription list which precedes it, was, I think, injurious rather than otherwise to the development of his poetical faculties. Injudicious commendation would seem to have crippled a mind and unsettled a judgment which might otherwise have attained to manly and vigorous proportions.'

In 1814 he went to Cambridge. He gained the Porson prize, and some other distinctions, and was subsequently elected Craven scholar, and finally Fellow of Trinity. Whether from the cause above suggested, or, as I think more probable, from temperament, if not from

hereditary disease, his career at Cambridge
was infructuous. It is no infrequent characteristic of such minds that their power lies
rather in the acquisition of knowledge than
in the employment of it. He, however, was
engaged to correct the press of a translation of
Milton's treatise 'De Cultu Dei,' discovered in
the year 1824, and committed by King
George IV. to the University of Cambridge
for publication. 'In the performance of his
task,' says his biographer, 'he considerably
overstepped the limits of his commission,
leaving upon the work the indelible impress
of his masterly scholarship and appreciation
of his author.' He also edited for his
friend Charles Knight, a 'Corpus Poetarum
Latinarum.'

He held his fellowship until the period
arrived at which it became necessary, under
the rules of the College, that he should either
take orders or resign it. After much anxious
struggle of mind he found himself compelled
to the conclusion, owing mainly, his biographer
believes, to his inability to accept the dogma
of the eternity of punishment, that he could

not conscientiously enter the Church. He accordingly relinquished his fellowship, and turned to the pursuits of general literature, for which, notwithstanding his learning and vast intellectual resources, he apparently possessed no great aptitude, for his support.

It was at this time that Praed introduced him to my father's acquaintance.

'When I first met him,' my father says in the notes from which I have quoted, 'he was indeed a most pitiable object; nervous to a degree which seemed to shake his whole frame when addressed by a stranger; almost blind, feeble, and ungraceful in his gait, he seemed to drag himself sideways like a crab. He dared not open his letters lest they should contain something unpleasant; and when he wrote one, it was with the greatest labour and repugnance. His conscience was so sensitive that every breath of opinion affected it; and he walked about in a state of perpetual torment. He once dined at my house, but so much affrighted had he been when he heard that two or three strangers were to be of the party, that I had had the utmost difficulty in inducing him to remain. It was not easy, indeed, to get him comfortably seated at table, for to have asked him to take down a lady would have caused him serious disquietude; and so absent was he, that during dinner he had to be kindly and carefully looked after. He became gradually more comfortable, but he went to bed, as he afterwards assured me, full of remorse for *gaucheries* which had been wholly beyond his control, and which had, of course, made no further painful impression upon others than one of concern at the disquietude which they had occasioned him.

'With all his peculiarities, however, there was,' says his friend Derwent Coleridge in a letter to Moultrie, 'about Sidney Walker an unmistakable air of refinement and superiority.' This spirit in him, which pervades all his poetry, was evidenced in an incident recorded in my father's notes.

'On one occasion,' he says, 'some of us had heard of a tavern called the Coal Hole, at which dramatic and newspaper wits were wont to assemble on one or two evenings in the week, and felt a curiosity to be present at one of these symposia.. Praed, his friend and *fidus Achates*; G. M. Fitzgerald, a clerk in the Board of Trade at that time ; Emerson, better known now as Emerson Tennent, and myself, made the party, which Walker with some difficulty was persuaded to join. We soon found that the entertainment was not to our taste, but so full had the room become that exit for a time was difficult. Walker looked nervous and ill at ease; and in reply to some jest of an actor of that day of the name of Rayner, attempted an expostulation. But this was not the worst. Who can paint his unfeigned surprise and horror when one of his most intimate Cambridge friends, who happened to be present, was presented to the company as a gentleman who had volunteered " to oblige " with the. then popular song of " The Dog's-meat Man." The whole thing was to Walker altogether intolerable. He struggled out of the room, and was with difficulty induced, by a promise of a cup of tea, to adjourn with our friends to my house, where he gradually recovered his equanimity and self-possession ;— sufficiently so, indeed, to administer to us, all round, an earnest reproof and remonstrance on the impropriety and indecency of countenancing such places of resort.

'Never was such a contrast,' continue the notes from which I am quoting, 'between two men as between Praed and Sidney Walker; yet Praed was almost the only companion in whose society Walker felt at ease. He was aware that Praed fully appreciated him, and knew of what he was really capable. He loved him for the genuine kindness of his disposition, and submitted to his good-humoured banter without exhibiting the slightest annoyance. I have seen them repeatedly in each other's company, and always on the same terms of affection and good-fellowship.'

Such was Sidney Walker in the year 1829-30. He survived nearly twenty years, but seems to have done little visible work during that time. The irresolution and inability to set himself in motion,—so often the accompaniment of great quickness and sensibility of mind,—which characterized his middle life, became so intensified towards the close as to leave him almost without any power of will whatsoever.   He believed, indeed, in his later days, that he was subject to the predominating influence and control of a 'spirit' which continually withstood him, and rendered him often powerless to carry out his ideas and to do work which he felt able and inclined to perform.   'What,' he says in one of his letters, 'can a man do who cannot open a book without being liable to have it, as it were, taken from him before he has read two pages!' Again, 'My demon, who, by the way, leads me a bitter life, is most unpropitious to letter-writing!'   Of this, his friend Derwent Coleridge says : 'Monomania would, of course, be the name given to this strange hallucination, but I could never myself detect the slightest symptom of cerebral disturbance.   It was impossible,' he adds, 'not to be reminded of the modern notion of spiritual possession, as an actual form or cause of insanity, or what passes for such at the present day.'

He retained to the last his wonderful memory; no fact, no word, no faculty seemed to have passed from him by disuse.   His remains are interred in Kensal Green.   'He left,' Moultrie adds, 'voluminous critical writings, of which some volumes of notes on Shakespeare were published after his death by the liberality of his friend Mr. Crawshay.' It is, however, by 'The Poetical Remains of William Sidney Walker, with a Memoir by the Rev. John Moultrie, Rector of Rugby : John W. Parker and Son, 1852,' that he is most likely to be remembered.

Of Winthrop Mackworth Praed, I find among my father's papers no further reminiscences than the foregoing short note in relation to Sidney Walker. He was one of the most valued and valuable of the contributors to the 'Literary Souvenir,' in which were first published, among others, three of his most popular compositions: 'The Legend of the Drachenfels;' 'The Legend of the Haunted Tree ;' and,— best remembered perhaps of all,—'The Belle of the Ball-room.'

Like all poetry which does not proceed from a very deep source, Mr. Praed's ' Vers de Société,' or lighter effusions, were susceptible of imitation ; and were, in fact, imitated so successfully by his friend Mr. Fitzgerald,

and not by him alone, that in the prepara-
tion of the collective edition of his poems,
many years after his death, his family and
most intimate surviving friends were often
greatly at a loss to eliminate the true from the
false, scattered as they were through the
magazines, annuals, and current collections of
the period.   My father's intimate acquaintance with the literature of that day, his
personal knowledge of the various writers,
and a quick discrimination derived from the
experience of many years, enabled him to have
the pleasure of rendering assistance to the
family in the recovery of many that were
unknown, and in enabling them authoritatively
to discard others which had been erroneously
attributed to Praed, assistance handsomely
acknowledged in Mr. Derwent Coleridge's
preface, which, however, he did not survive to
read.   It was the last of those literary recreations in which he loved to employ the leisure
of his later years.

CHAPTER XXIX.

SELECTIONS FROM POEMS OF EARLIER LIFE.

THE following selection from some of the poems written by my father in earlier life, to which allusion is made in the foregoing narrative and illustrative correspondence, is subjoined for convenience of reference.

TO OCTAVIA,

THE INFANT DAUGHTER OF THE LATE JOHN LARKING, ESQ.

(Written in his twentieth year.)

FULL many a gloomy month hath passed,
　On flagging wing, regardless by,
Unmarked by aught, save grief, since last
　I gazed upon thy bright blue eye,
And bade my lyre pour forth for thee
Its strain of wildest minstrelsy?

For all my joys are withered now,
    The hopes I most relied on thwarted,
And sorrow hath o'erspread my brow
    With many a shade since last we parted :
Yet, 'mid this murkiness of lot,
Young Peri, thou art unforgot !

There are who love to trace the smile
    That dimples upon Childhood's cheek,
And hear from lips devoid of guile
    The dictates of the bosom break :
Ah, who of such could look on thee
Without a wish to rival me !
He must be of a stubborn heart,
    And strange to every gentler feeling,
Who from thy glance could bear to part
    Cold and unmoved, without revealing
Some portion of the fond regret
That dimmed my eyes when last we met !

Sweet Bud of Beauty ! 'mid the thrill,
    The sickening thrill of hope delayed,
Peril, and almost every ill
    That can the breast of man invade,
No tender thought of thine and thee
Hath faded from my memory :
For I have dwelt on each dear form
    Till woe, awhile, gave place to gladness,
And that remembrance seemed to charm,
    Almost to peace, my bosom's sadness ;

And now, again, I breathe a lay
To hail thee on thy natal day!

Oh, might my fervent prayers prevail
    For blessings on thy future years,
Or innocence, like thine, avail
    To save thee from affliction's tears,
Each moment of thy life should bring
Some new delight upon its wing:
And the wild sparkle of thine eye,
    Thy guilelessness of soul revealing,
Beam ever thus as brilliantly;
    Undimmed, save by those gems of feeling,
Those soft, luxurious drops that flow
In pity for another's woe!

But vain the wish; it may not be;
    Could prayers avert misfortune's blight,
Or hearts from sinful passion free
    Here hope for unalloyed delight,
Then, those who watch thine opening bloom
Had never known an hour of gloom:
No; if the chastening stroke of Fate
    On guilty heads alone descended,
They would not sure have felt its weight,
    In whose pure bosoms, sweetly blended,
Life's kindliest social virtues move
In one unfailing tide of love.

Then since upon this earth joy's beams
    Are fading, frail, and few in number

And melt like the light-woven dreams
　　That steal upon the mourner's slumber;
Sweet one! I'll wish thee strength to bear
The ills that Heaven may bid thee share:
And when thine infancy hath fled,
　　And Time with Woman's zone hath bound thee,
If, in the path thou 'rt doomed to tread,
　　The thorns of sorrow lurk and wound thee,
Be thine that exquisite relief
That blossoms in the springs of grief!

And like the many-tinted bow,
　　That smiles the showery clouds away,
May Hope, Grief's Iris here below,
　　Attend and cheer thee on thy way,
Till full of years, thy cares at rest,
Thou seek'st the mansions of the blest!
Young Sister of a mortal NINE!
　　Farewell! perchance a long farewell!
Though griefs unnumbered yet be mine,
　　Griefs, Hope may vainly strive to quell,
'Twill half unteach my soul to pine,
If there be bliss for thee and thine!

KIRKSTALL ABBEY.

LONG years have passed since last I strayed,
  In boyhood, through thy roofless aisle,
And watched the mists of eve o'ershade
  Day's latest, loveliest smile;
And saw the bright, broad, moving moon
Sail up the sapphire skies of June!

The air around was breathing balm;
  The aspen scarcely seemed to sway;
And, as a sleeping infant calm,
  The river flowed away,
Devious as error, deep as love,
And blue and bright as heaven above!

Steeped in a flood of golden light,
  Type of that hour of deep repose,
In wan, wild beauty on my sight,
  Thy time-worn tower arose,
Brightening above the wreck of years,
Like FAITH amid a world of fears.

I climbed its dark and dizzy stair,
  And gained its ivy-mantled brow;
But broken, ruined, who may dare
  Ascend that pathway now?
Life was an upward journey then;
When shall my spirit mount again!

The steps in youth I loved to tread,
　　Have sunk beneath the foot of Time;
Like them the daring hopes that led
　　Me, once, to heights sublime;
Ambition's dazzling dreams are o'er,
And I may scale those heights no more!

And years have fled, and now I stand
　　Once more beside thy shattered fane,
Nerveless alike in heart and hand,
　　How changed by grief and pain,
Since last I loitered here, and deemed
Life was the fairy thing it seemed!

And gazing on thy crumbling walls,
　　What visions meet my mental eye;
For every stone of thine recalls
　　Some trace of years gone by;
Some cherished bliss, too frail to last,
Some hope decayed, or passion past!

Aye, thoughts come thronging on my soul,
　　Of sunny youth's delightful morn;
When free from Sorrow's dark control,
　　By pining Care unworn,
Dreaming of Fame, and Fortune's smile,
I lingered in thy ruined aisle!

How many a wild and withering woe
　　Hath seared my trusting heart since then;
What clouds of blight, consuming slow
　　The springs that life sustain,
Have o'er my world-vexed spirit past,
Sweet Kirkstall, since I saw thee last!

How bright is every scene beheld
　In youth and hope's unclouded hours;
How darkly, youth and hope dispelled,
　The loveliest prospect lowers :
Thou wert a splendid vision then ;—
When wilt thou seem so bright again !

Yet still thy turrets drink the light
　Of summer evening's softest ray,
And ivy garlands, green and bright,
　Still mantle thy decay ;
And calm and beauteous as of old,
Thy wandering river glides in gold.

But life's gay morn of ecstasy,
　That made thee seem so passing fair,
The aspirations wild and high,
　The soul to nobly dare,
Oh, where are they, stern ruin, say !
Thou dost but echo,—where are they !

Adieu !—Be still to other hearts
　What thou wert long ago to mine ;
And when the blissful dream departs,
　Do thou a beacon shine,
To guide the mourner, through his tears,
To the blest scenes of happier years.

THE DEATH OF THE FIRST-BORN.

My sweet one, my sweet one, the tears were in my
    eyes
When first I clasped thee to my heart, and heard
    thy feeble cries;
For I thought of all that I had borne, as I bent me
    down to kiss
Thy cherry lips, and sunny brow, my first-born bud
    of bliss!

I turned to many a withered hope, to years of grief
    and pain,
And the cruel wrongs of a bitter world flashed o'er
    my boding brain;
I thought of friends, grown worse than cold, of per-
    secuting foes,
And I asked of Heaven if ills like these must mar
    thy youth's repose!

I gazed upon thy quiet face, half blinded by my
    tears,
Till gleams of bliss, unfelt before, came brightening
    on my fears;
Sweet rays of hope that fairer shone 'mid the clouds
    of gloom that bound them,
As stars dart down their loveliest light when mid-
    night skies are 'round them.

My sweet one, my sweet one, thy life's brief hour is
    o'er,
And a father's anxious fears for thee can fever me
    no more!

And for the hopes, the sun-bright hopes, that
      blossomed at thy birth,—
They too have fled, to prove how frail are cherished
      things of earth !

'Tis true that thou wert young, my child, but though
      brief thy span below,
To me it was a little age of agony and woe ;
For, from thy first faint dawn of life thy cheek
      began to fade,
And my lips had scarce thy welcome breathed, ere
      my hopes were wrapt in shade.

Oh, the child in its hours of health and bloom that
      is dear as thou wert then,
Grows far more prized, more fondly loved, in sick-
      ness and in pain ;
And thus 'twas thine to prove, dear babe, when
      every hope was lost,
Ten times more precious to my soul, for all that
      thou hadst cost !

Cradled in thy fair mother's arms, we watched thee,
      day by day,
Pale like the second bow of Heaven, as gently waste
      away;
And, sick with dark foreboding fears we dared not
      breathe aloud,
Sat, hand in hand, in speechless grief, to wait death's
      coming cloud !

It came at length; o'er thy bright blue eye the
    film was gathering fast,
And an awful shade passed o'er thy brow, the
    deepest and the last;
In thicker gushes strove thy breath; we raised thy
    drooping head;—
A moment more,—the final pang,—and thou wert
    of the dead!

Thy gentle mother turned away to hid her face
    from me,
And murmured low of Heaven's behests, and bliss
    attained by thee;
She would have chid me that I mourned a doom so
    blest as thine,
Had not her own deep grief burst forth in tears as
    wild as mine!

We laid thee down in thy sinless rest, and from
    thine infant brow
Culled one soft lock of radiant hair, our only solace
    now;
Then placed around thy beauteous corse, flowers,
    not more fair and sweet,
Twin rose-buds in thy little hands, and jasmine at
    thy feet.

Though other offspring still be ours, as fair per-
    chance as thou,
With all the beauty of thy cheek, the sunshine of
    thy brow,

They never can replace the bud our early fondness
    nurst;
They may be lovely and beloved, but not, like thee,
    the FIRST!

The FIRST! How many a memory bright that one
    sweet word can bring,
Of hopes that blossomed, drooped, and died, in life's
    delightful spring;
Of fervid feelings passed away, those early seeds of
    bliss
That germinate in hearts unsered by such a world
    as this!

My sweet one, my sweet one, my fairest and my
    First!
When I think of what thou might'st have been, my
    heart is like to burst;
But gleams of gladness through my gloom their
    soothing radiance dart,
And my sighs are hushed, my tears are dried, when
    I turn to what thou art!

Pure as the snow-flake ere it falls and takes the
    stain of earth,
With not a taint of mortal life except thy mortal
    birth,
God bade thee early taste the spring for which so
    many thirst,
And bliss, eternal bliss, is thine, my Fairest and my
    First!

TEN YEARS AGO.

I.

TEN years ago, ten years ago,
　　Life was to us a fairy scene,
And the keen blasts of worldly woe
　　Had sered not then its pathway green;
Youth and its thousand dreams were ours,
　　Feelings we ne'er can know again,
Unwithered hopes, unwasted powers,
　　And frames unworn by mortal pain:
Such was the bright and genial flow
Of life with us,—ten years ago!

II.

Time has not blanched a single hair
　　That clusters round thy forehead now;
Nor hath the cankering touch of Care
　　Left even one furrow on thy brow.
Thine eyes are bright as when we met,
　　In love's deep truth, in earlier years;
Thy rosy cheek is blooming yet,
　　Though sometimes stained by secret tears;
But where, oh where's the spirit's glow
That shone through all,—ten years ago!

III.

I, too, am changed, I scarce know why;
　　I feel each flagging pulse decay;
And youth, and health, and visions high,
　　Melt like a wreath of snow away!

Time cannot sure have wrought the ill;
  Though worn in this world's sickening strife
In soul and form, I linger still
  In the first summer month of life;
Yet journey on my path below,
Oh, how unlike,—ten years ago!

IV.

But, look not thus; I would not give
  The wreck of hopes that thou must share,
To bid those joyous hours revive,
  When all around me seemed so fair:
We've wandered on in sunny weather,
  When winds were low and flowers in bloom;
And hand in hand have kept together,
  And still will keep, 'mid storm and gloom;
Endeared by ties we could not know,
When life was young,—ten years ago!

V.

Has Fortune frowned!—Her frowns were vain,
  For hearts like ours she could not chill;
Have friends proved false!—Their love might wane
  But ours grew fonder, firmer still!
Twin barks on this world's changing wave,
  Stedfast in calms, in tempests tried,
In concert still our fate we'll brave,
  Together cleave life's fitful tide;
Nor mourn, whatever blasts may blow,
Youth's first wild dreams,—ten years ago!

22—2

VI.

Have we not knelt beside his bed,
　And watched our first-born blossom die;
Hoped, till the shade of hope had fled,
　Then wept till feeling's fount was dry!
Was it not sweet in that sad hour
　To think, 'mid mutual tears and sighs,
Our bud had left its earthly bower,
　And burst to bloom in paradise:
What, to the thought that soothed that woe,
Were heartless joys,—ten years ago!

VII.

Yes, it is sweet, when Heaven is bright,
　To share its sunny beams with thee!
But even more sweet, 'mid clouds and blight,
　To have thee near to weep with me;
Then dry those tears, though somewhat changed
　From what we were in earlier youth,
Time, that hath hopes and friends estranged,
　Hath left us love in all its truth;
Sweet feelings we would not forego,
For life's best joys,—ten years ago!

MY OWN FIRESIDE.

Let others seek for empty joys,
　At ball, or concert, rout, or play;
Whilst, far from Fashion's idle noise,
　Her gilded domes and trappings gay,

I while the wintry eve away,
  'Twixt book and lute the hours divide;
And marvel how I e'er could stray
  From thee,—my own fireside!

My own fireside! Those simple words
  Can bid the sweetest dreams arise;
Awaken feeling's tenderest chords,
  And fill with tears of joy mine eyes.
What is there my wild heart can prize,
  That doth not in thy sphere abide;
Haunt of my home-bred sympathies,
  My own,—my own fireside!

A gentle form is near me now;
  A small, white hand is clasped in mine;
I gaze upon her placid brow,
  And ask, what joys can equal thine?
A babe, whose beauty's half divine,
  In sleep his mother's eyes doth hide;
Where may Love seek a fitter shrine,
  Than thou,—my own fireside!

What care I for the sullen roar
  Of winds without, that ravage earth!
It doth but bid me prize the more
  The shelter of thy hallowed hearth;
To thoughts of quiet bliss give birth;
  Then let the churlish tempest chide,
It cannot check the blameless mirth
  That glads my own fireside!

My refuge ever from the storm
　Of this world's passion, strife, and care;
Though thunder-clouds the skies deform,
　Their fury cannot reach me there;
There all is cheerful, calm, and fair;
　Wrath, Envy, Malice, Strife, or Pride,
Hath never made its hated lair,
　By thee,—my own fireside!

Thy precincts are a charmed ring,
　Where no harsh feeling dares intrude;
Where life's vexations lose their sting;
　Where even grief is half subdued;
And Peace, the halcyon, loves to brood.
　Then, let the world's proud fool deride;
I'll pay my debt of gratitude
　To thee,—my own fireside!

Shrine of my household deities;
　Bright scene of home's unsullied joys;
To thee my burthened spirit flies,
　When Fortune frowns, or Care annoys!
Thine is the bliss that never cloys;
　The smile whose truth hath oft been tried;
What, then, are this world's tinsel toys,
　To thee,—my own fireside!

Oh, may the yearnings, fond and sweet,
　That bid my thoughts be all of thee,
Thus ever guide my wandering feet
　To thy heart-soothing sanctuary!

Whate'er my future years may be,
  Let joy or grief my fate betide;
Be still an Eden bright to me,
  My own,—my own fireside!

THE YOUNGLING OF THE FLOCK.

WELCOME, thrice welcome to my heart, sweet har-
    binger of bliss,
How have I looked, till hope grew sick, for a
    moment bright as this?
Thou hast flashed upon my aching sight when
    Fortune's clouds are dark,
The sunny spirit of my dreams,—the dove unto
    mine ark!

Oh no! not even when life was new, and Love and
    Hope were young,
And o'er the firstling of my flock with raptured
    gaze I hung,
Did I feel the glow that thrills me now, the yearn-
    ings fond and deep,
That stir my bosom's inmost chords, as I watch thy
    placid sleep!

Though loved and cherished be the flower that
    springs 'neath summer skies,
The bud that blooms 'mid wintry storms more
    tenderly we prize;
One does but make our bliss more bright, the other
    meets our eye,
Like a radiant star, when all beside have vanished
    from the sky.

Sweet blossom of my stormy hour, star of my
    troubled heaven,
To thee that passing sweet perfume, that soothing
    light is given ;
And precious art thou to my soul, but dearer far
    that thou,
A messenger of peace and love, art sent to cheer
    me now.

What though my heart be crowded close with
    inmates dear if few,
Creep in, my little smiling babe, there's still a niche
    for you !
And should another claimant rise, and clamour for
    a place,
Who knows but room may still be found, if it wears
    as fair a face ?

I listen to thy feeble cry, till it 'wakens in my
    breast,
The sleeping energies of love,—sweet hopes, too
    long repressed ;
For, weak as that low wail may seem to other ears
    than mine,
It stirs *my* heart, like a trumpet's voice, to strive
    for thee and thine !

It peals upon my dreaming soul sweet tidings of the
    birth
Of a new and blessed link of love, to fetter me to
    earth,

And, strengthening many a fond resolve, it bids me
    do and dare
All that a father's heart may brave, to make thy
    sojourn fair.

I cannot shield thee from the blight a bitter world
    may fling
O'er all the promise of thy youth, the visions of thy
    spring ;
For, I would not warp thy gentle heart, each kindlier
    impulse ban,
By teaching thee, what I have learned, how base
    a thing is man.

I cannot save thee from the griefs to which our
    flesh is heir,
But I can arm thee with a spell, life's keenest ills
    to bear ;
I may not Fortune's frowns avert, but I can bid
    thee pray
For wealth this world can never give, nor ever take
    away.

From altered Friendship's chilling glance, from
    Hate's envenomed dart,
Misplaced Affection's withering pang, or 'true
    Love's' wonted smart,
I cannot save my sinless child ; but I can bid him
    seek
Such Faith and Love from heaven above as leave
    earth's malice weak.

But wherefore doubt that He who makes the smallest
　　bird His care,
And tempers to the new-shorn lamb the blast it ill
　　could bear,
Will still His guiding arm extend, His gracious plan
　　pursue,
And if He gives thee ills to bear, will grant thee
　　courage too.

Dear youngling of my little fold, the loveliest and
　　the last,
'Tis sweet to deem what thou mayst be, when long,
　　long years have past;
To think, when time hath blanched my hair, and
　　others leave my side,
Thou mayst be then my prop and stay, my blessing
　　and my pride.

And when the world hath done its worst, when life's
　　fever-fit is o'er,
And the griefs that wring my weary heart can never
　　touch it more,
How sweet to think thou mayst be near to catch my
　　latest sigh,
To watch beside my dying bed, and close my glazing
　　eye.

Oh ! 'tis for offices like these, the last sweet child is
　　given,
The mother's joy, the father's pride, the fairest boon
　　of heaven;

Their fireside plaything first, then of their failing
    strength the rock ;
The rainbow to their waning years,—the Youngling
    of their Flock !

THE SLEEPING CUPID OF GUIDO.

A SKETCH FROM THE WELL-KNOWN PICTURE IN THE
GALLERY OF EARL FITZWILLIAM.

I.

'Tis summer's softest eve ; the winds are laid,
The jarring sounds of day-life are at rest,
And all is calm and soothing ; not a shade
Mars the blue beauty of the skies : the west,
Gathering its hues of splendour from the crest
Of yonder setting sun, is changing fast
From sapphire to bright gold ; old ocean's breast
Is one broad plain without a cloud o'ercast :
'Tis day's divinest hour, its loveliest, and its last.

II.

Tired of his sport, the wreck of human hearts,
There, on his mother's couch in slumber bound,
The God of Love reclines ;—his idle darts,
Those ministers of woe, lie scattered 'round :
But that he guards, amid his dreams profound,
With so much jealous care, his unstrung Bow,
How might we now his vaunted strength con-
    found ;
From his own quiver pay the debt we owe,
And, with one keen, bright shaft, pierce our uncon-
    scious foe !

III.

But who would wound a breast so passing fair !
Look ! in immortal beauty where he lies :
His flushed cheek pillowed on his hand ; his hair
Clustering, like sun-touched clouds in summer
　　　skies,
Around his glorious brow ;—his twice-sealed eyes
With silken-fringèd lids, like flowers that close
Their dewy cups at eve ;—and lips whose dyes
Rival the crimson of the damask rose,
Wreathed with a thousand charms, all sweetness and
　　　repose.

IV.

Hush ; for a footfall may disturb his sleep ;
Hush even your breathing, for a breath may break
His visioned trance !   But no, 'tis deep, most deep ;
The last low sigh of evening fans his cheek,
And stirs his golden curls ; the last bright streak
Of parting day is fading from the west ;
Dim clouds are gathering round yon mountain's
　　　peak,
Yet still he sleeps ; and his soft-heaving breast,
Bright wings, brow, lips, and eyes, are redolent of
　　　rest.

V.

Love, O young Love, how beautiful thou art !
The brightest dream that ever poet feigned
May scarce compare with thee !   What though
　　　thy dart
The blood of many a gentle breast hath stained ;
What though thy godlike powers thou hast pro-
　　　faned,

And proved to some an evil deity ;
Yet, in thy softer moods, hast thou sustained
Full many a sinking heart ; and thoughts of thee
Have often stilled the waves of this life's stormy sea !

VI.

Thou art, indeed, omnipotent,—divine !
And the wide world is vocal with thy name ;
Princes and peasants bow before thy shrine ;
Whilst gentle Woman, in all lands the same,
For good or evil, oftenest swells thy fame !
Noble and serf, the despot and the slave,
(For even the slave, if Love his homage claim,
May wear a double chain), thy shafts must brave,
And own thy mighty power to ruin or to save !

END OF VOL. I.

BILLING AND SONS, PRINTERS, GUILDFORD AND LONDON.